THE DEATH DEALER

HEATHER GRAHAM

THE DEATH DEALER

MIRA®

MIRA

ISBN-13: 978-0-7783-2532-1
ISBN-10:   0-7783-2532-6

THE DEATH DEALER

www.MIRABooks.com

Printed in U.S.A.

First Printing: April 2008
10 9 8 7 6 5 4 3 2 1

To the New World School of the Arts,
especially Ms. Graham, teacher of Creative Writing and English,
who knows enthusiasm is the biggest part of the game;
and Mr. Jim Randolph "The God of Theater,"
who keeps himself and his kids real,
who knows there's a big bad world out there
but keeps a thumb on caring.

And for Beth Fath, a parent with quiet dedication;
and Debbie Benitez, who has helped keep me sane
and informed on more than one occasion!

Quoth the raven, "Nevermore!"
—Edgar Allan Poe

PROLOGUE

It's not easy being a ghost.

You would think that it would be the most natural thing in the world. There you go—you're dead. Live with it.

But it's far more difficult than you would ever imagine.

It begins with *why?*

Oh, we all know the theories. A death by violence. Something left undone. Someone to be protected, someone to be warned—someone to be avenged.

Vengeance? Once you're a ghost? Great stuff.

But that wasn't my situation. My killer perished split seconds before the light of life faded from my own eyes. It wasn't that I hadn't loved life—I had. There were those left behind whom I cherished deeply.

The great love of my life, Matt Connolly, had gone before me, however. And he was there to greet me when I arrived.

"Crossed over," as they say. Except there's the thing—you haven't actually crossed over. You're existing in a vague and shadowy world where, often, you see something truly horrible about to take place—and you don't have the power to stop it.

I'd known something of what would occur. I had almost died

before. I had felt the power of the light that beckons—an invitation to heaven? I don't know the answer to that yet.

Because that time I lived. And this time I stayed.

As a ghost.

And I know that I've remained behind for a reason, though I haven't a clue as to the specifics. But at least, unlike some, I'm pretty sure I *do* have a purpose.

I've come across many of my kind who are far more lost than I am, having had a strange relationship with them after my near-death experience and before I departed the life of flesh and blood. There's Lawrence Ridgeway, Colonel Lawrence Ridgeway, a charming fellow, with his perfectly trimmed beard and muttonchops.

Sadly, he can't accept the fact that the Civil War has been won. He was a brave soldier who came to New York during the terrible draft riots of the eighteen-sixties. No matter how often I try to explain things to him, he's forever keeping guard over his long-gone prisoners. Matt, too, has tried to point out to him that there are no prisoners present, but poor Colonel Ridgeway simply can't accept that fact. I'm afraid he's doomed to haunt one particular hallway here in Manhattan's historic Hastings House forever, a sad and tragic figure who'll never find closure.

Marnie Brubaker died in childbirth. She's a sweet and charming creature, and she loves the children who pass through the house. Children tend to be more open than adults to visits from my kind. Marnie likes to play games with the little ones. When they're falling asleep on a parent's shoulder, she sings lullabies. Every once in a while, one of them gets scared by her presence and screams bloody murder, which puts her into a funk for weeks to come. All she wants is to offer is love and comfort, but some people, even kids, just don't want solace from a ghost.

There are those, like Colonel Ridgeway, who will go on repeating their last action over and over again. Then there are those who learn to move around the physical worlds. Passing through walls. Appearing and disappearing at will. Moving objects. The truth of it is, we ghosts can learn to do all kinds of things, so long as we have the will, the patience and the stamina.

I was the victim of a killer who first took the lives of others, before he took mine. But there's no pain in my world, especially not for me. Because Matt's here with me, and that's really all that matters. He died the night of my almost-death, and he stayed behind to warn me. To save me. But my salvation wasn't to be. In the end, I died to save Genevieve O'Brien. And so far, at least, I've been successful. But as a social worker, she's one of those people who won't rest in her quest to help others, and that can put her in danger sometimes.

Then there's Joe Connolly, Matt's cousin. He's a private detective and a super guy. A tough guy.

But no one's so tough that he can defy death. Life's not like the movies. Most of the time, the bad guys can aim, so Joe can use some protection, whether he knows it or not.

I believe Matt and I have stayed on because of either Joe or Genevieve. Or maybe both. It's our job to make sure they—and maybe others—stay safe.

Nope, being a ghost isn't easy. In fact, it's damn hard work protecting people when most of the time they can't even see you and don't think they need protection, anyway.

Take Joe. He has a thing about going to the graves of the people he couldn't save—including Matt's and mine. Sometimes he brings flowers. Sometimes he just sits in deep thought. And sometimes he talks. Then he looks around, hoping that he hasn't been overheard. I imagine that it would be difficult to obtain new clients if word got out that he was insane. But everyone out there has his own way of coping with loss. For Joe, it's talking to people at their grave sites.

That's how we became involved in the Poe Killings.

And that's how Joe became involved with Genevieve again.

She was a child of privilege, but even after she'd almost lost her own life, she couldn't stop herself from investigating problems.

Including murder.

CHAPTER 1

The crash occurred on the FDR. Strange thing, Joe had just been driving along Manhattan's East Side and thinking it was amazing that there weren't more accidents on the busy—and outdated—highway when, right in front of him, a crash caused the car a few lengths ahead of him to slam into someone else. The sounds of screeching tires, shattering glass, grating steel and several massive impacts were evidence that the domino effect had come into play. Someone almost stopped in the aftermath of the first collision, but then that car was pushed into the next lane, and the driver coming up didn't have time to stop. He slammed into it hard and careened into the next lane. The car that hit that driver bounced over the median and into the oncoming traffic going south.

Joe somehow made it off to the side, threw his car into Park and hit 9-1-1 on his cell phone. He reported what he saw and his position, dropped the phone and hurried out to help.

The car that had caused the initial crash was fairly far ahead of him, but there was a line of disabled vehicles stretching back from it almost to where he was.

The people in the car closest to him were fine, and so were the people in the next vehicle, and the driver of the third probably had nothing more than a broken arm.

The smell of gas around the car that had hopped the median was strong, though—a bad sign.

People had stopped all around, talking, shouting, while other drivers were trying to get around the wreckage no matter what.

"Hey, it's going to blow up!" someone called to Joe as he approached the car. He lifted a hand in acknowledgment but kept going. He wasn't a superhero, he'd just worked lots of accident scenes when he'd been a cop, and an inner voice was assuring him that—death-defying or not—he had time to help.

The car was upside down. There was blood coming from the driver's head, which was canted at an awkward angle. The man's eyes were closed.

"Hey. You have to wake up. We've got to get you out of there. I'm going to help you," Joe told him.

"My niece," the man said. "You've got to help my niece." He grabbed Joe, his grip surprisingly strong.

"Trish," the man said.

Then Joe saw the little girl. She was in the back. Not really big enough for the seat belt, she had slipped out of it and was on the roof—now the floor—with silent tears streaming down her face.

Joe said with forced calm, "Come on, honey. Give me your hand."

She had huge, saucer-wide blue eyes, and she was maybe about seven or eight and just small for her age, he decided. "Trish," he said firmly. "Give me your hand."

He sighed with relief when she did so. He managed to get her out, even though she had to crawl over broken glass on the way. As soon as he had her in his arms, someone from the milling crowd rushed forward.

"Get the hell out of here now, buddy!" the man who took the child told him. "The car is going to blow."

"There's a man in the car," Joe said.

"He's dead."

"No," Joe said. "He's alive. He talked to me."

Joe was dimly aware that the air was alive with sirens, that evening was turning to night. He was fully aware of the fact that he didn't have much time left.

Flat on his stomach, he shouted to the man who had taken the child from him. "Get them back—get them all back!"

"Trish?" the man in the car said.

"It's all right. She's out. She's safe. Now, get ready, because I'm releasing your seat belt. You've got to try to help me."

He did his best to support the guy's weight after he released the seat belt, but it was a struggle. An upside-down crushed car didn't allow for a lot of leeway, especially when it was about to explode.

But he got the man out. He could only pray that he hadn't worsened his pain or any broken bones.

"Help me!" he roared, once he had the man away from the car.

The same Good Samaritan who had taken the child came rushing up. Together, they started to half drag and half carry the man from the wreckage.

Just in time.

The car exploded, flames leaping high over the FDR. They would have been easily seen over in Brooklyn, and probably even halfway across Manhattan.

The blast was hot and powerful. He felt it like a huge, hot hand that lifted him, the victim and his fellow rescuer, and tossed them a dozen feet so that they crashed down hard on the asphalt.

Joe rolled, trying to take the brunt of the impact, knowing he was in far better shape to accept the force than the victim of the crash.

For a moment he didn't breathe, since there was nothing to breathe but the fire in the air.

Then he felt pain in almost every joint, and the hardness of the

road against his back. He became aware of the screams around him,
which he hadn't heard before; the blast had sucked all the sound
out of the air along with the oxygen.

"You all right, buddy?" he asked the man who had helped him.

"Yeah—you?"

"Fine."

The next thing he knew, there was a young EMT hunkered
down in front of him. He tried to struggle up.

"Take it easy. Don't move until we're sure you haven't broken
something, sir," the med tech said.

"There's nothing broken. I'm good," Joe told him. "The guy
who helped me—"

"He's being taken care of."

"The man in the car—I think he was hurt pretty bad," Joe said.

"We, uh, we got it," the med tech told him. "And," he added
gently, "the girl is fine. Everyone's already talking about how you
saved her life."

"Great, good," Joe said. "But the man needs—"

"Sir, I'm sorry to tell you, but he's dead."

"I thought he had a chance."

The med tech was silent for a minute. "You did a good thing," he
said very softly. "But that man…he died on impact, sir. Broken neck."

"No—he talked to me."

"I think maybe you hit your head, sir. That man couldn't have
spoken to you. I'm sure his family is going to be grateful you got
the body out, but he's been dead since the first impact. Honest to
God. It was a broken neck. He never suffered." As he spoke, the
med tech got a stethoscope out; apparently he wasn't taking Joe's
word that he was okay.

Joe had his breath back. He pushed the stethoscope aside and
sat up, staring at the med tech. What did the kid know? He wasn't
the coroner.

"He was alive. He spoke to me. I wouldn't even have seen the girl if he hadn't told me she was in the car."

"Sure."

Joe knew damned well when he was being humored. "I'm telling you, I'm fine."

He knew the EMT was all good intentions, but he was just fine—except for this kid trying to tell him that the man had died on impact.

"Sir, let me help you," the med tech said.

"You want to help me? Get me the hell out of here," Joe told him. *"Fast."*

"Just let me get a stretcher."

"Sure," Joe said, figuring anything that would get the guy out of the way was fine.

As soon as the med tech went off for a stretcher, Joe took a deep breath and made it to his feet. Damn, it hurt. Well, he'd been pretty much sandblasted when he skidded down on the roadway, and he wasn't exactly eighteen anymore.

He saw that there was no way in hell he would be leaving the scene in his own car. But it wasn't blocking anyone, so the thing was just to start walking, to get away.

He did. It was easier than he'd imagined, but then, he was walking away from a scene of chaos, and everyone's attention was on the wreck, not on one lone pedestrian. He could hear voices—most alarmed and concerned, some merely excited—surrounding him as he escaped the scene. More and more cop cars and ambulances passed him.

He headed south along the shoulder, and at last he followed an entrance ramp down to the street, where he hailed a taxi. The driver didn't even blink at his appearance. Hey, this was New York.

He suggested a route to Brooklyn that didn't involve the FDR.

He got home eventually, where he showered and changed, then went out into his living room and turned on the television, looking for the local news.

The accident was center stage.

"Twelve were injured and are being given care in various area hospitals," the attractive newscaster was saying. Her face was grave. "There was one fatality. Adam Brookfield was killed when his car flipped over the median. The medical examiner reports that Mr. Brookfield died instantly, though a heroic onlooker, who fled the scene, carried the man's body from the automobile just instants before the car exploded. That same man rescued Mr. Brookfield's six-year-old niece, Patricia, who is doing well at St. Vincent's Hospital, where her parents are with her."

The woman shifted in her chair to look into a different camera. The somber expression left her face. She smiled. "This weekend, we welcome the All American Chorale Union to Kennedy Center, and for those of you with tickets, remember that tonight's the night for the special showing of ancient Egyptian artifacts at the Metropolitan Museum of Art. All those pricey meal tickets will pay for more archeological research right here in New York. And now…"

Joe no longer heard her. He was irritated.

That man, Adam Brookfield, had been alive; he had spoken to Joe. It was bull about him dying on impact. He couldn't have spoken if he'd been dead.

Joe glanced at his watch. It would be hours before he could reasonably go for his car, which meant it would probably be towed anyway. Screw it.

He had been on his way to attend tonight's fund-raiser at the Met when he'd gotten sidelined by the accident, but now he decided he no longer cared. He was heading to Manhattan and a bar that had become one of his favorites.

★ ★ ★

"Congratulations, she's just beautiful, Senator," Genevieve O'Brien said to Senator James McCray and his wife. They had been showing her pictures of their new grandson, Jacob. She had done the right thing, "oohing" and "aahing."

Frankly, the baby looked like a pinhead at the moment. As bald as a buzzard. Squinched up and...newborn.

But the senator was a supporter of the Historical Society, and had a paid great deal for his meal and a walk through the museum. Naturally she was going to say all the right things about his grandchild. Of course, if she'd met him on the street, she still would have said the same things, she realized.

She damned digital cameras.

The senator had not had just one picture but at least a hundred.

"You need to get married and have children yourself, young lady," James McCray said.

His wife elbowed him. She'd suddenly gone pale.

Genevieve sighed and tried not to show her feelings in her expression, but she was so weary of this. Anything that so much as hinted of sex was considered taboo around her. She'd been the victim of a maniac who'd been stalking New York's streets and targeting prostitutes, the same prostitutes Gen worked with. Everyone knew what she'd been through and that it was a miracle she was alive.

She had stayed alive because she had realized quickly that her attacker was actually incapable of sex. She had played on his own psychological makeup, providing the bolstering and ego boosts that he needed, and though she had been a prisoner and abused, she wasn't suffering as shatteringly from the experience as the world seemed to think she should be. If she faced an inward agony, it was knowing that someone incredible, her friend Leslie MacIntyre, *had* died.

"I would love to have children one day, Senator, Mrs. McCray," she said cheerfully. "When the right person to be a dad comes along. You enjoy that beautiful baby. But now, if you'll excuse me, I need to see to a few things."

Yes, she needed to see to an escape.

She walked quickly into a side hall, opened only for the convenience of the Historical Society, which was hosting the event. There was a bench, and she sat on it.

He hadn't shown.

She let out a sigh, wondering why she had even thought Joe would show up. He was a fascinating guy, intrigued by almost everything in the world. He hadn't come from money, but if anyone out there knew that money really wasn't everything, it was her. Joe was one of those people who *lived* life, and he'd done well enough for himself. He could look like a million dollars in a suit. Definitely a striking guy.

And her friend, she thought.

When he wasn't avoiding her.

She smiled to herself. If she was in trouble, if she needed rescuing, he would be right there. Thing was, she didn't need rescuing. And she didn't *want* to need rescuing, either.

Her smiled faded.

She *did* want help.

She had hoped he would show tonight because she wanted to ask him about the current worry dogging her life.

A murder.

The media had dubbed it the Poe Killing, because the victim, Thorne Bigelow, had been president of the New York Poe Society, a readers and writers group whose members studied the works and life of Edgar Allan Poe, and called themselves the Ravens, and the killer had left a note referring to the famous author.

She looked around the room. Most of the members were involved with things that were considered either literary or important educationally in the city of New York. There were several of the Ravens here tonight; like her own mother, they also supported various groups interested in history and archeology. Among them she noticed newspaper reporter Larry Levine, who had come to cover the event. Then there was Lila Hawkins—brassy and outspoken and very, very rich. Quite frankly, she was obnoxious, but she did do a lot of good things for the arts in the city. Just a few minutes ago, Gen had seen Lila with Barbara Hirshorn, another Raven and the complete opposite of Lila; Barbara was so timid, she had difficulty speaking to more than one person at the same time.

She had noted that even Jared Bigelow had made a brief appearance with Mary Vincenzo, his aunt, on his arm. He was gone now, and she hadn't had a chance to speak to him. He had shown up just to support the cause tonight; he was still in mourning for his father.

From her seat on the bench she could hear the booming voice of Don Tracy, the one Raven who'd taken Poe to the masses. He was an actor, a good one, even if he'd never become a household name. He loved the stage and had performed Poe's works on numerous occasions.

None of them seemed to be frightened by the note that had been found with Thorne's body.

Thorne Bigelow had been a very wealthy man. A well-known man. And though murder happened all too often, it was the sad truth that a murder with a hook—like a victim who was regularly in the headlines and a mysterious note making reference to a long-dead storyteller and poet—intrigued the media more than most deaths did.

It was only happenstance that Thorne Bigelow had been a very rich Raven. The Ravens didn't demand that a member be wealthy, published on the topic of Poe's life and works or world-renowned, though sometimes they were. Thorne Bigelow had written a book on Poe that was considered to be the definitive work on the man. Bigelow was honored far and wide for his knowledge.

And he had been poisoned. Poisoned with a bottle of thousand-dollar wine.

He loved wine, perhaps even to excess. And he had died of it. À la Poe.

"The Black Cat."

Or perhaps "The Cask of Amontillado."

The killer didn't seem to have been too *precise* about which story he meant Bigelow's death to parallel. He *had* made his intentions clear in the note he'd left at the scene, though.

Quoth the raven: die.

The police were pretty much at a standstill, though why the media were harassing them so strongly about the case, Genevieve wasn't certain. Thorne Bigelow had only been dead a week. She knew from personal experience that bad things could go on for a very long time before a situation was resolved. If it hadn't been for her family's wealth and her own disappearance, the sad deaths of many of the city's less fortunate might have gone unsolved for a very long time.

But Bigelow was big news.

"My darling, there you are!"

Genevieve looked up. Her mother—it was still strange to call Eileen *Mother,* when she had grown up believing that she was her aunt—was standing before her. Eileen, only in her early forties now, was stunning. Her love for Genevieve was so strong—not to mention that without her persistence, Genevieve would surely be dead now—that it was easy to forgive the lies of the past. Especially since Genevieve knew what family pressure was like, and that her mother had been far too young to speak up for herself when Gen had been born.

But Eileen Brideswell had finally decided that a New York that embraced reruns of *Sex and the City* would surely forgive her a teenage, unwed birth. What she might once have been damned for now passed without notice by most in the city.

And after all, Genevieve had loved Eileen all her life.

"Here I am," Genevieve said cheerfully.

"He didn't show," Eileen said.

"No."

Eileen hesitated. She was very slim, and had classic features, the kind that would make her just as beautiful when she turned eighty as she was now. But at the moment, her expression was strained.

"What?" Genevieve asked, suddenly worried by what she saw in her mother's eyes.

"There was a terrible accident on the FDR."

Genevieve leapt up. "When? Joe uses—"

"About an hour ago. The reports are just coming out now. One man was killed—don't panic, it wasn't Joe—and a number of other people were injured."

Genevieve sat back down and fumbled in the pocket of her black silk skirt for her cell phone. "That bastard better answer me," she muttered.

"Joe Connolly," came his voice, after three rings.

She could hear music in the background. An Irish melody. He was at O'Malley's, she thought.

"Joe, it's Genevieve."

"Hey. You still at your big soiree?" he asked.

"Yes. I thought you were coming."

"I couldn't make it past the traffic."

She let out a sigh. All right. That might be a legitimate excuse.

"Ah."

"I'm at O'Malley's."

"Yes, it sounded like O'Malley's."

He was silent. It felt like an awkward silence. Was she being too clingy? Good God, did she sound disapproving, as if she were his wife or something?

Stop, she warned herself. She had to be careful of expecting too much from him. It had seemed, after she was rescued, after Leslie had…died, that they were destined to be close. The best of friends, needing one another.

But then it was as if he had put up a wall.

She gritted her teeth. She needed him now. Cut and dried. Needed his professional help. He was a private investigator. Finding people, finding facts, finding the truth. That was what he did. And she needed to hire him. She wasn't asking any favors.

"Well, have fun," she said.

She clicked the phone closed before he could reply.

Eileen looked at her. "Don't worry, dear." Her mother sat down beside her and patted her knee. "It's all going to come out fine."

"Mom…" The word seemed a bit strange, but Genevieve loved to use it. "Mom, I'm worried about *you* now. You're a Raven, and…"

Eileen sighed. "Oh, darling, don't worry. I'm a fringe member, at best. Poor Thorne. I like being a member, I love all the reading and discussing we do, but…honestly, I'm just not worried."

"Mom, he was *murdered.*"

"Yes."

"By someone who apparently wasn't impressed with his work on Poe."

"And I've never written a book," Eileen assured her.

Genevieve sighed, rising. "But you *are* a Raven."

"Along with many other things."

"Can't help it. I'm worried about you. Henry is driving you home, right?"

Eileen frowned. "Yes, of course. What about you? Are you leaving, too?"

"I'm going to drop by O'Malley's."

"Oh." Eileen frowned worriedly.

"I'll be all right," Genevieve assured her. "I'm in my own car, but I know where to park. I'll let security see me out and I won't leave O'Malley's without someone to walk me to my car. Okay? I'll be safe, I promise. Hell, I think they ask your approval before they hire anyone at O'Malley's."

Eileen laughed, but there was a slight edge to it. "I do not tell them who they can and can't hire. I've simply always enjoyed the place, and I'm a friend of the owners."

"And I'm safe there," Genevieve said very softly.

Eileen still appeared worried, Gen thought. Then again, these days she was worried every time Genevieve was out of her sight.

But Genevieve had gone back to living in her own apartment. Not that she didn't adore Eileen or love the mansion. She just loved simplicity—and her independence.

It was sadly ironic that they both seemed to be frightened for each other these days, just when they had become so close.

She couldn't help worrying about Eileen in the wake of Thorne's murder, though. Eileen was a Raven, and though the police discounted the idea, it seemed to Gen that Thorne had been killed specifically because he was a Raven, not just because he was a published Poe scholar.

Admittedly, it was quite likely the book that had brought him to the killers attention, and it was true that Eileen had never written a book. She had way too many charities and women's clubs to worry about to devote much time to being a Poe fan.

Still, the connection made Genevieve uneasy, and she wanted Joe involved.

That was it, cut and dried.

Or was it so cut and dried?

Maybe she was lying to herself; maybe she wanted to see Joe for personal reasons, too. God knew there was enough about him that was easy to see. He was intelligent, funny, generous and a little bit rough around the edges. Sexy and compassionate. A hard combination to resist.

And he was in love with a dead woman.

She tried to dismiss the thought. She and Joe were just friends precisely because of what had happened. They had seen one another through the hard times and come away good friends.

Yes, she had a multitude of emotions raging within her where Joe was concerned. But what was becoming a growing fear for her mother's safety was the driving force in her desire to see him now.

She rose, kissing her mother's cheek. "I'll be at O'Malley's. I'll call when I'm leaving, and I'll call when I get home, all right?"

Eileen flushed, then nodded. "Did you enjoy the exhibit?"

Genevieve nodded. "I think we raised a lot of money. I think Leslie would have been happy." Leslie, who had been either gifted or cursed with extraordinary powers, had been an archeologist. She had loved history; she had revered it. Tonight had been planned in her honor, and they were going to use some of the funds raised this evening to respectfully reinter some of the bones Leslie had dug up on her last dig, the one that had ended up costing her life.

Genevieve dropped another quick kiss on her mother's cheek, then hurried out.

The night was a little cool, making her glad she had chosen a jacket rather than a dressier stole. Not so much because it was warmer, but because it would fit in a hell of a lot better at O'Malley's.

The attendant brought her car, and in minutes, she was taking the streets downtown. As she drove, she turned on her radio.

She was in time to catch the news, and the topic was that evening's accident on the FDR, which was still being sorted out. There were brief interview snippets with several of the survivors, and Gen sat up straighter, alarmed, at the sound of one name.

Sam Latham.

CHAPTER 2

Sam Latham.

Another Raven.

Coincidence?

How many millions of people were there in the city?

Gen frowned as the newscaster went on to talk a bit about the man that had been killed, though she was relieved to hear that his young niece had been saved by a man who had left the scene after rescuing the little girl and pulling her uncle's body from the car moments before the explosion that had destroyed it.

Joe?

How many millions of people in the city? she taunted herself.

No way.

That would be too much of a coincidence.

But Joe should have been on the FDR right around that time, on his way to the Met.

As she neared O'Malley's, she noticed a number of people on the streets and was grateful to see that the lights in the area were bright. Maybe she was more spooked by what had happened to her than she'd thought. She parked, pleased to find a spot right outside the bar.

At the door, she hesitated.

She'd been coming here what felt like all her life. It was an authentic Irish pub, and her family was authentic New World Irish. This was pretty much the first place she had come after she was rescued, and it was one of the few places where she had felt truly comfortable, one of the few places where people hadn't stared, where she hadn't felt as if she needed to describe her ordeal in detail, so that people would save their pity for the dead women and not waste it on her.

She wasn't uncomfortable about going into O'Malley's.

She *was* uncomfortable about confronting Joe.

What if he was with a woman? He might not have skipped the Met just because of traffic.

Then she would sit at the bar, have a soda and chat with the bartender. She didn't know who was on, but whoever it was, she would know him. Just as she would know a dozen of the old-timers who came here. Guys who had long since retired. Perhaps they had lost their wives, perhaps they'd never been married, but they liked to come to O'Malley's. It was comfortable. The beer was good, the food was tasty and the prices were reasonable.

No matter what was up with Joe Connolly, she would be fine.

She pushed open the door.

Joe wasn't with a date. At least, she didn't think so. He was leaning against a bar stool, shirtsleeves rolled up, tie loosened.

"Hey, Joe." She walked over to him.

Joe was a regular at the pub, too. She knew that he spent a lot of time here because he liked it. Because the beer was good, and the food was tasty and the prices were reasonable. But it was still more her place than his, she told herself. Even if he fit in just fine.

He was playing darts with Paddy O'Leary and Angus MacHenry. Regulars. Neither one of the octogenarians really drank much. She usually found them drinking soda, water or tea—hot Irish breakfast tea, always with sugar and milk.

She greeted both of them as she got closer.

The older men paused to kiss her cheek and offer her giant smiles. "Y' doin' okay?" Angus demanded.

"On top of the world," she assured him.

"Y' sure, lass?" Paddy demanded, searching out her eyes.

"I'm just fine."

She'd been saying the same thing for a year now, but with Angus and Paddy, it was all right. They asked after her every time they saw her, took her word that she was doing fine and moved on.

Joe threw his dart. It was just shy of a bull's-eye. He walked over, and also offered a hug and a kiss on the cheek. It was awkward, though. As if he were simply going through the expected motions.

They were friends, she told herself. Like she was friends with Paddy and Angus.

Except that Paddy and Angus could have been her great-uncles, while Joe was young and straight and pretty much the perfect man.

Too damned perfect.

"Aren't you supposed to be up at the museum, girl?" Paddy asked.

"I *was* at the museum," she said. "Now I'm here." She smiled to take any sting out of the words.

"Ah, a great night, eh?" Angus asked, rubbing his white-bearded chin.

"It was a very good night," she agreed. Then she hesitated. "I need to speak with Joe," she said. "I don't mean to mess up your game or anything."

"Ah, don't be silly, child," Paddy told her.

"Get on over there with the girl, Joseph Connolly," Angus said cheerfully. "Ye can knock the socks of the both of us old geezers later."

Joe arched a brow, but he didn't complain; he just reached for his jacket and said, "Certainly, gentlemen. I'm delighted to speak with Genevieve. At any time."

His words were polite, almost gallant, but then, Joe was always polite. It seemed to come naturally to him.

But he seemed distant. He indicated an empty booth, and she took a seat. He sat across from her and ordered "another beer" as soon as the waitress arrived. Gen asked for a soda and frowned. Joe had apparently had a few drafts already.

"Are you driving?" she asked him.

He shook his head. "Nope. Don't worry. I came by subway. You know me."

Do I? she wondered.

"So how was the party?" he asked her.

"Great. I actually think you would have enjoyed it."

He shrugged. "I'm sorry. I intended to come."

She nodded. "My mother wanted to see you." Oh, that was horrible. Laying a guilt trip on him when she knew how much he liked Eileen.

"How is she?"

"Fine. Not as worried as I think she should be."

He arched a brow. "Ah. The 'Poe Killing.'"

"You don't appear to be too concerned, either."

Again, he shrugged. It bothered her that he seemed so distracted. "I wish I could lose sleep over every terrible thing that happened, but I can't. We all need to keep a certain distance. It's the key to sanity and survival."

"I want you to take the case."

He drummed his fingers on the table for a moment. "Gen," he said softly, giving her his attention at last, "your mom isn't one of the key players in that organization. She doesn't write about Poe. Hell, she belongs to a zillion clubs, most of them trying to make the world a better place. I can't see her as a target." His argument was rational, and the same one Eileen had given her.

"You can't know that," Genevieve said.

He inhaled, looking off into the distance. "Gen, I'm thinking about heading out to Vegas."

She was stunned, and upset that his sudden announcement hurt her so badly. Sure, he was tall. Rugged, handsome. Frigging charming, even.

But she had led a life that didn't include a lot of wild dating, and that was by choice. If she had wanted…well, there had been plenty of willing men out there, if for no other reason than that she was rich. She had just thought that…

She shook her head. "Fine. Move to Vegas," she said with a shrug. "But take this case first."

"Gen, I'm willing to bet this murder was committed by someone who just wanted to kill Thorne—the Poe angle was just a convenient smoke screen."

"Prove it."

He looked away for a moment.

She leaned forward urgently. "Joe, did you know that Sam Latham was driving the first car that got hit in that accident on the FDR today?"

"What?" He looked at her with a frown.

"Sam Latham. He's a member of the New York Poe Society, another Raven."

"And I'll bet that at least two-thirds of the other people involved were all members of some society or other. We're social creatures. Usually," he added.

She shook her head, irritated. "Joe, the New York Poe Society is not a huge group. The local membership is pretty small. Both Thorne Bigelow and Sam Latham are…were on the board. As is my mother."

For a moment, at least, that seemed to pique his interest.

"Joe, there are only nine other board members, and two are Bigelow's family members. Jared, his son, and Mary Vincenzo, his sister-in-law. Then there are Brook Avery, Don Tracy, Nat Halloway, Lila Hawkins, Larry Levine, Lou Sayles and Barbara Hirshorn.

There were twelve in all, but Thorne is dead. And now Sam is in the hospital."

"Genevieve…it was an accident. I'm sure I don't know Poe's stories as well as the Ravens do, but since he died in the middle of the nineteenth century, I don't think any of his characters murdered anyone with a car. Somebody was probably driving recklessly, might have been drunk, might have been an asshole, but it was an accident."

"Or maybe the driver was pretending to drive recklessly, but he was really trying to hit Sam."

"No," he told her firmly. "I saw it, and it was an accident."

"You saw the whole thing?"

He hesitated. "I saw a lot of it."

"A lot of it?"

He didn't answer her at first. It was as if he hadn't even heard her. He was frowning, as if he were deep in thought.

"Joe?"

"I told you, I saw most of it. And before that…before that, I saw the guy who probably caused it. He could have hit any car on that highway. He was driving like a maniac."

"Did you get a look at him?"

"A saw a car weaving through traffic, and my instinct was to stay the hell away from it. Genevieve, I'm not a traffic cop."

He was irritated, which surprised her.

"What did the car look like?" she asked.

He shook his head, still looking irritated. "Some kind of sedan. Black, dark blue, maybe dark green."

She wasn't sure why, but she was certain he was angry with himself, and not with her.

Because he should have noted the car. He should have known the exact color, make and model. He should have gotten the license plate. He was an ex-cop, and in his own mind, he thought he should have done all those things, because the driver had ended up killing someone.

"It *was* you!" she exclaimed suddenly.

"What?"

"It was you." She knew it beyond a doubt, without need for verification. Oh, yeah. It sounded just like Joe, saving a life, then walking away. The man hated the limelight.

"I was not driving drunk!" he said indignantly.

"I'm not talking about the driver," she said.

A curtain seemed to drop over his eyes, along with a lock of his wheaten hair.

"What was me?" he asked warily.

"The missing hero."

He waved a hand in the air, his gray-green eyes as expressionless as steel.

"What are the odds? I'm not sure myself. Eight million who live in the city, how many million more when the work force is at its peak? During rush hour—"

"It was you," she said. "There were eyewitnesses, and you'll be identified eventually." She saw his hand where it lay on the table and grabbed it. He winced. She turned it over. There was a big scrape mark on his palm.

"Look, I really don't want a media frenzy. You understand that."

"Yes, I do," she said quietly. Life could be so odd. She had met Joe when he and Leslie MacIntyre had discovered the horrible pit in the subway tunnel where she had been taken after she'd been kidnapped by the monster who'd been stalking the streets of Lower Manhattan. His other victims had wound up dead. Leslie had been killed in the showdown.

Joe had been devastated.

But that day he and Genevieve had formed a certain bond. Maybe because they were both broken in a way.

Genevieve wasn't certain if she had made it through because she had been smart, because she had stroked the killer's ego or only because her instinct for survival had been desperate and strong. She had relied on herself in the awful days when she had been a prisoner, and in the aftermath she had created a block against those memories.

What had been harder to handle had been the press. Finding the right words to say at all times. Her uncle—who had raised her as his own child—had been a fierce taskmaster. She had been born to privilege, and he had taught her to be responsible. He had made her tough, had expected her to work hard and then harder.

After the rescue, she had been treated as if she were as fragile as a thin-shelled egg, though she had told the truth about her ordeal. Even so, rumors had found their way into the press that were more horrible than anything she'd been through, and for much too long she had been an object of pity. She appreciated that people could be compassionate, but she loathed being pitied, loathed the possibility that she might end up in the papers again.

She looked at Joe. "But it *was* you, on the highway, who saved that child, right?"

"Keep your voice down."

"Joe, my voice *is* down."

"I won't be able to work if this gets out. Come on, please. Don't say anything to anyone."

She lowered her head, smiling. Leave it to Joe. It was all about the work. She forced the smile to go away. "Take this case, Joe."

He groaned. "Are you blackmailing me?" he demanded.

Her smile deepened. She hadn't thought of that, but it wasn't a bad idea. "Maybe. Now, come on, I'll drive you home. It's late."

"No, but I'll see you home."

"Joe, you've had a few."

"I meant that I'll drive *with* you to your place and take a cab from there."

"I'm okay, Joe. I carry Mace now, and I can take care of myself," she said firmly.

Hmm. She was touchy, she realized. Friends saw friends home all the time.

Maybe being defensive was a good thing if he thought that he needed to look after her. She definitely didn't want *his* pity or to have him as a guardian. She was tough enough to take care of herself. She had proven it. She had survived. And she meant to keep doing so. She had thrown herself into self-defense classes, and she spent hours on a treadmill, getting fit.

Running.

As if she could outrun the past.

"I know you can take care of yourself, but I'd still like to see you to your place. And I'd like you to promise you'll keep your mouth shut about me helping out at the accident," he said firmly.

"Joe, I'll keep my mouth shut. And you can see me home," she told him gravely, "*if* you promise to take on the case."

"I don't understand why you're so afraid, Gen. Really. I simply don't believe your mother is a target."

"Joe..." She hesitated. She didn't know herself why she was so concerned. Her mother hadn't been a close friend of the dead man. Eileen and Thorne had been casual acquaintances, at best, brought together only by their membership on the board.

But she *was* scared. Bone-deep frightened. It was something that had just settled over her, and she wouldn't be comfortable until the killer was caught.

"Please. The cops aren't getting anywhere."

"Give them time."

"In time," she told him, even though she herself had been thinking earlier that the press should cut the cops some slack, "somebody else could die."

He lifted his hands, staring at her, shaking his head.

"Eileen hasn't been threatened in any way, has she?"

"No."

"Genevieve..." He lowered his head for a moment, then shook it again. "Gen, it's only been a week, which is no time at all. You've been watching too much television. A murder like Thorne Bigelow's isn't solved in a one-hour episode."

"I know that," she said sharply.

"Then..."

"Joe, this is what you do for a living. I want to hire you."

He sighed. "I'd be stepping in where people are hard at work already. I don't know that I could find out anything new."

"You don't know that. Maybe you *could* do something. Before somebody else gets killed. That's just it, Joe. Someone else could die."

It was strange, but just then Kathryn, their waitress, came by, her eyes wide. "Man, what a night for the bizarre!"

"Why? What happened?" Genevieve asked.

Joe was studying Kathryn with apprehension.

The waitress shook her head. "There's always one in every crowd, you know? Someone who just has to stick their nose in and make a tragedy worse."

"What are you talking about?" Joe asked.

"The psychic," Kathryn said.

"What psychic?" Joe demanded.

"Go look at the television," Kathryn said disgustedly. "There's a reporter talking to her right now, actually. Just turn around and you can see. It's that Robert Kinley, and he's with some so-called psychic named Lori Star, who claims that some guy named Sam Layman or Latham or something was supposed to die in the accident, and that it was the Poe Killer behind it."

"How could she know that?" Joe asked, his expression darkening.

Kathryn shrugged. "She said she just *knows* it. And she says she knows more, too."

"See?" Genevieve said.

"Oh, *please!*" Joe said.

"Joe, I'm telling you, it makes sense. That's why I'm afraid," Genevieve pressed.

"She is convincing," Kathryn admitted. "She says that in a few days, someone else will die."

"A Raven?" Genevieve breathed.

"She didn't say. Just go watch. All she said was that the Poe Killer will murder someone else."

Genevieve slipped out of the booth first, but she was quickly followed by Joe.

The woman, who was at the accident scene talking to the well-known anchor, was attractive enough. She just seemed to be slightly…rough around the edges. Her voice was clear, though, and her grammar was good. She didn't have an identifiable accent.

She also seemed to know how to play to the camera. She was direct and dramatic, without overplaying her cards. "It's true," she whispered to the camera, wide-eyed.

"Most people would say that's impossible," the anchor told her. There was slight scoffing in his voice. Nothing direct. He was too professional for that.

"It was as if I were there," the woman said. "As if I were driving."

"And you said that you felt heat and anger?"

"Yes. It was as if I were someone else, and I could feel that person's feelings."

"Were you a man or a woman?"

She shook her head. "I don't know. But as I said before, I do know this. It was the Poe Killer. And I know this, as well. He, or she, intends to kill again—soon."

"Thank you, Miss Star." The anchor turned his full attention to the cameras. "Truth or fiction? What's in store for New York? Well, first things first. The police are busy cleaning up the FDR, and it's going to be a long ride home for anyone on that highway tonight."

Another anchor picked up from the studio, and Genevieve turned to look at Joe, but he was already turning away.

"Kathryn, I'll take another beer, please," he called.

CHAPTER 3

Before he even opened his eyes, Joe winced.

His head was pounding.

What in the hell had made him drink so damned much beer? He hadn't even gone for the hard stuff, which he should have. No, he had just started inhaling the beer because of...

The accident.

It was ridiculous. He'd seen lots of accidents. He should have felt good; a little girl had been saved because of him.

But he didn't feel good.

He felt unnerved.

Because a dead man had spoken to him.

And things hadn't gotten any better after that.

A psychic. A self-proclaimed psychic solving the whole damned thing while somehow not solving anything at all.

Lori Star? Like hell. She might as well have called herself Moonbeam.

He went ahead and groaned, thinking that voicing his pain might make him feel a little better. It didn't.

Hell, no. Because he'd awakened *thinking*.

And all he could think about was the fact that a dead man had spoken to him, and then, as if that hadn't been bad enough, the news had dragged a damned psychic out of the woodwork. She knew, she just *knew*, that the driver of the car had been after Sam Latham.

No, they hadn't dragged her out of anywhere. She'd come forward, claiming to be eager to help the police.

She couldn't identify the car, of course. Because it was as if she had been the one driving it. She had been in his would-be head as he—or she—went after Sam Latham's car. And then she'd finished up with the dramatic revelation someone else would be murdered within days.

Later newscasts had delved into the truth about the woman, but too late for him. Genevieve had looked at him with her huge blue imploring eyes. And he'd known right then that he was on the case.

Though he dreaded it. *Dreaded it.* And he didn't know why, other than that it had something to do with that freakin' psychic.

It had turned out that Lori Star was an aspiring actress, as well as a supposed psychic. No wonder she'd been so good in front of the camera. But there would be those out there convinced that it was no act, that she was right, that the accident had been no accident.

Even if she *was* right—and he sure as hell didn't see how she could be—he was sure that all she had done was look at a few facts and take a lucky guess. She was definitely not a psychic. She just wanted her fifteen minutes of television fame.

And he was so angry because…

Because he had known Leslie. And he hadn't believed in her at first, when she claimed to talk to the dead. But she had been legit.

And this girl sure as hell wasn't.

He opened his eyes. He wasn't at home, but he already knew that. He was at Genevieve's. She hadn't let him take a cab; she'd insisted he stay on her couch. Lacking both the will and the physical coordination to find a cab willing to go to Brooklyn at that hour, he had shrugged and agreed. And fallen asleep. Or passed out. One or the other.

He'd been doing all right last night, considering what he'd gone through with Leslie and her ability to commune with the dead, until that damned psychic had shown up on television. And then he'd started calling for the beers hard and fast.

Now, of course, he was ashamed of himself. Only cowards drank because they'd been spooked. And what a fool he'd been, besides. As far as talking to a dead man went, there was surely a logical explanation for what had happened. One, maybe the EMT had simply been wrong and Brookfield hadn't died on impact. Or maybe, as Freud might have suggested, Joe had created the man's voice as a tool to tell him to look for survivors in the car. There. That made sense—so long as he didn't think about the fact that his inner voice had known the girl's name.

And the fact that Lori Star was an annoying fraud seeking the spotlight. Well, hell, that made sense, too. She was just trying to get work.

So here he was, having had way too much to drink, sleeping on Gen's sofa. It was a nice one, too. Antique, but restuffed and reupholstered. She loved things that were old and had a story. She and Leslie would have been great friends.

The thought made him wince and shut his eyes.

When he opened his eyes again, his face lined with tension, she was there.

Gen, not Leslie.

Thank God he was seeing the living, at least.

That caused a moment's guilt to trickle down his spine. *Leslie…I would love to see you. Your face…*

But that wasn't really true. He didn't want to see ghosts.

No problem. This was Gen in front of him, and she didn't seem to be judging him for his night of imbibing, even if she probably didn't understand it.

He didn't intend to explain.

Let her think that it was because he had been a witness to such an awful accident, or because he could have died when the car blew up.

"Good morning," she said gravely, handing him a glass and a couple of aspirin.

He looked at her, arching a brow.

"Trust me," she said. "They work for a hangover." She shrugged. "And no, I don't spend my life fighting hangovers. A lot of people thought I'd wind up on drugs or alcohol after the kidnapping, and this was a tip my doctor gave me."

"Thanks," he said briefly, swallowing the pills with the glass of water she'd provided.

He didn't really want to look at Gen. He felt too much like the dregs of humanity to want to face her.

There wasn't anything not to like about her, of course. Genetics had made her beautiful—Eileen, at forty-plus could still turn heads. Gen had the same perfect features, perfect skin and more-than-perfect build. She had rich auburn hair that looked more lustrous than silk and more wicked than sin. And her eyes...

Just saying they were blue didn't do them justice. They were the blue of the infinite sky, the blue of the deepest sea. Blue that could hint at darkness, blue that spoke of wisdom, even though she was only twenty-odd years old.

They were eyes that had seen a lot. The child of privilege, she had wanted to help those who hadn't been born with silver spoons in their mouths. She hadn't jetted around the globe, hobnobbing with the rich and useless. She had gone to school, gotten a degree and gone into social work.

She had survived for weeks in the underground lair of a psychotic killer.

She was strong. She was...

She was alive because Leslie had taken the bullet meant for her.

He pushed that thought from his mind. Genevieve sure as hell hadn't wanted that to happen, and he knew it. And Leslie had been gone nearly a year now. He liked to think that she was back with Matt, at last, but he didn't really believe it. He could have sworn that he had once seen them together on a little rise in the cemetery where they were both buried.

Again, Freud would have helped him out.

He had seen them there because he *wanted* to see them there.

"You should feel better soon," Gen told him, breaking into his morose thoughts.

Better than he deserved, she might have said.

But of course, she didn't.

He leaned back, studying her. She was already up and showered, smelling both fresh and subtly exotic, rich tendrils of her amazing hair curling over the casual black sweater she was wearing over jeans. He noticed her hands—delicate, refined, manicured, but not fussily so; she kept her nails filed and polished, but at a reasonable length. And she wasn't encrusted with jewels; she wore a simple claddagh ring on her left middle finger, gold studs in her ears and a plain cross around her neck.

She could easily have covered herself in furs and diamonds. Instead, she didn't even buy designer sunglasses; he knew because she had laughingly told him once that she seemed to lose a pair a week, so it made sense to buy them off the street vendors.

And in fact, she knew the streets.

Once upon a time she hadn't been regularly recognized. Despite her family's wealth, she'd kept far from the public eye and worked for a pittance helping to get prostitutes off the streets.

What the hell was not to like about her? he asked himself silently, wondering why the question left him feeling so irritable.

"I'm all right," he said gruffly.

She grinned, looking away. "Right. Real men don't get loaded on too much beer."

He groaned aloud and started to rise.

"Hey, I'm sorry," she said quickly. "Look, I know that what you saw must have been really terrible. I can't even imagine," she assured him.

Couldn't she? he wondered.

Dead was dead.

Did it matter if death came with gallons of blood, mangled steel and mangled flesh? Or a neat little bullet hole that left a person looking as if she were at peace, merely sleeping.

She had seen enough, he thought.

And she had somehow risen above it all.

He felt even more like a lout, if that were possible.

"You have every right," he agreed.

"That woman was a jerk," she said. "Lori *Star?* I doubt it. I don't know where she was getting her information, but I'm sure she's not in touch with helpful spirits or anything like that."

The way Genevieve looked at him, he knew that she was thinking about Leslie, too. She had known that her kidnapper had been determined to kill Leslie; she'd been at the top of his list.

Because Leslie had known things. She had seen things. He wasn't certain that *psychic* was the word to describe her, but whatever she'd been, she'd been for real.

He waved a hand in the air. "Hey, I was a horse's ass last night, and it was inexcusable," he said.

"No, once you weren't so angry, you were kind of cute."

Kind of cute? Great. Just what he'd always wanted to be. A kind-of-cute drunk.

"Well, thanks for your forgiveness. And your couch."

"Think nothing of it."

"I need to get going."

"Joe, there's a meeting tonight," she informed him, her eyes somber.

"A meeting?" Heaven help him, did she think he needed AA?

"Of the—the Ravens."

He looked at her quizzically. "On Saturday night? Date night?" His tone was mocking; he was stalling her, he knew. "Must be a wild bunch," he said.

"Joe, we're going."

"No."

"Joe, you promised last night that—"

He lifted a hand. Damn, she was persistent.

"I said I'd take the case," he told her. "And I'll go to the meeting. But *you* aren't going."

"Of course I am!" she said indignantly.

"No."

"Yes."

"Genevieve—"

"My mother is going to be there, Joe. There's no way I'm not going to be there, too."

He fell silent. What the hell was the matter with these people? If they all believed that Thorne Bigelow had been killed because he was a Raven, wouldn't anyone sane think that perhaps they shouldn't meet until the killer had been apprehended?

"It's just stupid for them to be meeting," he snapped.

"Stupid or not, it's happening," Genevieve said. "Besides, *you're* the one who said that the whole Poe thing is a smoke screen."

"I said it *could* be a smoke screen."

"That…woman said that another Raven would be dead in a matter of days."

"Gen…" He winced, lowering his head. He wasn't sure if he was feeling the temple-pounding headache of a killer hangover, or a sense of mixed anger and dread. Gen was surely the most stubborn human being he'd ever met. She was like pit bull on behalf of the underdog or any cause she believed in. She rushed in where the sane wouldn't go.

But he wasn't angry with her, only upset that people liked to play so casually with the fears of others by claiming to know the future.

He lifted his chin, eyes on fire, and pointed a finger at her. "I said I'd take the case, and I will. But you'll listen to me."

"I always listen to you, Joe," she said softly. That unnerved him.

Oh, yeah, she listened, in a perfect case of point noted—and rejected.

"Joe, honestly, I have to go tonight."

"And you think the Ravens are just going to discuss some favorite masterpiece by Poe?"

She shrugged. "I'm sure they'll talk about the murder."

"We're not members. Are you sure they'll let us in?"

"Members are always free to bring guests. It's simply a matter of paying for their meals. And can you imagine anyone trying to tell my mother that she's not welcome to bring her daughter and a friend?"

Gen had a point. Eileen had the power to open a lot of doors.

He stood up. The world didn't rock. A shower would fix him, he decided.

"All right, I'm going home, but I'll be back in time to go to the meeting with you. And you'll stay here until I come back for you."

"Joe…" She said his name in a soft whisper, accompanied by a weary sigh. "I am not a hothouse flower. I've been taking care of myself in the city for some time now. I do not intend to stay cooped up in my apartment all day."

He arched a brow. "It's a really nice apartment."

She flushed. It *was* a nice apartment. She lived here because of Eileen; the building was supposed to have the best security system in the city.

"Joe—"

"Give it a rest, Gen. I'll be back in a couple of hours. Depending on traffic," he added dryly, wondering how long it would take to reclaim his car at the impound lot.

"Oh?"

"Yeah. If we're going to this meeting, let's do a little Poe research first, huh?"

She stared back at him, a slow smile curving her lips, a light entering her eyes.

Damn, she was a beautiful woman.

"Oh, Joe, that's great!"

She leapt up and threw her arms around him. Her scent was intoxicating, and the feel of her warm body as she crushed herself against him was like a taste of heaven.

He unwound her arms and stepped back. "You, uh, you stay here till I get back, promise?"

She looked at him with a frown.

"Just this morning, Gen, please? Until I get a handle on this."

"I'm not a Raven. It's my mom we're worried about, remember?"

"Gen?"

"Yes, fine."

He started out.

"Joe? You don't have your car," she reminded him. "You can take mine. It's in the garage."

He was certain that the garage fee in this building was probably more than most Americans paid for an apartment. But he couldn't take her car. It was time to rescue his own.

"I'll just grab a cab for now."

"I can call you a car—"

"And I can run out to the street and snag a cab. I'll be back soon," he promised.

Genevieve didn't mind spending a few hours in the apartment. In fact, she loved the apartment and liked killing time there. What she *did* mind was being told that she needed to stay somewhere, anywhere, even though she knew that she should be grateful she had friends who cared.

At least he intended to involve her in the investigation, although he definitely wasn't happy about how things had played out last night. He was never happy if he wasn't in control. Not so much of others, but he was the kind of man who wanted to be in control of himself at all times, and getting drunk was anything but.

Restlessly, she paced the room. The morning would go slowly. She was sure of it.

She put a call through to her mother, just to say hello and tell her that she and Joe would be taking her to the meeting that night.

"I'm afraid it won't be much of a meeting," Eileen warned. "All they'll do is talk about poor Thorne." She hesitated at the other end of the line. "I suppose a lot of them are frightened, after what that psychic said."

"But you're not," Genevieve chided.

"Of course not." There was another slight silence, then a gasp. "Oh, Genevieve! Perhaps you shouldn't come."

"Mother, stop."

"But, darling, after all you've been through, do you really want to be around a bunch of people talking about murder?"

"After all I've been through, I take great delight in going wherever I choose to go."

"But—"

"We'll pick you up at six-thirty," Genevieve said.

"Genevieve, I can get there by myself."

"We'll pick you up at six-thirty," Gen repeated.

"At least you'll be with Joe," Eileen said.

"Right. At least I'll be with Joe," Genevieve agreed, though she was more than a little irritated by her mother's words. Even her own mother felt she needed protection.

Genevieve rang off and wandered over to her desk, where she brought the front page of the paper up on her computer, curious to see if anything new had been written about Thorne's murder.

The headline and the main story were on the accident that had taken place on the FDR. She read the story, then clicked a link and watched the video that had been taken by a chance onlooker. Unfortunately, nothing in the story or the video told her anything that Joe hadn't.

Genevieve drummed her fingers on the desk. Sam Latham had been in that accident.

And so had Joe.

She hesitated, then picked up the phone again. This time she called St. Vincent's.

Sam was in a regular room and able to see visitors.

Again she hesitated. Then she glanced at the clock. She could get to St. Vincent's and back in plenty of time. She wouldn't take her own car. She would have Tim, the morning security guard, call for car service, and the driver could just wait for her while she was at the hospital. She could be back in no time.

Even as she made the arrangements, she felt guilty.

She told herself that she didn't owe anyone anything, that she was a free woman who could come and go as she pleased. Even so, she felt guilty.

After all, she'd promised.

But it was broad daylight, and she needed to see Sam Latham.

But she had *promised*.

As her mind warred with itself, the phone rang. She was going to let the machine get it, but she heard Joe's voice and picked up.

"Hey."

"Hey," he returned. "Listen, I forgot I had an appointment. I'll be a few hours longer. Is that okay with you?"

"I'm sure I can fill the time somehow," she told him.

"Okay. Let's say I'll be back around two or two-thirty."

"Perfect," she told him.

Okay, so she still felt guilty. But, really, the promise had been made during the last conversation, when he wasn't going to be gone nearly so long. That had to make it null and void. She had said that she would find a way to fill the time, and she would.

She left her apartment, making sure to lock up, and hurried to the elevator.

If he'd been blindfolded, he would have known where he was.

No matter how much antiseptic was used, no matter what kind of air filtration was in place, a morgue smelled like a morgue.

Even in the entry rooms.

Joe was grateful to be in good standing with the police. He didn't even need to show his credentials when he arrived; Judy, at the desk, knew him well.

"Hey, gorgeous," he said.

"Hey, handsome."

"You're too kind."

She was a big woman, round and rosy-cheeked, fiftysomething and always pleasant. She was the perfect person to meet the public in such a place.

"Hey," she said, laughing. "The living always look handsome to me."

"Ah, shucks, be careful or all these compliments will go to my head."

"Better be careful—your head could swell up like a balloon if I really got going," she teased. "But you're not here to flirt."

"No. Judy, 'fraid not. I need to know who was on the Thorne Bigelow autopsy."

"Oh, that was Frankie."

Not many people could have used such a casual reference.

Frankie was Dr. Francis Arbitter, one of the most renowned members of the medical examiner's office. He was a down-to-earth guy, but his expertise had earned him a reverence over the years that made most people speak of him with awe.

"Is he available?"

"I'm sure he'll see you."

A phone call sent him through the double doors and down the hallway to autopsy room number four.

Francis Arbitter was alone. There was a corpse on a Gurney, but a sheet covered the torso and limbs. There was a huge gash on the head of the middle-aged, bearded man who lay there, but there was no sign of blood. The body had been washed for the exam that was about to take place.

Frank was at his desk, munching on what appeared to be a ham and cheese on rye. "Joe!" he called with a smile, and he rose. He was a tall, well-muscled man who looked like he should have been playing fullback instead of solving mysteries at a morgue. But his tousled, thinning hair and Coke-bottle glasses gave him a little bit of the mad-scientist look that was more befitting to his chosen calling.

"Sit, sit," he said, drawing up a chair from behind one of the other clinically clean desks in the room.

Joe took a seat. He'd been in plenty of morgues, but he never became as accustomed to working with the dead as Frank, who got right to the point.

"If you just wanted to shoot the breeze, you'd have called to meet for a beer somewhere. So what's up? I'm guessing it's the Thorne Bigelow murder."

"Good deduction," Joe said.

"Well, speaking as Dr. Watson here, I'd have to say I learned something from Holmes," Frank said shrewdly. "You've worked for Eileen Brideswell before. She knew Thorne, so I assume she intends to use her resources to help the police find the murderer. After all, she has a lot at stake."

Joe decided not to correct him and explain that he wasn't working for Eileen but had been pretty much forced to take the case by Genevieve. He wasn't surprised that Frank had made the assumption that his appearance had to do with the case, but he *was* surprised that Frank seemed to think that Eileen had a lot at stake.

He nodded, watching Frank. "Yes, I'm here about Bigelow."

"His son picked up the body the other day. Personally. What with the Bigelow money, he certainly didn't have to do it, but the kid came in here crying like a baby. Well, hell, he's not a kid, really. He's got to be about thirty."

"I guess you never get so old that you don't feel the loss of a parent."

"No." Frank shrugged. "I talked to him. He's on the warpath himself, wants to know who killed his father, and why."

Joe stared at Frank, and Frank grinned and shrugged.

"Okay, you and I both know that the Bigelow money and power drew lots of enemies. But, hey, I'm not a cop. I turn over my findings, and the cops take it from there."

"And what did you find?"

"That the man's love for a good glass of wine did him in."

"So his wine was definitely poisoned?"

"Definitely. He hadn't eaten in hours. From the timing, I got the impression he was probably about to go out for dinner. That it was the aperitif before the meal."

"What was it?"

"Rosencraft 1858. A very rare burgundy," Frank said.

Joe almost smiled. "I meant the poison."

"Arsenic."

"I thought arsenic poisoners usually dosed their victims more slowly?"

"Arsenic poisoning was popular in the past. Centuries ago.

People got sick, and eventually they died. But a large dose is just as effective—and quicker."

"Was there anything else? Any sign of a struggle? Bruises, gashes, defensive wounds?"

"Not a thing," Frank told him.

Joe was silent. Frank shrugged. "'Quoth the raven—die.'"

"There's nothing about poisoning in 'The Raven,' is there?"

"No, but there is in both 'The Black Cat' and 'The Cask of Amontillado.'"

"I do the autopsy, Joe. That's it. After that, I let the cops do their work."

"Who caught the case?" Joe asked.

"Raif Green and Thomas Dooley. They're both good guys. Neither one is green. They've been working murders together for almost ten years."

"Yeah, I know them both," Joe said. He knew them well, and he liked them both. That was a relief. Neither was the type of hot-head to get antsy because a P.I. was on the case. They were both workhorses who had come up through the ranks, seen everything, grown weary and kept at it anyway. Good cops, they were con-strained by the department's budget and tended to be pleased when someone like him could throw some private citizen's funds at a case.

"There's a break for you," Frank said.

"Yeah, thanks, I'll give Raif a call. I know him best," Joe said as he rose. "We'll have to grab a beer soon, Frank. I don't want to keep you from your work now, though."

"Don't worry. Old Hank isn't going to get any deader," Frank told him.

Joe glanced over at the body on the Gurney. If it weren't for the gash, "Old Hank" could have been sleeping.

"A fall?" he asked skeptically.

"Oh, yeah. You bet. He *fell* right into his buddy's broken-off whiskey bottle."

"Sad," Joe said.

"It's always sad," Frank said. "That's the thing—death is sad. Except..."

Curiously, Joe turned back to him. "Except?"

Frank shrugged. "Every once in a while, I get someone in here who was dying of cancer or something. I cut them open, and it's horrifying what disease does to them on the inside. But on the outside, hell, sometimes it's as if they're actually smiling. Like death was a release from god-awful pain." He shrugged. "You get used to it. Then again—hell, you should know this—you *never* get used to it. And if you did, you'd suck at your job."

"Dr. Arbitter?"

A young woman was standing in the open door.

"Connie?" Frank said.

"They need you in reception."

"Be right back," Frank told Joe.

Joe started to protest. He needed to get going. But Frank had already gone to see to whatever business had summoned him away.

Joe looked over at the body, and suddenly the corpse's head turned, and the grizzled old man opened his eyes. *Hey, you. Yeah, you, buddy. You can see me, and you can hear me. You tell Vinny I said* fuck *you! You tell him he's going to get his. He can get that crack-freak friend of his to pay his bail, but he's going to go down out on the streets. You tell him. He ain't going to have a moment's peace. You tell him, you hear me? Damn you, you hear me?*

Joe felt frozen, staring at the corpse.

This was bullshit.

It was all in his mind.

Hell, he must have had even more to drink last night than he'd thought.

The door behind him swung open again. He spun around. Frank had returned, muttering. "With all today's technology, these clerks still can't spell. Who the hell mistakes the word *breast* for *beast?*"

Joe looked back at the body.

It was just a corpse again.

Old Hank couldn't get any deader.

"Joe? You all right?" Frank asked. "Hell, man, you're as white as if you'd seen a ghost."

Joe forced a laugh. "Like you said, Frank. Old Hank can't get any deader. I take it the cops have whoever did this to him?"

"Dead to rights. A low-life drug dealer. Not that Hank was your model citizen. He bought it during a barroom fight with a guy named Vincent Cenzo."

He'd just had to ask, Joe thought.

"So, Joe. I'm sorry, where were we?" Frank asked.

"Finished," Joe said, offering his hand.

"Beers are on me," Frank said as they shook.

"Sounds good. See you soon."

"You bet. You need anything else, don't hesitate to call."

Call. Yup. Next time, he would just call.

"See you, Frank. Thanks."

He felt like a swimmer who had seen a shark and needed to stay calm. He tried like hell not to go running out of the autopsy room.

He managed to push his way through the doors like a normal person, then walked quickly down the hall. He even managed a goodbye and thanks for Judy at the desk.

Then he burst out into the light of day and joined the throng of people rushing around in the Saturday afternoon sunshine.

He was almost running...

And then he stopped.

Because there was no way for a man to run away from his own mind.

★ ★ ★

What a beautiful day.

He walked and walked, wishing he had a hat to tip to passersby. It was nearly summer, but the usual heat and humidity weren't plaguing the city today. No rain clouds marred the heavens. No unhealthy miasma hung around the buildings, and a pleasant breeze swept through the giant forests of concrete and steel. It was simply a perfect day.

He visited St. Mark's Square, where he paused, thinking that politicians, stars, geniuses, men of letters, heroes, patriots and enemies of the state had once walked this way. He closed his eyes and imagined a long-ago city.

What a beautiful, beautiful day. It was just good to be out. To love New York. To love the world.

To bask in pleasure.

Someone walked by him with a boom box blaring, gold chains making a strange clanking sound against the plastic casing. The man's arm sported a tattoo.

Ah, yes. The gangs of New York. Ever present. Then and now.

A little Yorkie passed him, yapping shrilly. He was tempted to kick the tiny beast into the traffic. Instead, he paused and said something complimentary to the dog's pudgy owner, who blushed and chatted. He moved on quickly then, afraid she was going to try to give him her phone number.

He passed a police officer strolling his beat, and nodded a greeting. The officer nodded and smiled in return.

As he walked at a leisurely pace, he passed an electronics store. A giant plasma screen took up most of the display window. The news was on, so he paused to watch.

His heart was filled with glee. He longed to laugh aloud. Instead, he watched gravely as other people grouped around him on the sidewalk.

The entire city was still pondering the death of Thorne Bigelow. Philanthropist.

Icon.

Brilliant man of letters.

Like hell!

Bastard. Braggart. Glutton. Idiot.

"What a horrible way to die," someone said.

"It's that book he wrote. He was killed because someone didn't like his book on Poe," a young woman said solemnly.

Her boyfriend slipped an arm around her shoulders. She was hugging something that looked like a mop. Maltese, Pekinese, some kind of "ese." What was it with people and their obnoxious little dogs ruining his Saturday morning?

"It could have been anything," the boyfriend said. "I mean, the man *was* a billionaire."

The man was a bag of hot air. Gas. He was one big fart.

"Tragic," he said aloud.

The boyfriend was shaking his head. "Did you know that one of the guys who got hurt in that pileup on the FDR was some friend of Bigelow's?"

The girl shivered. "And that psychic said somebody else is going to die."

"Think psychics really know the future?" he asked, turning to the couple.

"Oh, yes," the girl said, and turned to look at him. Maybe a little too closely. "There are real psychics out there. People who see things. Who knows if that woman, that Lori Star, is really one of them, though. I mean, I never heard of her. She hasn't written a book or anything. Anyway, it's all so tragic, don't you think?"

"Tragic," he repeated, shaking his head.

And he moved on somberly, his head lowered.

His grin wide.

Yes, it was a beautiful day.

His grin suddenly faded.

It was bull. There weren't really people out there who could see the future, who had second sight, who could share experiences as if they were in another person's body and just...*know* things.

Were there?

He kept walking, pensive.

Maybe it wasn't such a beautiful day after all.

CHAPTER 4

"Thanks, guys, for taking the time to meet me," Joe said.

They were at Gino's Salads and Sandwiches, near One Police Plaza.

Times had changed. Once upon a time, Raif Green would have been wolfing down a hamburger anywhere that served up hot, greasy food. Tom Dooley would have chosen corned beef on rye.

But, as he had discovered when he called Raif, Tom Dooley had suffered a heart attack two years ago. No doughnuts for these cops anymore.

Raif had opted for the Greek salad, while Tom was nibbling his turkey, low-fat Swiss, lettuce and tomato on wheat, as if by taking small bites he could make the sandwich last longer.

Thomas Dooley was a big man. He'd lost weight since Joe had seen him last, but he was still six-four and just shy of three-hundred pounds. Raif wasn't really all that small or thin—five-ten and one-eighty, maybe—but next to Tom Dooley, he looked like a midget.

Both men were in their early forties.

Both still had their hair.

They were like Laurel and Hardy in size and appearance, but there was nothing comedic about the work they did.

"Hey," Raif said. "It's Saturday, we should be off, but here we are—

working. You know, this may be a democracy but Joe Schmo in the streets gets knocked off and it's nine to five. Bigelow…well, he was a big cheese. No one is off until we solve this one." He cast Joe a crooked grin. "At least we can eat light and fit, with you picking up the tab. There's the problem with heart-healthy. It's expensive."

"I'd kill for a fry," Tom said. His round face was deceptive. He looked so amiable, but in an interrogation room, he was about as amiable as King Kong on steroids.

"So, one day, order some fries," Raif said.

Tom shook his head. "My wife would kill me."

"Is your wife here, Tom?" Raif demanded.

"I swear, that woman should be the detective. She's got surveil-lance everywhere," Raif said, shaking his head. "Hell. She's got eyes in the flipping lettuce, I swear."

"We're getting old. Talking about food," Raif said to Joe.

"The way of the world," Joe assured him. "Your wife just wants you alive, Tom."

"Yeah," he said sheepishly. "Man, this is rabbit food, though."

Joe nodded sympathetically, and asked, "What's your take on the Poe angle? Motive or smoke screen?"

"So far?" Raif wiped his mouth with his paper napkin. "So far, we don't have a hell of a lot to go on. What you saw in the papers is pretty much what we have. I wanted to conceal the note, but there was a leak—not a big surprise, there were uniforms all over the place before we got there. The crime-scene guys had a night-mare, trying to figure it all out. First the son gets there and gets hysterical, then the sister-in-law…and the butler, to boot. Everyone decides they're going to save him. People calling 9-1-1, med techs all over. It looked like he'd had a heart attack or something."

"What's the deal on the butler?" Joe asked.

Raif shook his head. "You think it might be as easy as *the butler did it?* I don't think so. He's a skinny old English guy, and he was totally shaken. His name is Albee Bennet. He was in tears when we interviewed him, and he didn't know a thing. He has his own little apartment in the building, and he was there napping when it happened. Never saw or heard anything."

"You believe him?" Joe asked.

"Yes," Raif said.

"I believed him, too. You know, it's that sixth sense you get about people after doing this job for so many years," Tom said.

"So, he was there. And the son?"

"First one on the scene. He'd been out. But he lived there— came and went all the time," Tom told him.

"What's your take on him?" Joe asked.

Raif shrugged. "His tears seemed real, too. Young guy, early thirties. We asked around, and it seems he and his dad didn't have any major problems."

"The sister-in-law?" Joe asked.

"Mary Vincenzo. His late-brother's wife," Tom said.

"You'll interview her, I'm sure," Raif said dryly. "But I don't see it. She's real thin, one of those nervous types. Wealthy in her own right. The brother left her part of the family fortune already."

"You should have seen them wiping their lips when they heard it was poison," Tom commented, shaking his head.

The concept of poison didn't in the least deter him from his enjoyment of his sandwich.

"Sorry, I just want to hear it beginning-to-end. The med techs were there? How soon did they discover that it was a crime scene, if everyone thought it was a heart attack?" Joe asked.

"Pretty darned quick, thanks to one of the bright boys with fire rescue," Raif informed him. "He stopped them from moving the body when he noticed it was cold. But, actually, they were right to think it. I mean, say your grandmother or someone in your house dies in the middle of the night, and you call 9-1-1. They're taught to try mouth-to-mouth. Even if you're sure they're dead. Anyway, the body is cold, and this kid is bright. And because it's an unexplained death, he tells the head guy on his team that they need the cops. The cops come, and then the medical examiner's office gets out there. Doc Arbitter is on, and he figures out it could be poison in the wine. So at least there's photo documentation of just about everything. Everything *after* the family and EMTs have moved everything to hell and gone."

"So was the note found?"

"Right on his desk. Just one piece of paper among a bunch of others—no one even noticed it at first. Looked like—and forensics proved—it had come right out of his own printer. Computer was dusted, of course, and there weren't any prints, so it had been wiped down," Tom told him.

"What was the timing? And why did the sister-in-law show up?" Joe asked.

"The son showed up first to tell his dad it was time to go. And he'd already been to get his aunt. They were all going to some dinner party. The butler didn't come out until after the son and sister-in-law arrived," Tom explained.

Raif continued the report. "When the son walked in, it looked like the old man had been drinking his special vintage wine, and then just keeled over."

"There was just one wineglass?" Joe asked.

"Just one," Raif said.

Tom waved what was left of his turkey-and-Swiss in the air. "In a nutshell, we think Bigelow was alone. He was due at that dinner party at eight, and he'd been dead about an hour when he was found. He had a visitor earlier, though. He last spoke to the butler around five and told him someone was coming before closing himself into his office. But whoever it was must have come and gone, because Bigelow was drinking alone."

Joe shrugged. "Either that, or the killer took his wineglass with him. Anyone check to see if a glass was missing?"

Tom flushed and looked at Raif.

"I don't know," Raif admitted, reddening.

"No one saw anyone come or go?" Joe asked.

"No one. The chauffeur was waiting for them out in the garage, sleeping behind the wheel, by his own admission," Tom said. "And, yes, we canvassed the neighborhood. No one saw anything."

"What about the—the other Ravens?" Joe asked.

"We've spoken with them. They all claim to have alibis, but we have a lot of legwork to do, checking them all out."

"Anything you can tell me about the family?" Joe asked.

Raif looked at Tom.

"Come on, you know I'm licensed, and I've been hired by an interested party," Joe said.

"Yeah, okay. We've got some files on the rest of the board. I'll fax 'em to you," Raif said. "I'd just as soon you not mention it around, though. Some guys on the force aren't all that fond of outside interest, you know?"

"I do know. And thanks," Joe told him. He hesitated, then asked. "What do you think about that woman on TV, the one who claimed to be psychic?"

Raif and Tom exchanged glances again.

Joe groaned softly. "Oh, Lord. You two believed her?"

Tom laughed softly.

Raif's lips twitched.

"What?" Joe demanded.

"Jerry Grant in vice has picked her up at least three times," he said.

"For fraud?" Joe suggested.

"Hell, no," Raif said. "Vice doesn't handle fraud."

"He picked her up for prostitution," Tom said. "I noticed that last night she was going by Lori Star. When the cops picked her up, she was going by Candy Cane."

"She did say she was an actress," Joe said dryly.

"Yeah. She's put on a few innocent acts at the station, all right," Raif said. "Still, we're going to talk to her."

"When?"

"Now, as soon as Tom Turkey here finishes his sandwich," Raif said.

"Mind if I tag along?" Joe asked.

"What the hell, we're on your dime today," Tom said.

Raif was staring at him. "You don't think it would bother you?" he asked. "Your cousin's fiancée…that Leslie MacIntyre. She was supposed to be the real deal."

"I should definitely go. I'll know the real thing when I see it."

Sam Latham was an all-around good guy. Thirty-six years old, married and the father of two young children. He worked in the editorial department of one of the major publishers, and he simply loved books, especially mysteries, and joined scholars everywhere in considering Edgar Allan Poe to be the father of the detective novel. Genevieve had met him through her mother, and though she couldn't say she knew him well, she had always liked him, his wife and their kids, Vickie, eleven, and Geoffrey, fourteen.

When she arrived at the hospital, she expected something more than what she found: a quiet hallway; Dorothy, Sam's wife, in the room with him; and a woman who introduced herself as his mother, Stella, returning with coffee from the hospital cafeteria.

No cops in the hallways, no one on guard.

Because apparently no one believed that Sam had been the intended victim of a killer. Despite the so-called psychic.

"Genevieve!" Sam said with pleasure, seeing her at the door. He had a cut below one eye, and the bruising that accompanied it, but other than that he appeared to be fine, though the sheets could have been covering other injuries.

"Sam, Dorothy…Mrs. Latham," she said after introductions were made.

His mother was probably around sixty-five. She had stunning silver hair styled to set off her tiny features. She immediately looked apologetic. "I'm so sorry. I didn't know Sam was expecting visitors. I could have gotten you a coffee."

"It's all right, but thank you so much for the thought," Genevieve said. She'd stopped downstairs for a flower arrangement, which Dorothy came forward to accept.

"How are you?" Genevieve asked Sam, as Dorothy added the flowers to the others filling the room.

"Fine," Sam said.

"He's such a liar," Dorothy said, distressed. "He goes into surgery tomorrow. For his leg."

"Oh, Sam, I'm so sorry," Genevieve said.

His mother cleared her throat. "Are you going to be here for a while, dear? I thought Dorothy and I might go grab something to eat."

"They won't leave me alone," Sam said with a groan.

Genevieve glanced quickly at Dorothy, who tried to appear impassive. Apparently Dorothy was more worried than the police were. Maybe she'd seen the psychic on TV.

"I'll be happy to stay and chat with Sam until you return," Genevieve said.

His mother flashed her a grateful smile; Dorothy gave her a kiss on the cheek. "Sam," Dorothy asked, "will you be okay?"

"Honey, go eat. Genevieve will guard me. She has a black belt now."

Gen didn't have a black belt. But she didn't contradict him.

The other two women left, and Genevieve took the chair by the bed. She looked at the IV drip, and the various tubes to which he was attached.

"Well, other than the hardware, you do look good," she told him.

He showed her a little clicker which had been hidden in his hand. "Morphine," he said, with a dry grin.

"Wow, Sam, I'm so sorry. It must have been a horrible accident."

"Yeah. A horrible accident," he repeated.

"But it *was* an accident," she said. "Right?"

He looked at her, as if suddenly realizing she had come for more than a simple visit. "I guess," he told her. "Genevieve, I didn't see anything. I was driving along, thinking about a new manuscript we'd just paid a small fortune for, and then…"

She could have chatted a while, talked more about his kids, pretended. But Sam wasn't about to pretend, so she wouldn't, either.

"Then…bang."

"Yep. Then…that sound. That awful impact," he said, shaking his head.

She inhaled deeply. "Well…you look good," she said, trying to sound cheerful.

He shook his head. "Genevieve, you're full of bull. I look like shit. And you're a nice person, and I'm sure you'd visit me no matter what, but you're worried because of Thorne Bigelow. You think someone wants to kill all the Ravens. Including your mother."

She didn't attempt to deny it. "What do you think?" she asked him.

"I don't know what to think," he said. "A couple of people reported a car driving erratically. The cops wanted to know if I had seen it, too."

"And did you?"

"I didn't. I was driving, then…wham. I was out. The air bag saved my life—that's why the bruises. But I was knocked out. The next thing I knew, I was on a stretcher with a microphone in my face while I was being stuffed in an ambulance. And they were shooting stuff into me, and I was grateful, because I managed to break a leg, despite the air bag."

She nodded, reached for his free hand and squeezed it. "I'm so sorry, Sam."

"I'm having a tough time seeing how anyone could have planned to murder me on the highway like that. He couldn't have any idea who he might kill, and he obviously didn't succeed in killing *me,* if that was even his plan."

"That's true." She hesitated. "But what if…?"

"What if…what?" Sam pursued.

"What if he didn't care if he killed a dozen other people at the same time?" she asked.

Lori Star. Candy Cane.

She lived in a rent-controlled building in Soho. When she opened the door to their knock, she kept the chain on as she looked out. Her eyes were wide, hopeful.

"Are you with another news station?" she asked.

Raif shook his head solemnly, showing his badge. "Sorry."

"Cops," she said with annoyance.

"Yeah, cops," Tom supplied.

She stared at Joe. "But you're not a cop," she said. Her voice had changed. It had turned low and sexy. Candy Cane, not Lori Star. How did she know? he wondered. Was she really psychic? Was it his manner? Or just a wild guess?

"Mr. Connolly is a private investigator, and he's with us," Raif said.

Joe blessed the fact that he'd managed to keep a great relationship with the NYPD.

The woman still had the chain on the door. "I didn't do anything illegal," she said defensively.

"We haven't come to arrest you," Raif said.

"Then you should go away," she suggested, and started to close the door.

Joe put out hand to stop it. "Miss Star, we really need to talk to you. Just for a few minutes."

He was convinced that she didn't have any extraordinary talents—not *paranormal* talents, anyway—but he still very much wanted to talk to her.

She stared at him with wide, powder-blue eyes. Then she sighed, closed the door most of the way and undid the security chain.

"Come in," she told them resignedly.

She was a small woman, thin, but cosmetically "enhanced" in the breast department, and pretty in a hard-edged way. She wasn't exactly a high-class hooker, but it didn't look as if she'd hit bottom yet, either. She had blond hair—enhanced, too, but decently done—and small, sharp features. As she let them in, he saw that she was wearing a silk kimono, but beneath it she had on sweatpants and a Mötley Crue T-shirt.

"Sit down, I guess," she said, indicating a sofa and two chairs in the living area, which was also the dining area and was connected straight to a typical studio kitchen.

He chose one of the chairs across from where she sat on the edge of the couch. Raif took the second chair, so Tom was left to sit next to her on the couch, perching uncomfortably a few feet away. She picked up a pack of cigarettes, shook one out and lit it.

"Do you mind?" she asked. "Say no—this is my apartment, and I can smoke here if I want to."

"It's your funeral," Raif said with a shrug.

"I still like the smell of smoke," Joe told her, smiling.

She flashed him a smile in return.

"How long have you been a psychic, Miss Star?" he asked politely.

She hesitated, a strange look on her face. "I'm really an actress," she said.

Tom made a choking sound. She flashed him a cold glare. "I've been an extra in three movies now," she said.

"Oh, yeah?" Tom asked. "Did you play a hooker?"

Joe shook his head, tempted to put a bag over the man's head. Tom was too used to interrogating suspects with whom it was necessary to take a hard line.

In this case, though, a hard line wasn't what was called for.

"Miss Star, please, we need your help," he said. He had been ready to dismiss the woman's claims himself, but something about the way she had looked when he'd asked her how long she had been a psychic had given him pause.

After all, who the hell was he to doubt anyone? He'd thought a corpse had spoken to him from a Gurney at the morgue.

She hesitated, looking at him. "Honestly?" she asked. And at that moment, there was something raw and young and vulnerable about her features that got to him.

She was scared.

"Yes, honestly."

She looked around at the three of them. "This is off the record, right? You guys have to keep what I say between us."

"If you know anything about an attempted murder…" Raif began.

She shook her head. "I don't know anything about an attempted murder. Except for what I saw. In my mind."

A shadow seemed to pass over Raif's eyes. From now on, he wasn't going to believe her. Tom seemed to have withdrawn, as well.

"What did you see, in your mind's eye, and how did it all happen?" Joe said quickly, before either of the other men could say anything to shut her down.

"I was here. At home. Getting ready for the night."

Tom made a choking sound again.

Joe flashed him a frown. "Were you here alone?" he asked.

She nodded. Then the words suddenly started spilling out. "I sat down here. Right here. On the sofa, like I am now. I lit a cigarette, and I was going to watch some TV before I went to change clothes. But then…it was so weird. All of a sudden it was as if I was in a car. As if I were really there. I could see the traffic in front of me. I was someone else. And I was gunning for a car. A green Cadillac. I knew the car. I knew where it was, because I'd been following it. It was as if I was me, but at the same time I wasn't me. It was as if I was a passenger in someone else's body. Oh, God, it was awful. As if I could feel all this hatred…I—the me that wasn't me—knew not to hit the car myself, but I'm—he's—a good driver and could make people swerve and stuff. So I…he…she…I don't know which…did, and then…wham. Crash. There was metal and glass, and a word in my head.…"

She stopped speaking. She was trembling, her face ashen. Either she really deserved her shot at Hollywood, or the fear she was feeling was real.

"Miss Star?"

She looked at him, as if she had forgotten that he was there.

"And the word? What was the word?" Joe persisted gently.

"*Nevermore,*" she said.

CHAPTER 5

"I'm going to the meeting tonight," Genevieve told Sam. "No matter what's going on. I can't help it—I'm worried about my mother. About all of you."

"Because of Thorne's murder," Sam agreed.

"I know he made plenty of enemies, and the Poe angle could just be the killer's way to throw people off track, but...well, what did you think of his book?"

"I think it was a good book," Sam said. "The man could write." He looked past her for a moment, then turned back to her and asked, "I take it you saw that 'psychic' on TV?"

She nodded.

"You believe in psychics?"

"I don't know what I believe."

She heard a sound then and turned around.

Joe was there, leaning against the wall, arms crossed over his chest as he watched her. She swore silently.

"Joe, hi. Come on in," Sam said.

She rose uneasily. "You two know each other?" she said.

"We met years ago," Sam said. "Joe and Matt Connolly were cousins." He stared at her. "But I guess you knew that."

"I never knew Matt," she said.

"Oh, right," Sam said uncomfortably. "Anyway," he said, "Joe and I actually go way back."

"A long way," Joe agreed pleasantly. "So how are you doing?"

"Hanging in," Sam said. He must have noticed the way Joe looked at Genevieve—as if she had committed a sin—because he looked curiously from one to the other.

She hoped she wasn't looking guilty. She shouldn't feel guilty. She hadn't actually lied to Joe.

As if trying to diffuse the tension, Sam asked her, "So Joe is working for you, right?"

"Yes," she said, meeting Joe's eyes.

"She's an amazing woman. She hires me, but she still likes to do all the work herself," Joe said dryly.

She forced a tight smile. "I thought I'd drop by to see a friend," she told him. "You did say you'd been held up."

"So I did."

"Hey, Joe, do you know if they've questioned all the drivers, trying to figure out who hit me?" Sam asked.

Joe nodded. "Not that it did much good. Apparently, if you're a crook in this city, you find a dark sedan with mud on the license plate so no one can read the number. A lot of people noticed a dark sedan driving dangerously. Some say it was blue, others say it was forest-green, and one man is positive it was black. What do you say?"

"No idea. I'm sorry I can't be more helpful," Sam said. "Really sorry."

Joe moved farther into the room to stand by the bed. "Sam, do you think the driver might have been gunning for you?"

Sam had nice brown eyes. They were intense as he stared at Joe, then Gen. "I'm praying not. I'm praying that someone else didn't die because of me, and that a dozen people aren't laid up in a hospital like I am—because of me."

"Do you think the Poe Killer is after more members of the society?" Joe asked.

"Hell if I know," Sam said bitterly, shaking his head. "That psychic says so, huh?"

Genevieve expected Joe to say something derisive, but he didn't. He just waited for Sam to go on.

"My wife is afraid it's true, though," Sam said. "Really. Afraid... Oh, God. I'm sorry, Genevieve, I shouldn't be talking to you about fear."

There they were. Back to her ordeal once again, she thought. Why wouldn't people let it rest?

"Sam, please," she said awkwardly, avoiding Joe's eyes. She knew he was angry with her for leaving the apartment.

Too bad. He would just have to get over it.

"There are many kinds of fear," she said to Sam. "And I'm afraid, too. Afraid for my mother."

"The police haven't said anything about needing to protect you, right?" Joe said to Sam.

"No. But Dorothy has decided that she wants to hire off-duty officers to guard my room," Sam said, shrugging. "I honestly don't know what I think, but God knows, I have time here to try to figure it all out. But if it's going to make Dorothy happy, I guess it's fine to bring in some security."

"That's never a bad idea," Joe said, to Genevieve's surprise. Had he changed his mind on his conviction that Bigelow's murder had nothing to do with Edgar Allan Poe and the Ravens?

Dorothy and Sam's mother returned just then. They both greeted Joe and spoke with him about hiring private security. He put through a call to a friend, and before he and Gen left the hospital, an off-duty officer was sitting in the hallway.

"I thought you were going to wait at your apartment for me," Joe said a few minutes later, as they got into his car after dismissing Gen's driver. He looked at Genevieve and saw that she was blushing slightly. Whatever she said, it would be an excuse, he knew. She obviously felt guilty. But then her chin lifted.

Guilty and defiant, he amended. Ah, yes, that was Genevieve. Then again, that defiance was part of what had saved her life.

"I *was* staying in and waiting, but then you called and said you'd be late. And I told you I'd find something to do to fill the time."

"Good one," he said.

"Hey, Joe, you're the one who said the whole Poe thing was a smoke screen."

He groaned. "Whether it is or isn't, don't you think you should be a little bit careful for a while?"

"It's my mother I'm worried about," she said. "She's the Raven, not me."

"Still…"

She gazed at him sharply. "What changed your mind?" she asked.

He was driving, but the traffic was light enough that he was able to look over at her before turning his attention to avoiding a kid on a skateboard who had just swerved into the street.

"Nothing has changed my mind," he said, knowing it was what he wanted to believe, rather than the truth. To accept the fact that he believed a two-bit hooker—*actress*—had experienced a genuine psychic vision was more than he was ready to admit.

And yet it appeared, even to him, that it might be true.

After so many years prying into the lives of others, he had a good sense for whether people were lying or not. And Candy Cane, or Lori Star or whatever her real name was, hadn't been lying.

Not only that, she was scared.

"So…" Genevieve asked, "where are we going?"

He cast a quick glance her way, a slight smile curving his lips. "I thought we should take a self-guided Poe tour. Just a pleasant walk around a few places our long-gone poet might have haunted. What do you think?"

She looked back at him, smiling quizzically herself. "You've acquired a new appreciation for the literary life and times of Edgar Allan Poe?"

"Don't be silly. I've always been an aficionado," he assured her.

Ten minutes later, he found a garage where he could park for a few hours without spending half a month's rent, and they started walking.

There was something special, almost magical, about Lower Manhattan, he thought. It had nothing to do with Wall Street and all the money that changed hands there, or even the vibrancy of the people who were always rushing around following their own agendas.

Maybe it was magical, he thought, because he had learned to see it through Leslie's eyes.

New York wasn't just Wall Street and big bucks, or the egos of celebrities and business moguls. Nor was it any longer the huddled poverty of the thousands of immigrants who had made their way here, first via Ellis Island and now via Kennedy Airport.

It was both, and it was more.

He and Genevieve walked. They toured the area around Lower Broadway, pausing at Trinity Church, looking toward the empty place where the World Trade Towers had once stood, which gave them both pause.

Finally they moved on.

"Are we actually on a *thinking* tour?" she asked him, curious and amused.

"I'm sorry. Does it feel like I'm just dragging you around aimlessly?" he asked her.

"Hey, I like to walk. Just so long as we're not walking because you don't want me going home by myself," she said.

He couldn't help but ask, "Is it so bad for someone to be worried about you?"

She looked away. "I don't want to spend my life being a burden, being someone others have to worry about all the time."

"Hardly a burden," he said gruffly.

And so they kept going.

"This has been my home my whole life," she said, "and I still love being here. I love to go into Trinity and St. Paul's. I love to go in and look at George Washington's pew, and wonder what it might have been like when we were a country fighting for its independence."

He flashed her a smile. "Yeah, cool, huh?"

And amazing.

They were near Hastings House, in fact, near the area where she had been held prisoner underground. He saw no deep-seated bitterness or fear in her eyes, and she had just told him that she had moved on, that she loved this part of town.

Was it true?

Whether it was or not, Lower Manhattan, the area around St. Mark's, and his small cottage up in the Bronx, were places where Poe had spent time when he was in New York.

"'The thousand injuries of Fortunato I had borne the best I could,'" he quoted aloud.

Genevieve arched a brow at him. "Is that word-for-word?"

"I think," he said with a shrug.

"So you know more about Poe than you've admitted?"

He offered her a sheepish grin. "When I was a kid, my folks bought a video of *The Raven*. The movie had little to do with the poem, but Vincent Price, Boris Karloff and Peter Lorre were magnificent. It was pretty silly, really. They turned the poem into a battle between magicians. But I watched it over and over, and then went on a Poe binge."

She laughed. "Maybe you should be a Raven."

They were on Nassau Street now. "I think it would have been right about here," Joe said.

Genevieve frowned. "What would have? I don't think Poe lived here."

"No, but not far away," he said, flashing Genevieve a smile. "No. I'm thinking about 'The Mystery of Marie Roget.' It was based on a real murder case that put New York City into a state of upheaval. Journalists had a field day. Politicians were shaken to the core...and Poe wrote his story. The girl who was killed lived on Nassau Street. Her name was Mary Rogers, and she'd worked at a cigar shop where Poe had almost certainly been. She was considered to be beautiful, and she was from a good family whose fortunes were in bad shape. Her mother opened a boarding house on Nassau Street. And it was from Nassau Street that she left...and never returned. The summer of 1841 was stifling. A steamboat ran across the river to New Jersey, and people went to escape the heat and the crowds. It was like going to a park to play. P. T. Barnum staged wild west shows over there, and people flocked to someplace called Sybil's Cave to drink the waters, which were considered to be restorative. Anyway, three men took the ferry over one day, several days after she disappeared, and as they were walking north along the river, heading for the pavilion at Sybil's Cave, they spotted something in the water. It was Mary Rogers. Poe turned Mary into Marie and he moved the whole thing to Paris. He had already written 'The Murders in the Rue Morgue,' and he wanted to use his Parisian detective, C. Auguste Dupin, to solve another mystery."

Genevieve was staring at him.

He shrugged. "Hey, it's common knowledge."

She laughed. "So common I didn't know it. I did see *The Raven*, though, and I loved it. And of course, I've read the poem. I've even been to his grave site in Baltimore," she admitted.

He turned and walked toward Broadway again. "Poe didn't live here when Mary Rogers was killed—he had left the city for a job in Philadelphia. But he lived here from eighteen-thirty-seven to thirty-eight, and there was a bookstore near here, owned by a Scot named William Gowans, where Poe spent a lot of time. Gowans was totally eccentric and only catered to those he considered serious readers. The shop where Mary Rogers worked was only a few blocks north, and Gowans roomed at the boarding house Mrs. Rogers kept. So they were all acquaintances, one way or another."

Genevieve cocked her head, looked at him with a slight grin tugging at her lips. "You're very serious about your Poe facts—for a man who said that that note was just a smoke screen."

"And it might be."

"Then why are we here?"

"Might as well get the feel for what's going on," he said.

He started walking faster, though he didn't realize how fast until he heard the sound of her footsteps as she tried to catch up.

"Joe?"

"Yeah?"

"There was poison in Thorne's wine. That doesn't have anything to do with 'The Mystery of Marie Roget.'"

"I know."

"Then...?"

"Right now, I'm just trying to get a feel for Poe himself, and his life and times."

"Ah."

"New York back then...the Five Points area was like a haven for thugs, drug dealers, murderers and thieves. I think the population of the city back then was about three-hundred thousand."

"Wow," Genevieve said dryly.

He laughed. "Okay, nothing by today's standards, but back then, it was huge. Just like now, people came here from all over to make a living. You know, if you can make it here, you can make it anywhere? Well, that's always been true before. So Poe came to New York with his sights on becoming financially secure and finding real respect for his talents. According to those who knew him, he was a fine literary critic—but a vicious one at times."

"The best critics are vicious at times, so they say."

Joe shrugged. He indicated the doorway to an old bar. The Dingle Room. A sign boasted that it had stood on the same street for over two hundred years, acting as a tavern for over one hundred of them.

"Think he might have lifted a beer or two here?" Genevieve asked.

"Maybe. Meanwhile, *I'm* thirsty. And hungry."

They went inside, and not only did the place appear to have been in business as a tavern for more than a hundred years, Joe wasn't sure it had been cleaned in all that time, either. But answering the question Gen had asked, there was a sign above the bar that read: *Edgar Allan Poe drank here. Imbibe and find your inner genius.*

Those words were followed by a hand-painted addendum that said: *At least, we think he drank here.*

"Just like Washington," Genevieve said.

"How?"

"He *slept* everywhere, and Poe *drank* everywhere."

Their waitress, a gum-cracking woman of about fifty, offered them a tired smile. "What'll it be?"

"What's good here?" he asked.

"Nothing," she told him honestly.

"A Coke—in a bottle—then," Joe told her. "Gen?"

She opted for the same, and then the woman smiled and told them that the home-style meatloaf and mashed potatoes were actually quite tasty, so they went ahead and ordered food.

"So…" Genevieve said, when the waitress had gone.

"So?"

"What were you doing all morning?"

"Talking to the police."

"And?"

"They don't have any answers."

"Do *they* think the Poe angle is a smoke screen?"

He tilted his head thoughtfully. "If they have any ideas right now, they're not sharing. And I think they would if they did. I know the two lead detectives on the case, and they're both solid guys, good at their jobs. The killer was careful and seemed to know how not to leave any clues he didn't want to. Maybe a professional, or maybe just someone who reads or watches television and has learned how not to leave trace evidence behind. There was no forced entry, and Bigelow apparently had a visitor earlier, so it's likely Thorne Bigelow knew his killer. But as far as the Poe connection goes, though he was killed via his beloved wine, he wasn't walled up."

"What about Sam Latham?"

He hesitated. "They're looking into the accident, as well, trying to find out exactly what happened. Lots of people apparently saw the same car I did, but no one can agree on the details of what it looked like, and no one caught the license plate. Maybe a better witness will come forward in the future."

It was inevitable that she asked him, "What about that psychic?"

And dammit, she knew him well enough to catch something in his hesitation.

"You think she *does* know something!" Genevieve exclaimed.

Luckily their meals arrived just then and saved him from having to answer.

But the minute their waitress moved on, Gen pounced on him again. "Well?"

He shook his head. "Who knows? I sure don't."

"I want to meet her."

"She *can't* know anything," he insisted.

"But I want to meet her anyway."

He glanced at his watch. It was already nearly six.

"Too late. We have to go pick up your mother and get to that New York Poe Society board meeting."

"Tomorrow, then," she told him.

He shrugged. "We can stop by and talk to her, if you like."

"Tomorrow, definitely. And you won't put me off. Promise me, Joe."

"Yes, all right, I promise. You can really be a pain in the...butt, you know."

"I work hard at it," she assured him solemnly.

"I'm not at all sure you need to make much of an effort," he said.

She shrugged, and silence fell between them.

"Hey," she said softly a little while later, and smiled a little crookedly.

"What?" He'd sounded gruff and impatient. He knew it.

"The meatloaf wasn't half bad."

He offered her a half smile in return. "Actually, I think it was more than half good."

When the check came, she reached for it, but he got there first.

"You agreed to take the case. We're talking about the case... working, so I should pick this up," she told him.

"I'll take the check," he said in a tone that brooked no interference.

"Chauvinist," she accused, but her tone was light.

"Exactly," he assured her.

"But you're on the clock."

"I'll bill you, then. But I'll still take the check."

A few minutes later, as they waited by the register for his credit card to be returned, he noticed the large wooden plaque over the doorway. It had a giant etched raven on the right side, with just a few words of Poe's immortal poem on the left.

Quoth the raven...

CHAPTER 6

Not everyone on the board of the venerable society was in attendance.

Thorne, of course, was dead.

Jared Bigelow, Thorne's son, and Mary Vincenzo, his sister-in-law, were understandably absent. Because Thorne's body had been held at the morgue, the funeral was planned for Monday, so both Jared and Mary had sent their regrets to Brook Avery, who was chairman of the board.

Sam Latham wasn't there, either. He was still in the hospital, but even if he hadn't been, he might not have been in the mood to attend.

Four missing. Eight in attendance, including Eileen.

Brook Avery was a tall, imposing man who was the publisher of a literary magazine. He had a full head of snow-white hair, broad, substantial shoulders and a muscular build, especially for a man of sixty-odd years.

As they gathered in a private room at the Algonquin, Joe noticed that, despite what Gen had said about guests being welcome, Avery was looking at him as if he were an interloper. But since Eileen Brideswell had insisted that they be there, the man limited his response to disapproving, even suspicious, stares.

Joe was happy to return suspicion for suspicion. In his mind, if the murder was connected to Poe, then everyone there, other than Gen and her mother, was a potential suspect.

Including Brook Avery.

Joe looked around the room and considered the attendees one by one, starting with Don Tracy. Because he had never done film or TV, his name wasn't well-known, but he was seldom out of work as an actor.

Nat Halloway was a banker. Fortysomething, thinning hair. An interesting prospect, he had managed Bigelow's investments.

Lila Hawkins was a perfect society matron, big-breasted, tall, with an imperious manner and voice. She was involved with charities all over the city. She didn't work; her family owned several large buildings on Park Avenue. Barbara Hirshorn was her complete opposite: thin, shy, nervous and a working woman, a librarian.

Lou Sayles was actually Louisa Sayles. She was retired from the school board, an attractive woman with silver hair and bright blue eyes. Rounding out the list was Larry Levine, a newspaper reporter. The best word to describe him was *medium*. Medium height, with medium-colored brown hair and light brown eyes and a medium build.

His work was much the same. He reported on events in New York. He wasn't bad, he wasn't great. He specialized in facts, ma'am, just the facts, nothing more. He was a solid reporter. He was not imaginative.

Joe knew about Larry Levine because he read the paper and because he had met him a few times through the years at social events with his cousin Matt.

He knew about the rest of the group, because Raif had kept his word and had faxed over his files on the rest of the board members. Meeting them face-to-face, however, was interesting.

Like Brook Avery, they were all happy to greet Genevieve, but they looked at him as if he were some kind of alien. Eileen had introduced him as Genevieve's friend; she didn't mention that he was a private investigator working the case. His line of work was hardly a secret, though; his name had been all over the media when Gen's rescue and the truth behind the killings had come out.

Larry Levine definitely knew his line of work. He greeted Joe curiously as the group mingled over drinks. "So, Connolly. You working this?" he demanded.

He shrugged. "I'm just keeping an eye on Genevieve."

"Good gig, eh?" Larry asked, looking appreciatively in her direction.

Joe couldn't help the tension and anger that rose in response to the other man's comment.

"She and her mother are fine people," he said, and changed the subject. "Very sad about Thorne Bigelow."

"You think?" Larry lifted his glass. "Can't say this too loud here, but Thorne was a pompous ass. Should anyone be murdered? Hell, no. But I doubt most people here are going to miss him much."

"People! Shall we get down to discussion?" Brook Avery called.

There was a moment's confusion as they all took seats around the large oblong table.

Joe was between Genevieve and Eileen. Brook Avery remained standing at the head of the table.

"Tonight's discussion is slated to focus on the financial feasibility of planning a tour to follow the route Poe took in the days before his death."

"Brook!" Lila Hawkins interrupted sharply.

He was clearly displeased, but he paused and said patiently, "Lila?"

"Surely you're joking!" she accused.

"I assure you, my dear Lila, I am not."

"Then you should be," she informed him. "Let's face it. We shouldn't be discussing business tonight. We should be discussing Thorne's death."

"Lila, what is there to discuss?" Brook Avery asked, then cocked his head meaningfully, indicating that they had guests in the room.

Lila Hawkins rose. She was clearly a woman who could stand her ground. "Oh, let's all stop pussyfooting around. Genevieve is Eileen's daughter. And Mr. Connolly—" She looked at him, and she had made it sound as if his name were a curse word. "—Mr. Connolly is here as a private investigator."

They all stared at him. It was obvious he was being given the floor to speak.

He shrugged. "I should think you'd all want to know exactly what happened to Thorne," he said quietly.

Lila spoke up again. "Of course we want to know. The question is, just how honest are any of us going to be? Tonight. Here and now. Amongst one another."

"I—I—I don't know what you could possibly mean, Lila," Barbara Hirshorn said. Her eyes darted around the room. "It was terrible, just terrible. The poor man was murdered."

"She means that one of us might have done it, my dear," Don Tracy said. Joe wondered if the man was capable of speaking without sounding as if he were delivering a speech on stage.

Barbara gasped, clapping both hands over her mouth.

The rest of them stared at each other, suddenly suspicious of people they'd known for years.

Then they stared as one at Gen—as if she had brought the real monster, because the real monster might be the truth—before turning to Joe again.

As they did so, he suddenly felt spotlighted, one degree removed from the people around him. It was almost like an out-of-body experience, as if this were just a scene in a film and he was watching it. A dead man had spoken to him, and then he himself had spoken to a girl claiming to be a psychic, and he had actually believed her. Which made all this totally unlike anything he had ever dealt with before.

Murder suddenly seemed so simple.

While death itself was not.

At last he stood. "You don't need to look at each other as if you've all suddenly turned into the devil," he said. "There are any number of other possibilities, and the police will be investigating all of them. Perhaps the murderer is counting on you all turning on each other. Perhaps he—or she—is hoping that the police will believe it's a member of the society. Nothing has been ruled out as yet."

"So why don't *we* try to rule out a few things?" Barbara asked.

Everyone was silent.

"Seriously, who here would have anything to gain by Thorne's death?" Larry demanded.

"No one," Eileen said evenly, glancing at her daughter. "No one," she repeated firmly. "I very much doubt any of us are in Thorne's will."

"But is murder always for personal gain?" Don Tracy demanded dramatically.

"Of course not. Think about Poe's stories. Characters were killed simply because they made the narrator crazy," Barbara Hirshorn said. "So…did Thorne drive any of us completely crazy?"

Lila let out a laugh that sounded like a bark. "Seriously?" she asked.

Barbara looked as if her feelings had been hurt, as if she thought that Lila was laughing at her.

But Lou Sayles set a hand on her arm. "Barbara, dear, I don't believe Lila was laughing at *you* but simply because, well, which one of us *didn't* he drive crazy?"

Nat Halloway cleared his throat. "He *was* a bit of a braggart," he said.

"Oh, come on. Jared isn't here to listen to what we're saying, so we might as well be honest. Braggart? He was obnoxious," Lila said.

"We shouldn't speak ill of the dead," Barbara said.

"Death doesn't change the truth," Larry said.

Don pointed at Larry and said, "Face it, Larry. You've always talked about writing a book on Poe, but Thorne went ahead and did it. You can't tell me you weren't at least a little bit jealous."

"I wouldn't have killed him for that," Larry protested indignantly.

"Really? So what would you have killed him for?" Lila demanded.

"I wouldn't kill anyone!" Larry said, his face suffusing with color.

"Oh, for heaven's sake," Eileen said.

"People, really, there's no need to start accusing each other," Joe told them.

"It's impossible not to talk about it," Lila said.

"I'm not suggesting that you stop talking about it," Joe said. "I just think there are more constructive conversations to have. So…Thorne Bigelow was a man who aggravated his friends. And when was the last time you each saw him?"

"I hadn't seen him since our last meeting, a month ago," Barbara said, relief in her voice, as if she now considered herself free from suspicion. "But, we would all have seen him the night he died. We were slated to attend a dinner to benefit a literacy foundation."

"So everyone would have been at that dinner?" Joe asked.

"Everyone," Eileen said. "Even Gen was going to go. With me."

Joe nodded. "Okay, he died a week ago. Barbara says she hadn't seen him in ages. What about the rest of you?"

"I had a meeting with him on Friday to discuss his finances," Nat Halloway admitted. "I left him alive and well."

Larry waved a hand in the air. "He was at the Whiskey Bar on Thursday night. I saw him there."

"I saw him at the Whiskey Bar, too," Brook admitted.

"Last month," Lila said. "I hadn't seen him since the last meeting."

"That's a lie," Brook said.

"What?" Lila demanded.

"You were at Dooley's Pub the Tuesday night before he was killed. I saw you there, and I saw Thorne there, too," Brook announced.

So much for this being a friendly group, Joe decided.

"Did anyone see him Saturday morning?" he asked. "Or do any of you know if he had any plans for Saturday morning or afternoon?" He wasn't expecting any of them to admit they had seen the man; what he was interested in was watching the interaction between them. There didn't seem to be any tight bonds here; it had already turned into every man for himself.

"I talked to him Saturday morning," Nat said. "I called him with the answer to a tax question he'd asked me. He was excited about the evening, because the society was going to give him an award. He was in a good mood."

"Did he say anything about seeing anyone before the dinner?" Joe asked.

"No," Nat said. "Just that Mary and Jared were both coming to his place, and that they'd all be going over together," Nat said.

"What about the butler? He was there, too," Larry said irritably.

"The butler?" Lila scoffed.

"Why would his butler want to kill him?" Eileen asked. "They got along quite well. Thorne paid him a very nice salary."

"Because he must have been wretched as a boss," Larry said.

"Oh, darling," Lila protested. "It's not the butler. That would be far too boring."

"Lila, a man is dead," Barbara reminded her. "This isn't the plot for a novel."

"And I still say it wasn't the butler," Lila insisted.

"Having a meeting tonight is pointless," Brook said with a sigh. "We should have cancelled. We're all too emotional."

Genevieve spoke up then. "Maybe being emotional isn't so bad. What if whoever killed Thorne really does have something against the Ravens? Aren't you all frightened?"

"Of course, we're frightened, darling!" Lila exclaimed. "But we can't let ourselves get carried away. I know Sam was hurt, but it's ridiculous to think someone was able to cause that accident just to harm him, then get away unscathed himself. Good God, simply getting on that wretched highway is dangerous. So, Mr. Connolly, what do you suggest we do next?" She stared at him pointedly.

"My suggestion is to do what everyone should always do—be careful. Don't park in dark garages, don't walk in dark alleys. Keep your doors locked," Joe said.

"Good advice," Lou Sayles said, and offered him an awkward smile. "But what happens when the danger comes from someone you trust?"

"There we go again!" Brook exploded. "Accusing one another."

"Be helpful to the police in any way that you can. The sooner Thorne Bigelow's murder is solved, the sooner you'll feel safe. And enjoy one another's...society again," Joe said. "No pun intended."

And yet, it was hard not to feel as if this entire thing weren't some kind of terrible joke.

The people here were...

Well, caricatures in a way, he thought. He had lived in New York City most of his life, and he loved New Yorkers. But tonight he felt as if he had walked in on a play satirizing the rich and the poor and everyone in between. They had the poor librarian, the angry columnist and several society matrons. Men who lived hard, men who thrived and men who were always thirsty.

A ripple of uneasy laughter reminded him of his last words.

No pun intended.

Too bad Thorne Bigelow's murder was anything but a joke.

"I feel better just for speaking honestly," Barbara said with a soft sigh.

"Why on earth would you feel better?" Lila asked. "All we've proven tonight is that we don't trust one another."

"Oh, come, Lila," Lou said. "I refuse to believe that any of us is capable of murder."

"Maybe not," Joe said, and all turned to stare at him. "But someone out there is. So, all of you, be careful."

"Yes, we all need to be careful."

The statement came from the doorway. Joe turned around to see that a newcomer had joined them.

Jared Bigelow.

He'd seen the man's picture in the papers and in the file Raif had faxed over. He was perhaps six feet in height, lean and wiry. He had dark, curling hair and a face with features so fine they were almost sharp. His eyes were deep set and dark. He was in his early thirties, casually dressed in chinos and a tweed jacket.

And he was not alone.

The woman standing behind him was in her late thirties or early forties. She was small and model thin. Her hair was blond and highlighted with an even lighter shade, and her eyes were enormous and a marbled blue-gray. She appeared both extremely artificial and extremely attractive at the same time, as if many things about her had been enhanced, but enhanced very well.

Mary Vincenzo, Thorne Bigelow's late brother's much younger wife. She had been in public relations before her marriage, according to the file Raif Green had sent. She had never changed her name.

The two newcomers walked into the room, and the others jumped to their feet and crowded around Jared, voicing the usual awkward and sympathetic words everyone came up with when someone died.

Genevieve, however, hung back, Joe noticed. As did Eileen. Interesting.

Only when the crowd around Jared had dispersed did they take the opportunity to murmur quiet sympathy. Joe found himself realizing that, despite all the jewels and silk, cosmetics, surgeries and expensive coiffures in evidence, there was no one in the room like Genevieve. Tall, slim, sleek and natural, everything about her whispered of innate perfection. He found himself glad for personal, as well as professional reasons that he had attended this very strange affair.

She had endured so much and was herself so strong. But no one should have to be alone after what she'd been through, and he would protect her.

"Please," Jared said, lifting a hand and stepping back to address the group. He smiled awkwardly. "I actually came here tonight to say the same thing to all of you that he…" he indicated Joe with a nod of his head "…that he told you. Please be careful." He grinned. "If one of you bastards didn't kill my father, or even if you did, we have to live with the fact that any one of us may be a target."

If one of you bastards didn't kill my father…

He had spoken the words lightly, Joe thought. Like a joke. But had he really meant them humorously?

Joe walked over and offered his hand to Jared. "Joe Connolly," he said. "I add my condolences on your loss."

"The private detective?" Jared asked him. "What are you doing here?"

"I've engaged Mr. Connolly," Gen said, stepping up. "To look into your father's murder—and to make sure that my mother and the rest of you aren't in any danger."

"But…this is a board meeting," Jared said.

"No, this is actually an accusation fest," Larry said huffily.

"Larry…" Barbara chastised.

"Seriously, right now it would be prudent for all of you to be careful. The police are investigating a number of possibilities, but until they have a suspect in custody, you all need to behave as if you could be next," Joe said.

"But this is a board meeting," Jared repeated, staring at Eileen Brideswell.

"Calm down, Jared. Anything that helps, right?" Mary Vincenzo said, speaking up at last.

"Yes, yes. All right. Well, get to it then, Mr. Connolly. Actually, I just stopped in to make sure everyone on the board was aware that we're having a special viewing of my father before the services Monday. Five o'clock, at Philips Mortuary. I hope to see you all there." Jared looked from one to another. "I hope you'll understand if I don't stay. Aunt Mary…?"

They started to walk away, and then Jared, with Mary on his arm, paused at the door and turned back. "Mr. Connolly?"

"Yes?"

"You'll be there, I assume? In your…professional capacity."

"Yes," Joe said. "I'll be there."

He felt Genevieve lay her hand on his arm, and he watched as Jared Bigelow noted her movement, a curious glint entering his eyes.

"Until then," Jared said, and left.

Joe was acting strange lately, Genevieve thought.

The distance between them suddenly seemed far too great, far greater than it ever had before.

They had dropped Eileen at home, and then he'd brought her to her place. Being Joe and ever the gentleman, he had seen her up to her apartment, his every move the epitome of courtesy.

But, to be quite honest, she didn't want courtesy any more than she wanted pity or to be treated like a fragile rose.

All of a sudden she realized the complete truth that had inexplicably eluded her until now.

In the days following her rescue and Leslie's death, she had been forced to find her own footing, to learn simply to go on again.

But since then, during the time they had spent together, she had begun to realize just how much she liked Joe. More than liked him.

He, of course, had been in love with Leslie, who in turn, had been in love with the fiancé, Joe's cousin, who had died before her. But if she had lived, would she have fallen for Joe in time? Or would she have fallen only for a shadow of her first love? Matt, like Joe, had been tall, with light hair, though Joe's was slightly darker, just as his eyes were greener. But Matt had been built with the same broad-shouldered strength. Maybe Joe would have wondered all his life if she had been truly in love with him, or only dreaming that he was someone else every time they made love.

Some questions could never be answered. Leslie and Matt were both dead now.

She found herself thinking of Shakespeare then, rather than Poe. Of *Hamlet*.

He is dead and gone, lady, he is dead and gone. At his heels a grass green turf and at his head a stone…

Yes, Leslie MacIntyre was dead, but did Joe still dream about her?

Perhaps Joe could never be serious about anyone—especially Gen herself, because she had been the cause of Leslie's death.

But not intentionally. Never intentionally. She would never have allowed someone else to die in her place.

Joe knew that. She knew he did. And dwelling on the events of that fatal night would only serve to drive her insane. What had happened, had happened. And no one but the murderer himself had been at fault. She hadn't needed therapy to recognize the truth of that. And she knew that Joe knew it, too.

So why was he so strange and distant these days?

And why did she insist on caring? Was she only hung up on him because he had been there in her darkest hour? According to Dr. Mowbry, women often fell in love with men they considered to be their saviors.

And he *had* saved her life. No doubt about it. But that wasn't why she had fallen for him. She was sure of that.

And now, here he was, and she didn't want him to be so gentle. She wanted him to crush her in his arms. She wanted to make wild, hot love with him. She didn't want him to see her as delicate or in need of protection. She was tempted to simply slip off her dress, fling her arms around him and do something so sensual and sexy that he couldn't resist her.

"So," she said, with just the right amount of curiosity and professional courtesy, "what did you think?"

She loved his rueful smile, she thought. Loved it when she had his full attention and could see on his face that certain dry amusement he felt for life, himself and everything around him.

"I felt like I walked into a play filled with outsize characters who had to prove themselves and their innocence within the confines of two hours and one intermission," he told her.

"Oh, come on, we're not that bad," she said.

"I didn't say anyone was bad."

He was hovering in the doorway. They'd already argued about the fact she had refused to stay with Eileen at the mansion, even though she was worried about her mother, and even though everyone was worried about *her,* despite the fact that, as she kept pointing out, she wasn't a Raven. This time around, *she* wasn't the one who had something to worry about.

But her mother had live-in help and an excellent security system, and she still needed her own place, her own independence.

So that, if she ever got up the nerve, she could just strip off her little black dress, and do something so exotic and sensual and sexual that he couldn't stand it and...

"I know Larry," Joe said. "He's not a bad guy. And your mother is a wonderful woman."

"See? Rich people aren't all bad," she heard herself say defensively.

He laughed easily and shook his head. "Gen, I never said they were. It was just tonight...that group. Let's face it, I think everyone there was afraid someone else in that room did it. Lila was all bravado. Barbara was all denial. Brook Avery was pure pretense. And then...Jared showing up so dramatically... It was...interesting."

"Did you learn anything?"

He hesitated. "I learned that no one there likes anyone else all that much, that no one liked Thorne, in particular, and that Jared Bigelow is sleeping with his aunt."

She gasped. "What?"

"Well, they aren't related by blood, are they?"

"No. Mary was married to Thorne's older brother, Steven. He was thirty-some years older than she is."

"A real love match, huh?" he said cynically.

"Supposedly it was a good marriage," she said.

"Sure. I'd probably be good for that kind of money, too," he said.

"You really are a skeptic, aren't you?"

"Oh, come on, Gen! You weren't just a little bit skeptical about that one yourself?"

"Maybe," she admitted.

He was laughing, and suddenly he seemed to be so easy with her.

"Okay, so she probably married Steven Bigelow for his money," she admitted. "That doesn't mean that people always marry rich people for their money." Why on earth had she said that? Could she be any more obvious about what was on her mind?

But he didn't even seem to notice. "I'm sure some women do fall in love with men who are older and richer," he said. "Just not in that particular case."

"And what made you so certain that they're sleeping together? Jared and Mary, I mean."

"The possessive way she hung on his arm. The way he looked at you, and the way she looked at him for the way he looked at you."

"You're reading a lot into the way people look at each other."

"Because there's a lot to be read into it."

"So do you think Jared killed his father, or his aunt killed his father or—"

"I think there are a lot of suspects," he assured her. "And a lot of motives. Greed and jealousy have both been strong inducements for murder over the centuries. Of course, tonight we were missing one of the traditional suspects."

"Who?"

"The butler, of course," he said, grinning.

She had to laugh. But then she assured him, "Bennet didn't murder Thorne, I can assure you."

"Bennet? You know him?" he asked her.

"Of course. My family and the Bigelows kind of run in the same circles, though I can't exactly say we were friends." She pointed a stern finger at him. "And don't you dare start in on rich people again."

"I wasn't about to."

She offered him a doubting sniff.

"So tell me about Bennet."

"Well, he's old."

"How old?"

"Oh, honestly, sixty-five, maybe. He's been with the family for as long as I can remember. You could talk to my mom. She would know more."

"Actually, I'd like to talk to Bennet himself."

"I'll go with you tomorrow."

"No."

"Why not?"

"You need to stay out of this."

"But I hired you,"

"Yes, and if you wanted to do everything yourself," he said irritably, "you shouldn't have."

"You need my help on this," she assured him.

"Oh?"

"Bennet likes me," she said. "He'll be happy to talk to you if you're with me. He won't be so thrilled if you're on your own."

"Genevieve, seriously—"

"If you don't let me help, I *will* start doing things on my own," she said softly.

He stared at her, frustrated.

She had him, and she knew it. He still had that protective thing going on, which wasn't what she wanted, but it would have to do for now.

"So what time are we going to see Bennet tomorrow?" he asked dryly.

She smiled. "I'll talk to him in the morning. He goes to church, and I'm taking Mom to church, so I'll see him there. So let's say about…one?"

He nodded, eyeing her cautiously, as if he had just realized she might be a species of dangerous animal he had misjudged.

"One o'clock, then," he said.

Joe stood there in the doorway for a moment, and she couldn't help staring at him. Joe, whose sandy brown hair fell over his forehead in such a casual and sexy manner, whose eyes seemed to reflect the world and his knowledge of it. Whose shoulders filled the doorway, whose jaw could be so hard and stubborn. Joe…

For a split second she thought that he was going to move forward. Come closer. Even touch her.

And finally he did.

He reached out—and tousled her hair.

"Tomorrow, then, kid. See you. And until then…."

"I know, I know. I'll be careful."

Then he was gone. And she locked the door—as he told her to do from the other side.

When she went to bed, she found herself staring at the ceiling and thinking about loss, about death.

Leslie's death. And the deaths of the prostitutes she herself had tried so hard to help. They had been nothing but disposable members of society to so many people, but she had known them as women with hopes and dreams. So much loss.

Then there was the loss she faced herself…

The loss of a life once filled with promise but now controlled by fear. Not hers, but everyone else's for her.

The loss of a life never really lived…

By the time her phone rang Sunday morning, Lori Star had given up expecting anything good.

At first the news media had embraced her, but then they had dropped her like a hot potato. Perhaps they had found out about her arrests; she didn't know. Apparently they now believed she was some kind of a fake. Which she usually was…

But not this time.

It had been terrifying when she had first felt the sensation of being somewhere else, being some*one* else.

Not just because it was like some sort of out-of-body experience, but because there was more to it. That sense of pure malice and…*evil* had been terrifying.

She was shivering just from that thought, that memory, when the call came through.

"Hello?"

"Miss Star? Miss Lori Star?" The voice on the other end was cultured, courteous.

"Yes?" Her response was wary, despite the caller's tone.

But on a different level, she already felt excitement. She just knew that this was someone who believed in her.

"I'm sorry for disturbing you on a Sunday morning, but I'm anxious to get out there with my story before anyone else beats me to it. I'm from the *New York Informant*. You've heard of it, I hope?

We follow up on the stories other papers leave behind when they rush off to cover the latest celebrity scandal. We like to stick with things and cover them in depth."

She sank down on her sofa, very glad that she'd been home to answer the phone.

"That's wonderful," she said, trying not to sound too eager. "And of course I'm familiar with the paper," she lied.

"We're also willing to pay, and pay well, when someone helps us with a story."

She tried to be careful with her reply and not let on how curious she was as to just what he meant by paying well. "Of course," she said simply, having decided not to ask how much. The amount he volunteered almost staggered her.

"Let's meet, then," he suggested. "And please don't mention that you're meeting me. I don't want any of my competitors to get wind that I'm talking to you."

"Don't worry," she said. "If anyone asks me," she said with a laugh, "I'll just tell them I'm off visiting an aunt."

"Perfect," her caller purred.

"Where should we meet?" she asked.

She didn't bother to jot down the address he gave her. She knew exactly where it was.

"How will I recognize you?" she asked.

"Don't worry. I'll recognize you."

New York City.

Talk about a mass of humanity.

People moved like ants. So many of them. So busy. All in such a hurry.

The mass of people crept and crawled, stopped and flowed. They congregated at street corners. They slid past one another. A light changed; a crossing sign flickered. And they moved in a giant mass, surging forward all at once, each individual following a personal agenda that led them to become a part of the massive back and forth.

Ants.

How many times had he walked in the city, in the country, on a sidewalk, through a house, across a yard, and seen ants? How easy it was—amusing, even—to step on a few and watch the confusion, the panic, of the others, as the instinct for survival took over and became the single thing that made them rush away.

Did one ant really even care when another one was stepped on by the harsh supreme being that walked above? Or did it only care about its own survival?

They were just ants. All of them, just ants.

And there *she* was.

One of the ants. Walking, stopping, moving again.

Would anyone really notice when she was stepped on by the supreme being above? Would they care?

Or would they just be afraid? Panicking. Scattering. Seeking, searching, running...

Desperate not to be stepped on themselves.

CHAPTER 7

Just as Gen had said, Bennet was in his sixties. Even so, he was as straight as a ramrod, with snow-white hair, with impeccable manners. And he wore a suit, complete with bow tie, to take care of the house.

Except, of course, he didn't really do the housework. He directed.

And he clearly had a soft spot for Genevieve. That much was evident from the minute he let them into the house.

He had pale eyes, a faded green. Still, they lit up like stars when he saw Gen.

"Miss Genevieve, you're looking well. Color in your cheeks, flesh on your bones...oh, not too much flesh," he assured her as he held her hands and looked at her from arms' length. He let out a sigh. "I'm ever so grateful things went...well, I'm quite grateful you're still with us, my dear."

"Thank you, Bennet," she said softly.

"Not like Thorny," he said.

Thorny, Joe noted. Interesting.

"And it may be my fault," Bennet said sadly, shaking his head. Then he stopped, his lean, wrinkled face instantly suspicious, eyes narrowed.

"You brought a friend, I see. And I know who he is," Bennet said.

Inwardly, Joe winced. It was a lot easier to do his job if no one knew what he was. Oh, well. Too late for that.

He extended a hand. "How do you do? I'm—"

"Lawrence Levine." Bennet started to say more, but then he drew himself up very straight and said stiffly, "Forgive my rudeness, Miss Genevieve."

So much for being full enough of himself to think the world knew who he was, Joe thought dryly.

"I'm not Larry Levine," he told Bennet, his hand still out. "I'm Joe Connolly."

"Oh." Bennet returned the handshake. "Sorry."

"Why did you think I was Larry?"

Bennet shook his head. "I don't know. I've never met him, but Mr. Bigelow talked about him all the time, so I just thought…" He sighed softly. "God rest his pompous old soul."

His words surprised Joe.

But Genevieve gave Bennet a light punch in the shoulder and said, "Come on, we all know you loved him."

"Aye, that I did," Bennet said, and suddenly the subtle undertone in the man's accent became clear to Joe. Though he was doing his best to impersonate a very proper English butler, Bennet was actually Irish. Did that mean anything?

Point noted and…

Shelved.

"Have you come to see Mr. Jared?" Bennet asked. "If so, I'm sorry, but he isn't here. He has his own place, you know. Although I suppose this is his place now, too. And I'm very much hoping he'll be keeping the house. It's a fine piece of property, it is."

"Actually, we've come to see you, Mr. Bennet," Joe said.

The old man looked at Joe again, studying him. "You're too young to be that reporter. But I *have* seen your face. You were in the papers, right? All that business with Miss Genevieve, right? You're that private detective."

"Yes," Joe said simply.

"Am I a murder suspect?"

"Of course not," Genevieve said.

But Joe said, "Sorry, but yes. Everyone associated with Thorne Bigelow has to be a suspect until they can be cleared. I hope you understand that it's nothing personal."

"Aye, I do, and God forgive me, but I was right here when it happened."

"Right here?" Joe asked.

Bennet waved a hand. "Come into the kitchen. It's my domain for the moment. I'll put some tea on."

"Tea sounds lovely, Bennet, thanks so much," Genevieve said.

A few minutes later, they were seated around the huge butcher-block table in the kitchen. Bennet told them, "Mr. Bigelow's office is still closed off. I haven't touched a thing in it. I believe I could now, but..." His voice faded away. Joe couldn't help but believe that the man had felt a genuine affection for his employer of so many years. "Not even young Jared has had the heart to go in there."

Joe looked up at the rafters where copper pots and utensils were handsomely displayed. It was a great kitchen, with a big fireplace and every conceivable appliance. Then he poured a teaspoon of sugar into his cup and stirred. "So, Mr. Bennet, you said you were here when it happened?"

"Yes."

"But you saw and heard nothing?"

"Nothing at all. My apartment is on the third floor, you see. What was once the attic, but it's been renovated. You're welcome to come up and see for yourself. Once you shut that door...well, a bomb could go off downstairs, and you wouldn't know."

Joe smiled. "I think I know what you mean."

Bennet stirred his own tea, then shook his head, looking distressed. "I talked to the police at length. Mr. Jared, of course, was distraught, and accused me of horrible things, but he apologized later. And the detectives cleared me. Who knows, maybe they figured I just wasn't literary enough to pull off something like this."

"What is your position now?" Joe asked.

"Well, I imagine Mr. Thorne left me something in his will, but who knows? Jared asked that I stay on for now, while he figures out what he wants to do. We're keeping everything the same. The maids come in each morning still. They just stay away from Mr. Bigelow's office. And his room," Bennet added softly. He shrugged. "It was clean when he was killed. The police went through it, of course, looking for any information he might have kept in his personal quarters, rather than his office, but they were very diligent about putting things back as they were, and there's been no reason for anyone to go back in and clean as yet."

"How and when did you know something had happened?" Joe asked him.

"I heard Jared screaming."

"But you said you couldn't have heard a bomb go off," Joe said lightly.

Bennet had the grace to offer a rueful smile. "You never heard anything like the way Mr. Jared was screaming when he found his father."

"So the two got along?"

"Argued like cats and dogs—but they lived for it," Bennet said. He leaned a little closer to speak more softly, as if they were surrounded by others and might be heard. "I think it was one of those other fellows. Jealous. Those men are fanatics. I mean, take the actor fellow. Don Tracy. He thinks he's Lawrence Olivier! He and Mr. Bigelow fought all the time whenever they had those Poe meetings here. To be truthful, I think Mr. Bigelow would have loved to be on the stage himself. Half the time, I think he *was* acting. Or trying to aggravate Mr. Tracy."

"Mr. Bennet, when was the last time you saw Mr. Bigelow?" Joe asked.

Bennet looked at him oddly. "Well, before the ambulance took him away, of course."

"I meant, when was the last time you saw him alive?"

"When I picked up his lunch tray that afternoon."

"And what time was that?"

"Let's see…I brought lunch up to him around one, and I picked up the tray at about one-thirty."

"And no one was here until Jared arrived?" Joe asked, knowing the answer but wondering what Bennet would tell him.

"No, no. He was expecting a guest, but he didn't tell me who it was, and he said I shouldn't worry, that he'd answer the door himself."

Good enough, Joe thought. That fit with what the detectives had said.

"And what time did Jared start screaming?" Joe asked. He had the notes on the initial investigation that Raif Green had passed on to him, but it was always interesting to see if the eye witnesses' memories stayed the same.

"I'd say it was about six-thirty. Somewhere around there. I didn't actually look at the clock."

"Someone dialed 9-1-1 immediately, right?" Joe asked.

"Of course," Bennet said.

"Was it you?"

"No. In fact, when I started running downstairs, I could already hear a siren."

"That's amazing," Genevieve said.

Yes, it was, Joe thought.

"But Mr. Bigelow was already gone?" Joe prompted.

"Stone cold, poor Thorny was stone cold," Bennet said.

"Stone cold?" Joe repeated curiously.

"Well, cold to the touch," Bennet said. "There was so much confusion, though. Jared was trying to resuscitate his father, and Mary, his aunt, just kept saying he had to stop, that Mr. Bigelow was dead."

"And when she said that…you touched him?" Joe said.

Bennet frowned. "I'm thinking…trying to remember exactly what I did. There seemed to be so much confusion. Um, no, no, I didn't touch him."

"Then how did you know that he was cold?" Joe asked.

Bennet frowned. Not like a man who had lied, but like a man who was genuinely confused. "I…I guess I did touch him," Bennet said. "I must have."

"Then?"

Bennet looked distressed.

"Joe…" Genevieve murmured, distressed.

He gave her a fierce frown.

"It might have been right when the paramedics came in," Bennet said. "Yes, that was it. The first young man asked if anyone had tried to revive him, and I said that his son had tried, and I touched Thorny then, and he was cold."

Joe finished his tea. "What about Mary? Mrs. Vincenzo?" he asked.

"What about her? She and Thorny always seemed to get along fine," Bennet assured him.

"No, did she touch him?"

Again, Bennet appeared perplexed. "I…no. No, I don't think so. She just kept crying, touching Jared, telling him to let his father be, he was dead. They were both so upset."

"How did they react to you coming down?" Joe asked, filing away the question of what had made Mary so certain that Thorne was dead.

"I'm not even sure they noticed me at first. Then Jared looked at me, and he shouted, 'Bennet, what the hell did you do to my father?' And of course I told him I'd done nothing, nothing at all. And I asked him what had happened, and he said they'd found his father keeled over on the desk."

"Keeled over on the desk?" Joe asked.

"Yes."

"So Jared moved him so he could do CPR?" And didn't notice that the man was "stone cold"? This case was getting more and more interesting by the moment.

"I suppose so. The man was beside himself. If he could have saved his father, he would have, believe me."

"It's kind of you to defend him," Genevieve said. "Considering he was so quick to accuse you of killing him."

"Jared was simply distraught, as I told you," Bennet explained.

"Did he keep accusing you when the police came?" Genevieve asked, looking at him sympathetically.

"No, no, I don't think so," Bennet said.

Joe seemed to feel he'd gotten all the information he could at that point, because he thanked Bennet for the tea and for being so forthcoming, and in a few minutes he and Gen were on their way.

"I'm not sure where you're going with your questions," Genevieve told Joe when they were back out on the street. "All of this must be on the record already."

"Yes."

"So?"

"You asked me to investigate," he said.

"But…"

"But what?"

"He's a nice old guy, and you were practically attacking him, as if you were the police."

"I would be willing to bet the police were much harder on him than I was."

"And they didn't arrest him, did they?"

"They don't have the evidence to arrest him. Or anyone, if it comes to that."

"We're just going in circles," Genevieve protested.

He arched a brow to her. "Want to fire me?"

"Of course not! I just…I just feel we should be doing more."

"And I feel," he told her, "as if you should be staying with your mother."

She let out a long breath of aggravation. "I will not let this situation put me back a hundred years, do you understand?"

"You said that you were worried about her," he reminded her.

"Yes, and when she's at home, she couldn't be safer," Genevieve told him. "Bertha never leaves the mansion, and Henry is there, too. And the security system is state of the art."

"Just like the one at Bigelow's mansion," he reminded her.

He was immediately sorry he'd spoken, as her face drained of color. "That's what's so horrifying. Bigelow must have known, maybe even trusted, his killer. How do you ever figure out who's lying?"

"You catch them in a lie," he said, and glanced at his watch. Sunday afternoon was waning. "I think I should take you home."

"No way," she told him. "I took you to talk to the butler. Now you can take me to talk to the psychic."

He knew her. Knew the dead-stubborn set to her jaw. They wouldn't be going anywhere or doing anything until he took her to see Candy Cane slash Lori Star.

"Joe, please." She set a hand on his arm. It was such a little thing, but it sent a jolt of electricity through him as strongly as if he'd been strapped into the chair at Sing-Sing.

"Yeah, yeah, let's go," he almost snapped. His voice sounded too deep, too husky, even to his own ears. He wondered if she really didn't know how she affected people, men—*him*—and if she was truly as blind to her own assets as she seemed to be.

Fifteen minutes later, they were knocking at Candy Cane's door. She didn't answer.

Joe was persistent, and he tried rapping harder. Down the hall-way, a young woman poked her head out.

"Knock it off, buddy," she said, then looked at the two of them and softened. "Sorry...I was just watching television. I didn't mean to bite your heads off."

"That's okay, we're sorry," Genevieve told her.

"Do you know where Can—where Lori is?" Joe asked.

"No, I'm afraid not."

Genevieve took a step forward. "Did you see her today? Did she say anything to you? I'm sorry to bother you, but it's really impor-tant that we speak with her."

The woman—who was probably only in her late twenties but already acquiring the pinched look of someone years older—took a long look at Genevieve. Then she smiled.

"Let me try to remember. I was just coming up from the laundry room when she was going out. She was all excited when she left," the woman said. "Um...she did tell me that it was a great day, and that she was going to go see a man about a horse. Then she laughed and said it was a race horse and she was going to be in the money."

"Really?" Genevieve said, frowning and looking at Joe.

Joe looked at Lori's neighbor, and something about the way he looked at her clearly made her defensive.

"She wasn't hooking," the woman snapped.

"I didn't suggest she was," he assured her.

"You two cops?" the woman demanded.

"No, no," Genevieve said quickly, and stepped forward, offering her hand. "I'm Genevieve O'Brian, and this is Joe Connolly. We just wanted to talk to Lori, that's all."

The woman's shoulders sagged, as if she didn't have the energy to be angry anymore. "She's really a sweet girl. She deserves a break."

"I'm sure she does," Joe said, and he was surprised to realize he wasn't being sarcastic. He had been stunned himself to feel that something about Lori Star's words had felt real and that she really had seemed like a nice kid.

The woman smiled. "I'm Susie Norman, by the way, and I'm sorry I can't help you." She brightened. "Next time I see Lori, I'll tell her you were here, though."

"Thanks," Joe said. He slipped a business card under Lori's door, then walked over and handed one to Susie. "Here's my number, in case you think of anything to help us find her. And thanks again."

When they reached the street, Genevieve looked at Joe expectantly. "What now?"

"Now I have to check on some alibis."

"Okay. Where do we start?"

He shook his head, looking at her with exasperation. "Genevieve, you hired *me* to do this job. That means *I* do the work, and *you* head on home and enjoy what's left of your Sunday."

"Joe, I've spent enough time closed up in my house. Where do we go from here?"

"I need to do some work on the computer and make some phone calls," he told her.

"I have a computer."

"And all my contact numbers and stuff are at my house."

"I'm willing to bet your contact numbers are in your phone," Genevieve told him.

No way out of it. He let out a sigh of vast exasperation. "Then you're coming to Brooklyn," he told her.

She smiled. "Fine."

Sunday in New York. It seemed as if every dog owner in the city was out. A poodle took issue with a Doberman. The owners sounded as if they were barking right along with their dogs as they accused each other of causing the problem. A Maltese went trotting

by with its owner, a shaggy-haired young girl. Both were oblivi-
ous to the shouting match as they walked by.

Joe hailed a cab for Genevieve's apartment, where they retrieved
his car. The Sunday traffic wasn't bad, and she seemed to enjoy the
ride, looking out the window, watching as they traveled over the
Brooklyn Bridge.

Joe realized that although they had been friends for over a year,
he'd kept his distance. She had never been to his place before.

He lived in an old brownstone. It was three stories, plus a basement, and he had the basement and the first floor. He even had a
reserved parking space, which was something of a coup in his
neighborhood, which was residential, but just a block off a com-
mercial boulevard, where he could go for coffee, or great Chinese,
Italian or diner-style American food whenever he chose.

But entering his place with Genevieve brought with it a stab of pain.

Leslie was the last woman he'd brought here.

And she had told him about the ghost in his basement, a Civil
War era musician who had wanted the work he'd left behind to be
found and performed.

Ghosts.

He'd spent his life being logical. He hadn't believed in ghosts. But
then he'd met Leslie and through her, a man named Adam Harrison
and some of his employees, a group of people who found it as natural
to talk to ghosts as it was to converse with strangers at a party.

But despite everything he had come to know about Leslie and,
through her, Adam Harrison and his group of paranormal investigators, he had fought against believing in any of it.

But then he had spoken to a dead man on the highway, and after
that, a corpse had looked up at him at the morgue and spoken....

Ridiculous. It was all ridiculous.

He'd been working too hard. Or not getting enough sleep. Hell,
maybe he actually needed to start drinking more.

"Make yourself at home," he told Genevieve.

He couldn't help watching her as she looked around his apartment.

And he couldn't help wondering if he didn't have a little bit of a chip on his shoulder where she was concerned. He'd always worked hard and made a decent income, and he was good at investing the extra, so finances weren't a worry. But Genevieve O'Brien was the kind of rich that went beyond most people's dreams, including his.

Still, she had chosen a life of service to others, even before her kidnapping. She had worked the meanest streets in town. She had tried to save prostitutes and their children. She had fought against heroin and crack addiction, and dealt with those who were down and out and even those suffering from AIDS. She had never given any indication that she was a spoiled rich kid just because her family had obscene amounts of money.

She smiled, her eyes meeting his. "Joe, this place is great. That's one of the most fantastic fireplaces ever."

"Thanks," he said. "Kitchen is there, so help yourself if you want something to drink. I've usually got beer, wine, soda. And food, if you're hungry. There's a TV over there, and a pool table downstairs, if you get bored. I'll be in my office, right down the hall."

"Thanks. And don't worry about me. I'm fine. Mind if I go through your CD collection?"

"Knock yourself out."

"Thanks."

He nodded, still feeling oddly awkward, and walked down the hall to his office. It was lined with oak bookshelves and three-drawer filing cabinets. His desk was an antique that might have belonged to Uriah Heap, if he'd been real and not a character in a book.

He put through a call to Raif Green at his home.

"Hey, Joe, got anything?" Raif asked as soon as Joe identified himself.

"No, sorry. I was hoping *you* might have something to tell *me.*"

"To tell you the truth…we basically have nothing," Raif admitted. "Except what we've known from the beginning. Thorne Bigelow knew his killer. He let the person in, and he was willing to sit there and drink wine with him or her. So we're looking at friends and acquaintances."

"What's your take on the butler?"

"Apparently, he 'buttled' very well," Raif said.

"But he was there the whole time," Joe pointed out.

"We don't have a thing on him. We searched the house, but there was no sign of poison anywhere, including in his quarters. Naturally we looked at his son, but there was nothing to prove he was there earlier. Same thing with the aunt. The two of them arrived together."

"Still, I'm assuming the son had the most to gain from his death?"

"Of course. We've talked to Bigelow's attorney, and except for some special endowments and individual bequests, Jared Bigelow inherits everything."

"I'm going to assume you've looked into the rest of the Ravens' alibis?" Joe said.

He heard Raif's sigh. "Yes, of course."

"Want to give me a list?"

"Larry Levine was at the paper."

"On the weekend?"

"Yeah, a doorman vouched for him. Brook Avery was at home, watching television. He spoke to a neighbor around three o'clock. Um, hang on. I'll get my notes." There was some shuffling. Joe could hear a woman's voice, calling Raif to dinner. He promised her that he'd be right there. Joe tried to imagine Raif Green's domestic life. Sometimes he seemed sad and burned-out, but he had kids at home. And a wife. He investigated murders every day, then went home to kids and homework and meatloaf.

Raif came back on the line. "Nat Halloway was working on his clients' files at his office. He was seen by a cleaning woman. Don Tracy, the actor…was rehearsing a one-man play. We verified his alibi with the director and the rest of the cast. Lila Hawkins was at a blood-donation center, seen by a dozen people around four o'clock. Barbara Hirshorn…home alone watching television. Verified by a neighbor, who saw Barbara when she went out for groceries. Lou Sayles was at an afternoon party for a retiring school-teacher. Out in Brooklyn Heights. Verified by half a dozen people. I think we've got them all covered. Oh, yeah, your friend. Eileen Brideswell. She was home, too, verified by Bertha Landry, her live-in maid, and Henry Grant, her…jack of all trades, I guess you'd call him. Besides, I can guarantee you that Eileen Brideswell is as law-abiding as they come."

"Thanks," Joe said. "But you know, Raif…"

"Yeah?"

"I'm not sure any one of those is a really good alibi, the kind that guarantees someone didn't slip out to Bigelow's place for a half hour or so."

"Yeah, I know," Raif said.

"So…"

"There are laws, Joe," Raif said. "I'm a public servant. I can't just barge into people's houses and search them without a warrant. I haven't got a thing to hold anyone on."

"What about the accident on the FDR?" Joe asked.

"What about it? That's Traffic's job. I can't do a damned thing when there's no one out there who can give me anything more than a dark sedan that was driving erratically. I can't connect that accident—even if Sam Latham is still in the hospital—to Thorne Bigelow's murder. And if we're talking Poe…"

"Yeah, yeah. Poe had no vehicular homicides in his stories. Got ya," Joe said.

"Of course, you're a private investigator…" Raif reminded him, letting the words trail off suggestively.

"And your point is…?"

"You're not subject to quite as much shit as I am."

"Great. Are you going to get me out of jail when they lock me up for breaking and entering, or whatever it is you're suggesting I do?" Joe asked.

"Joe, I'm not suggesting you do *any*thing illegal," Raif protested. "Not that you couldn't push the boundaries a little if you needed to."

"Gee, thanks."

"The thing is…"

"What?"

"Well, if Bigelow *was* killed because of the Poe thing…"

"Then you think the killer will end up striking again before he's caught, is that what you're saying?" Joe asked.

"Sadly, yes," Raif said.

Joe heard the woman's voice calling out to Raif again. "Go eat your dinner before it gets cold," Joe said.

"Yeah, thanks, I will. Don't forget, Joe, if you get anything…"

"You know I'll call you," Joe promised, and hung up.

He pulled out a map of Manhattan and started going through alibis one by one. Brook Avery lived uptown; if he was where he said he'd been, getting down to Bigelow's place would have taken a while. Joe put his name on one list. On the other hand, Larry Levine's office was relatively close to Bigelow. He could have slipped out easily. His name went on a second list.

Joe kept going. Don Tracy. The theater was close enough, too. Don's name went under Larry's.

He put Jared Bigelow and Mary Vincenzo on that list, too.

Along with the butler.

Lou Sayles had the best alibi. He put her name on the list with Brook's. Lila Hawkins, big, pushy Lila, had been uptown at the blood-donation center. Her name, too, went on the "improbable" list. He hesitated when he got to Barbara Hirshorn. She was afraid of her own shadow, but her home was near Bigelow's. He didn't really see her as a potential killer, but he put her name on the "follow up first" list anyway.

He drummed his fingers on the desk, then decided to start with Jared. Why not go for the obvious?

The butler had been an easy choice, but if the butler hadn't done it...

Patricide was as old as history. And Jared Bigelow was the one who would profit the most from his father's death.

Edgar Allan Poe, so they said, was the father of the detective story. And he and his Monsieur Dupin had used "ratiocination," or rational deduction, as their method of investigation.

So, rationally, who benefitted? And who not only had motive but opportunity?

He skipped over Poe and thought about Sherlock Holmes, who always told Watson that you needed to get rid of the impossible, and then what was left, no matter how improbable, had to be the truth.

Joe groaned softly, looking at his notes.

So far, *nothing* seemed to be impossible.

Not even talking to dead people.

CHAPTER 8

Genevieve's cell phone rang and she answered it absently. "Hello?"

"Oh, thank God!" It was her mother's voice.

Gen smiled. "Mother, I'm fine."

"I tried calling the apartment," Eileen said, as if that were a perfectly acceptable explanation for sounding so worried.

"I'm with Joe."

"Oh? That's wonderful." Her mother adored Joe, Gen knew.

Yes, and why not? Without him, she might not be here.

"Hey, I'm the one who should be calling, and panicking about you," Genevieve reminded her mother. "Promise me that you won't go anywhere alone. Or with any of the other Ravens," Genevieve said sternly.

"Those people are my friends, you know. Most of them. Well, some of them," Eileen said.

"One of them could be a killer."

"And poor Thorne might have been killed for some other reason entirely," Eileen reminded her. "But never mind, I didn't call to argue with you."

"No, you called to check up on me," Genevieve said with a laugh.

"Do you blame me, dear?"

"Never," Genevieve promised.

"Well, I'll let you go, now that I know you're all right. Enjoy the rest of your day with Joe."

"Sure. And thanks," Genevieve said, then rang off.

Enjoy her day with Joe?

He was in his office; she was here alone.

But at least she was *here*. For whatever good that did her.

Restlessly, she stood. He had a great CD collection, and an appreciation for music that went beyond eclectic and on to boundless. He had the classics, from Pavarotti to Wagner, country, soul, rhythm and blues, rock, even some trance. She put in a Buddy Holly CD and tried to relax.

No good. She was too restless.

He'd told her to make herself at home. Since she wasn't hungry or thirsty, the kitchen held no great allure, so she decided to explore the basement.

It had been finished, and now it was perfect for intimate entertaining. That made her think about the way Joe thought about *her*. He had a dual vision of her.

Little rich girl.

And damaged goods.

What could she do to change that?

Perhaps it couldn't be changed. Perhaps...

Perhaps he simply didn't find her attractive, she told herself.

Here she was, thinking about Joe, about being damaged, about the past, wondering why he wasn't making a move on her, when he was upstairs doing exactly what she had asked of him: working on the case.

And then something very strange happened.

She didn't close her eyes, but it was as if she were seeing something else besides this room. Almost as if she herself *was* someone else.

She was walking down the street, anxious and excited. She was going to meet someone, and that someone was going to change her life. It was all very hush-hush, because it was so important. Someone was going to take a chance.

On her.

For her.

This was her chance to be rich and famous. Well, he was going to pay her well, so rich, anyway.

And if things went the way they should…

She was almost at the place where they'd planned to meet, and she hoped he wouldn't be late. That he would be there waiting for her.

She knew she hadn't been followed.

That no one knew where she was.

She was about to see a man about a horse….

Genevieve blinked. She was in Joe's basement again, staring at the pool table. For a moment, her hands shook. What the hell had that been? She couldn't believe she was seeing things.

Oh, great. Damaged goods to begin with, and now she was going crazy. No. She was *not* going to allow herself to crack.

She ran up the stairs. Joe was still in his office. He hadn't heard her; he obviously didn't know anything was wrong.

Because nothing *was* wrong.

She turned up Buddy Holly, then headed back to the basement, determined not to worry about her love life—or complete lack thereof—anymore.

Joe sighed, rose and stretched, surprised at how long he'd been at his desk. He walked out to the living room.

Buddy Holly was playing on the stereo, but Genevieve was nowhere to be seen.

He noticed that the door to the basement stairway was open. Then he heard a series of clicking sounds and realized she was downstairs, playing pool.

He walked down to join her, and on the way he noticed the brick wall and remembered how Leslie had told him that he would find music there if he tore it out. She hadn't felt ready to admit that she talked to ghosts then, so she had just told him that she did a lot of research in the course of her work and had happened to stumble across some information about his building.

Yeah, right. Accidental research, right where he happened to live.

He remembered their conversations, too. How he had thought she simply needed time to get over Matt, because it had seemed clear that she was drawn to him. Well, she was with Matt now. Whether there was an afterlife or only a dark void, they were together.

"You all right?" Genevieve asked. She was standing by the pool table, her cue in hand, staring at him, and he realized that he must have been standing there, lost in thought.

"Yeah, sure, fine."

"Find out anything?" she asked.

"No." Eager to take his mind off his thoughts of a moment ago, he picked up a cue stick himself. "I'll rack 'em," he said.

She watched while he gathered and set the balls. "Break?" he asked her.

"Sure."

She was an exceptional player. She almost cleaned the table with her break.

"I didn't know rich kids got to be such sharks," he told her teasingly.

He was surprised when she paused, smoothing back a stray lock of her glorious auburn hair, and said, "I really wish you would quit that," she said.

"What?"

"Staring at me as if I grew up on another planet," she said.

"Sorry."

He stared at the brick wall, picturing the day Leslie had been there. She had talked to dead people. And *he* had talked to a dead man on the FDR. No. The medics must have been wrong. The guy had somehow survived long enough to save his niece.

But what about the morgue?

He'd been tired. Mind playing tricks.

"Joe?"

"Yeah, sorry."

She set her cue stick down. "I'd like to go home now, if you don't mind."

"We're in the middle of a game."

"No. You're in the middle of your memories. And that's all right. But I'd just like to go home."

He nodded. "Sure."

She was silent during the drive back to her place. Dusk was falling, and it seemed to have thrown a dark shadow over her. Over them.

As they neared her apartment, she said, "You can just drop me off in front."

"Not in this lifetime," he told her.

"There's a doorman on duty."

"Not good enough," he said.

"Joe, I…don't want or need to be protected."

"And I won't work this case unless you're careful and take every precaution."

She lifted her hands in a gesture of futility.

He parked the car, and walked with her past the doorman and the security guard on duty downstairs, and then up to her apartment.

When she opened her door, he just stood in the hallway, inhaling the scent of her perfume, light and evocative of summer breezes somewhere far from Manhattan.

Like the scent of her hair. Clean and inviting…

"You have to stop sleeping with her, you know," she told him softly, turning to face him.

"What?"

"Leslie."

"I never slept with Leslie," he heard himself say, and his words were far more curt than he had intended.

"But she's haunting you anyway," she said.

"Leslie is dead. Like Matt," he said.

"And I'm alive because of her," she said.

He shook his head. "I'm not sleeping with Leslie, even in my dreams," he said.

He was surprised when a slight smile curved her lips. "No?"

"No."

"You're sure?"

He frowned. "Gen…this is awkward."

"It shouldn't be," she whispered, something he couldn't define in her tone.

He shook his head, feeling lost, a little bit confused and more than a little bit dazed by the scent of her perfume, her hair…her nearness.

What was there not to like about Genevieve?

What was there not to *want* about Genevieve?

Blue eyes, intelligent, direct, seductive, alluring… That hair, like dark auburn fire, as soft as silk. Her height, her shape, slim and perfectly curved. She was erotic and enticing, everything God had intended for a woman to be, but he had somehow kept his distance in the past because…

Because of everything she had been through.

He suddenly felt as if he couldn't think, couldn't speak, but he tried. "I…I cared about Leslie, yes. Very much. But she was still in love with Matt. And now…I like to think that they're together now." He hadn't realized that he was touching her, but he was. His hands were on her shoulders. And she was close, actually leaning against him. He could feel the warmth of her. Every breath he took was filled with the scent of her.

"So you're really not sleeping with her in your dreams?" she whispered.

"No."

"Then maybe you want to sleep with me. In the flesh."

Oh, Lord.

"Genevieve…"

He felt alive in a way he hadn't felt in what seemed like eons. Fire was racing through his veins. He could feel her heartbeat. Her every breath.

"Gen…after everything you've been through…"

She clutched his hand, bringing it to her heart, her breast. "I'm alive, Joe. I'm not broken, not dead and I need to feel alive. Please…" She winced, almost backing away from him, but he wouldn't let her. "Talk about awkward. Here I am, throwing myself at you, and you're turning me down. I'm sorry. You don't have to—"

Enough.

He bent and kissed her. At first she was surprised. Then his mouth softened over hers, and she responded, rising on her toes, pressing against his body. Each cell in his body seemed to feel her slightest touch. Her mouth parted beneath his, wide, wet, deliciously decadent. She kissed with her tongue, erotic and sweet, the kind of thing that made a man forget everything in the world except her kiss. And she was still holding his hand against her breast. He kept kissing her, tasting her lips, playing with her tongue, seductive, suggestive….

He picked her up. She was tall for a woman, but small against his size. He knew the layout of her apartment and carried her to her bedroom, where he simply placed her on the bed, before lying down beside her.

There was no neat, leisurely discarding of their clothing. The buttons of her blouse simply gave way to the ministration of his fingers as they slipped beneath the hem, stroking over the tautness of her abdomen to the fullness of her breast. Her bra was an annoyance that somehow went away as soon as he found the hook. And then his face was buried between her breasts, ministering to them with hot, wet kisses, tender and hungry, subtle and raw. And then her jeans disappeared. The snap first, then the zipper lowering, his hand sliding down to cradle her hip, dislodging the denim, then caressing her skin as it moved lower, until the jeans, along with the little string panties beneath them, were gone.

His shirt hung open, and his own pants lay on the floor, tangled with hers, though he had no idea how they'd gotten there. His black briefs hit the floor, as well, and then she was crushed against him, the tip of her tongue sliding over his flesh. He groaned, his erection suddenly painful, but then he was lost in the sensation of her fingers on his flesh. Suddenly the two of them were a tangle of lips and tongues and teeth, and they were touching, touching....

He'd always thought that he would be so tender, so careful, if the thought of making love to her that had teased his imagination had ever come to fruition.

Her kidnapper had been impotent and cruel, and she had survived by playing to the man's ego. Because of that, he *should* have been slow. Careful. Tender.

But she was like a lava flow in his arms, radiant, electrifyingly hot, her touch boldly erotic. She was a writhing cascade of carnal beauty and desire in his arms, and he couldn't be gentle, couldn't take the time for tender, as his senses sent him spiraling out of control. Later he would remember straddling her, kissing her lips and looking into her eyes, those dark pools of half-lidded blue, and then his mouth was caressing her breasts, and his fingers were sliding between her thighs, his body adjusting to her exquisite length as he slid against her. Then his lips were moving lower over her abdomen, to the concave mystery between her thighs. When she cried out and arched against him, he moved again, driving himself into her, so aroused that he felt as if he was about to crawl out of his own skin. The world came down to nothing but the two of them, their naked, hot, wet flesh, their hunger and need, and then, cataclysmically, a combustion of muscle, sinew and flesh as he felt her climax, then followed her as if rockets had flared in the night.

And then...

He felt guilty. Torn.

But then she touched his face. Touched it so tenderly, as he slipped down by her side, cradling her against him.

"Joe," she said softly. And then, "Thank you. Thank you for being so...normal."

God, he didn't want to lose his heart so quickly. He may have lost his mind, but the world was still real, and they were who were they were, and normal or not, they were both still damaged.

"Normal?" he teased softly. "*Normal?* Do you know how to flatter a guy, or what? How about, 'Oh, Joe, you were incredible'?"

She laughed then, snuggling more tightly against him, and said, "Oh, Joe. You *were* incredible."

"Except I had to coach you to say so," he said.

They lay together for a while, just breathing, just being... And then her delicate hands with their talented fingers were on him again and she whispered, "If you're just as good a second time, I promise you won't have to tell me what to say."

It was enough.

They made love again then, heedless of everything dangerous that might be lurking in the night.

He couldn't help it; he had to ask.

"If you're so psychic, how come you didn't see this coming, huh?"

The girl hadn't been part of his original plan, but she hadn't given him any choice. She'd wanted her moment in the public eye, her fifteen minutes of fame.

Well, now her name would be blazoned across dozens of head-lines. She would make the news again, this time in a spectacular way. She should really be thanking him.

She hadn't been the one slated to die this way. He'd intended to go after someone else. Someone not only young and beautiful, but with a name and face so easily recognizable that the city would be in an absolute uproar.

"You will go down in history, my dear," he told her. She had been such an easy mark, her desire for fame and fortune blinding her to any possible danger.

She didn't look at all grateful for the favor he was doing her, though.

Her eyes were bulging, and she kept making little mewling noises behind the gag. He was actually a little bit sorry, but not sorry enough to stop.

He had an agenda, and he couldn't let her get in the way of it any more than she already had. Now it was time. Time to finish her off.

She kept struggling, but he'd been careful. No one would ever find any of his DNA under her fingernails, nor would they find his fingerprints, even if they could actually lift them off skin these days. Every killer left something behind or took something away, they said.

Not him.

He knew how to be careful.

Still…poison was much better. And so easy. You simply slipped it into the bastard's wine, he drank it and then he died.

Strangulation, on the other hand…

He'd never figured it would be so hard. Everything leading up to it had been easy. She'd fallen for the idea that they needed to keep their meeting secret. She'd been willing to slip into the dark with him, go wherever he wanted to go. Even getting on his boat and going out on the water…

Such a sap. Such a fool.

She's jumped at the offer when he'd suggested the champagne

to seal their deal, but she hadn't gotten as drunk as he had thought she was. She wanted to live. He had her bound and gagged, but she was still struggling, and...

Those eyes!

He thought he might see her awful, bulging eyes forever.

And then, at last, they closed.

She stopped struggling, and the rest was easy. Distasteful, but easy. He hadn't done so well the last time, hadn't been able to carry out his literary parallel to the full extent he would have liked to. In this day and age, walling up old Thorne wouldn't have been easy.

He couldn't really use Poe as his road map. Not without chancing being caught.

So he would just do his best to follow the master's model.

In this case, Genevieve O'Brien would have made a much more appropriate victim. She was far lovelier than the original cigar girl, Mary Rogers, not to mention Lori Star. But Lori had been too nosy, and though he didn't believe in psychics, someone else might, so she had had to become his Marie Roget.

Finally he was done, and he sent to her body to a watery grave. Of course, she would be discovered. It was, in fact, absolutely necessary that she be found.

As he headed back to the hustle and flow of life in New York, he contemplated the fact that he hadn't done a bad job. In fact, he was feeling quite satisfied with his efforts, even gleeful.

This was going to be fun.

Then he paused, arrested by a flash in his mind's eye. Those bulging eyes.

But for a minute, they hadn't belonged to the whore, the would-be psychic, Lori Star. They had been *her* eyes. The eyes of the beauty he had originally intended to take the victim's part in his reenactment of Poe's brilliant original. They had been the eyes of Genevieve O'Brien. Beautiful and blue.

Watching him.

Seeing him.

Knowing him for who—and what—he was.

Genevieve!

She was at his side, Joe told himself. There in her bed.

Sleeping.

He, too, had been asleep. No, it hadn't been a dream, it had been a nightmare, a look into the hellish pit of his imagination.

He had seen her face, and she'd been looking at him with those brilliantly blue eyes of hers.

Looking at him…in accusation.

And then those perfectly blue eyes had begun to bulge, her face growing red as it was suffused with blood, her throat darkening with the deep black and blue of bruises.

She was choking. Being choked. By the hands he could see around her throat. Powerful hands, squeezing, tightening, stealing her breath…stealing her *life*.

It had only been a dream, he told himself again. They were still in her bed, and she was next to him.

But she wasn't sleeping. She sat up suddenly, staring ahead blankly into the shadows of the room.

"Gen?" He was bathed in sweat, but already the Technicolor horror of the dream was fading.

She didn't hear him at first.

"Gen?" he said again.

She blinked, then shuddered and turned to him. Tousled hair framed the delicate features of her face, and she smiled. "Hey," she said softly.

"Hey," he said back.

She lay down beside him again, as if nothing were wrong in the world.

Was anything wrong?

"Are you okay?" he asked.

"Fine," she said, but she sounded hesitant as she added, "How about you?" He realized instantly that she was referring to what had transpired between them, that her question had nothing to do with what had been *his* nightmare. After all, people didn't share their dreams, their nightmares, not even if they had been intimate.

He shook off the dream. It was just a result of stress, he told himself. Just like thinking he'd heard the dead speak. No matter how embarrassing it was, he was going to have to go see a shrink. How many cases had he worked on in his life? How many corpses had he seen? So why now?

Yeah, a shrink was definitely in order.

He reached out, slipping his arms around her. "I'm fine. I haven't been so fine in a very long time," he said.

Her smiled deepened. "Can you stay...through the night?" she whispered.

"Just try to get rid of me," he told her.

Her eyes, so deep, so blue, so *trusting,* were on him.

He held her closer, and for a moment there was nothing between them but warmth. Contentment. Closeness. There was something so good about just being together, touching.

Later in the night, they made love again. And when they slept again at last, it was as if they were meant to fit together. The only thing that marred the feeling for him was...

Fear.

Dear God, he thought, please, don't let me lose her, too. We've come through so much. She's survived so much. Please...

CHAPTER 9

Jared Bigelow was waiting when Joe entered his office.

He had a floor in a Midtown building where Bigelow, Inc., ran its investment business. Most of the family money had been in real estate, but online investigation had shown Joe that Thorne had weighed other options and diversified into computers and several other high-tech concerns. He'd been president, but apparently he'd left most of the day-to-day management to his son for many years. He'd allowed himself the freedom to indulge his love of Edgar Allan Poe and to write the book that had brought him so much acclaim. And possibly led to his death.

A secretary let Joe in to see Jared, who indicated, without rising himself, that Joe should sit. There was a long sofa across from Bigelow's desk, but Joe opted to pull over a chair from the far side of the room; he wanted to be close enough to read the man's eyes.

"What is it? Why are you here?" Jared asked.

"To talk about your father's death," Joe said, as if the answer should have been obvious. "I'm assuming you want his killer caught," he went on easily.

"Of course, I do," Jared snapped.

"Then you shouldn't mind helping me out."

Jared sighed, and for a moment he didn't look like such a blustering jackass, Joe thought. "Look, my father was *murdered*. The police questioned me for hours. Do you think I'm an idiot? I'm obviously the first suspect on anyone's list. I inherited his money and this company, for one thing. But I loved my father, *and* we worked well together. You can question everyone from now until eternity, and they'll tell you the same thing."

Joe nodded. "Look, I know you talked to the police. And I know it has to be hard to lose your father, then have to deal with all the questions, knowing that people suspect you. But it will help me a lot if you just go over everything one more time. Everything that happened once you found him."

Jared Bigelow sat back in his chair, tapping a pencil against his desk and looking up at the ceiling, as if he could better recreate what had occurred.

"We were supposed to go to dinner."

"You, your aunt and your father."

"Yes."

"And your aunt was with you when you got to your father's house?"

"Yes, I picked her up first."

"She lives closer to you than your father did?"

"Different direction," Jared said. He shook his head, then shrugged. "We got there. I have a key, so I unlocked the door and went in. I called for my father, but he didn't answer. I went into his office and…he was slumped over. I thought at first that he'd just collapsed…maybe had a heart attack. I went a little crazy."

"You tried CPR?"

"Yes."

Joe was still trying to figure out how Thorne had ended up slumped over when the paramedics arrived, given that Jared had admitted to trying CPR on him, but he decided not to derail the man by asking about it now.

"And your aunt called 9-1-1?"

"Yes, I guess."

"You didn't call them, right?"

"I don't…I don't think so. I remember seeing my father…my aunt being there…and then Bennet coming down. And sirens, and then a lot of people." He looked at Jared. "That's all I remember," Jared said.

"Where was the wineglass?"

"What?"

"Your father's wineglass. Where was it?"

Jared frowned. "It was…on the desk. His desk."

"Where?"

"On the left, near the edge. What the hell does it matter?" He sounded aggravated again.

"I'm not sure."

Jared cleared his throat. "Well, then, if that's it…I have to get through today, and then his memorial service is tonight."

"And his burial?"

"He's being cremated."

"I see."

"So?" Jared Bigelow asked impatiently. "Is there anything else?"

"Just one more question," Joe said.

"And that is?"

"How long have you been having an affair with your aunt?" Joe asked easily.

The pencil dropped from Jared's fingers. His face turned a mottled shade of crimson and he stood up, enraged. "Get out. Get out of my office, and don't come back."

"It had to be a man," Lila Hawkins announced.

She had decided to drop in on Eileen Brideswell for lunch. And Genevieve hadn't been about to let Lila Hawkins anywhere near her mother without being present herself. It didn't matter that Bertha was going to be preparing the food, and that she wouldn't leave Eileen alone for a minute. Genevieve intended to be there.

From there, it had somehow turned into a ladies' lunch. Lou Sayles and Barbara Hirshorn were both there, too, as they all congregated around Eileen's balcony table. Henry and Bertha hovered nearby, determined to keep an eye on Eileen at all times.

"Lila, he was poisoned, so why are you so sure his killer was a man?" Eileen asked.

"And why do we have to keep rehashing this?" Barbara asked.

"We haven't even held Thorne's memorial yet," Lila said. "I think it's only natural that we're talking about it."

"Well, I still don't see why you think he had to be murdered by a man," Lou said.

"A man did it. I just know it," Lila said.

"Pity you don't know what man," Genevieve said, drawing one of Lila's reprimanding stares.

"Lila, historically, women who commit murder often use poison," Eileen said.

"Really?" Barbara Hirshorn demanded, looking horrified. "That's just too terrible. I can't believe a woman could have hurt the poor man."

"Killed him," Lou corrected.

Lila shook her head. "It was Larry Levine. He's always been jealous of Thorne. You know, sees himself as the real writer, while Thorne was just a businessman. Poor Thorne. It's a pity he ever wrote that book. It was his downfall."

"Lila, it's reckless of you to accuse Larry this way," Eileen said firmly. "And we have no idea if Thorne's book was really a factor or not."

For a moment they all paused, looking at one another awkwardly.

"Do you think that…Mary Vincenzo…could have…?" Barbara asked in a whisper.

"No," Lila said firmly. "I don't. I think they need to look at Larry. Hard."

"Does Larry know that you think he's the killer?" Barbara asked nervously.

"Oh, good heavens, I'm not foolish enough to accuse him publicly," Lila said. "What I'm saying here is just between us…and Genevieve, of course. Although I strongly suspect some of our words will be repeated to that private investigator you hired." She pointed a finger at Genevieve. "All right, maybe I'm saying this because I *know* it will be repeated, and there's where he should be looking. Tell that young man he needs to tear apart everything in Larry Levine's life. I promise you, Larry is—or was, anyway—viciously jealous of poor Thorne."

Genevieve held her tongue. Lila had talked about *pompous* Thorne when he'd been alive, but now he was *poor* Thorne.

"I'll tell Joe what you suspect, Lila," Genevieve said. "And I'm sure he'll investigate Larry." *Along with everyone else,* she added silently.

Lila nodded, as if pleased, and things were just as they should be. "Keep an eye on him at the service tonight. Keep a close eye on him," she warned gravely.

"Of course, Lila," Genevieve said.

At first, the service for Thorne Bigelow could have been any memorial. The prayers were said, and the mourners looked duly sad.

Both Raif Green and Tom Dooley were there, but they remained at the rear of the church, just watching.

When the prayers were over, Jared tearfully talked about his father's brilliance and his love for literature. Then Mary Vincenzo spoke about her brother-in-law's philanthropic work. Afterward, Jared stepped back to the podium and invited any of the mourners who had something to say to come up, starting with those who had been in his father's beloved society.

And with that, the service turned into a Poe convention.

Brook Avery came up and read from "Annabelle Lee." Then Don Tracy did a dramatic reading of "The Raven." Nat Halloway, though awkward and stiff, announced that he was reading from a story that was a favorite of his, as well as Thorne Bigelow's, "The Masque of the Red Death." Larry Levine was just as awkward, but he stumbled through a passage from "MS Found in a Bottle."

Lila Hawkins came up and briefly said that the community would mourn such a colorful man, and that the perpetrator of the crime must be caught. Lou Sayles spoke fondly of a man she would miss. Eileen was just as kind and brief. Sam Latham, though he remained in the hospital, sent his condolences through a coworker.

Barbara Hirshorn was shy and hesitant, but she commended Thorne Bigelow on all he had done for the literary community. When she finished, there was only scattered applause, because by then people were getting tired, and some had even slipped out.

Joe noticed, however, that one person was soundly clapping.

Albee Bennet, the butler.

He caught Joe watching him and smiled sheepishly. Later, as they were filing out of the church, he stopped Joe, who was with Genevieve and Eileen, and said, "That poor shy woman. I had to clap. I mean, the whole place went crazy over that egomaniac Don Tracy, but she was the one who really deserved the applause."

"That was very kind of you," Eileen told him sincerely.

And then they were all outside. Raif and Tom had respectfully disappeared before the end of the service, Joe noticed, as he watched Jared escorting Mary toward a limousine. Jared turned and stared back at Joe, and it was a bitter and resentful stare. Then he and Mary got into the limo, which drove smoothly away.

But Joe noticed that, as it started down the street, it was being followed.

Apparently the cops were still keeping an eye on Jared and his aunt.

He made a mental note that tomorrow he would try interviewing Mary Vincenzo. She never appeared quite as assured as Jared. She might well be the one to give him a clue to Jared's guilt or innocence.

"Thorne would have been horrified," Lila Hawkins announced, coming to stand beside them.

"Why?" Eileen asked, surprised. "I thought it was a lovely ceremony. A bit long, but Thorne would have enjoyed all the readings in his honor."

"I meant he would have been horrified that Jared isn't having a reception, that he isn't inviting people back to his father's house."

"Maybe he's still too upset," Eileen suggested.

Lila let out a snort and turned to Gen. "Did you mention Larry Levine to Mr. Connolly?" she asked, then looked meaningfully at Joe.

"There hasn't been time," Genevieve said, then quickly told him about Lila's suspicions.

"Is there some reason why you suspect him, especially?" Joe asked.

"He was always so jealous," Lila said.

"I'll certainly look into Larry's whereabouts at the time," he said.

"Good. And now, since nothing is on offer, I'm off," Lila told them. "Good night."

"Did you gain anything from this?" Genevieve asked him as they walked over to his car together.

"Maybe," he told her.

"What?"

He grinned. "I'm not sure yet. We'll have to see."

"Lila is very suspicious of Larry, but..."

"But?"

"Well, I think it was my mother who mentioned that women tend to use poison to commit murder."

"Historically speaking, that's true. Poison is generally thought of as a woman's weapon," Joe agreed.

"So do you think…?"

"I wish I knew what to think," he told her softly.

They drove Eileen home. Henry and Bertha were there to see that she got safely inside. When they got to Genevieve's apartment, Joe parked and went with her to her door. Once there, he hesitated.

"You're not leaving, are you?" she asked softly.

"Not if you don't want me to," he told her.

"I don't," she said, and smiled.

It was incredible, being with her. She was an exquisite lover, giving, exciting, tender, wild. He cared about her deeply, had been in danger of falling in love with her from the moment he had first seen her, as traumatic as it had been. Now, on only their second night together, they had already slipped easily into a close relationship, as if they were longtime lovers. He was physically exhausted and emotionally content when at last they slept.

There was no reason for the dream—the nightmare—to come again, but it did.

He was looking at her face, the perfect, sculpted beauty of it, and into her eyes. Those eyes, bluer than blue, filled with vibrancy, brilliance and life.

And then…

Then everything changed. Her eyes were suddenly huge and bulging, the red of broken capillaries spilling out around the blue, and bruises, blue and black, circled her neck, taking the form of handprints against the pale flesh of her throat….

"Joe!"

He heard her calling to him, but he was gasping, desperate to stop her murder but unable to figure out how. He couldn't see who was threatening her; he could only see the certain death that was facing her. He could only see her death…

As it happened.

"Joe!" she called again.

He awoke with a start. She was next to him, her hands on his shoulders as she shook him awake.

He stared at her for a long moment before registering the fact that he was awake, and she was alive and well and at his side and that he had been experiencing a nightmare once again.

He didn't speak at first, just put his arms around her and pulled her against him. He felt a thundering and knew that it was his own heart.

"Joe," she repeated again, struggling to free herself enough to look up and meet his eyes. "Joe, what is it?"

I keep seeing you die, he thought, but he had no intention of saying the words aloud. Instead, he shook his head to clear it. "Nightmare," he told her gruffly.

She seemed perplexed. Her hair spilled around her face, like soft flames in the shadows. "Maybe I should fire you," she said.

He shook his head, his eyes dead set on hers. "You can fire me if you want to, but I won't leave."

She smiled. "You…you really *are* incredible, Joe."

"Thanks. I'm good out of bed, too."

Her smile deepened, and she settled down at his side. As he drew her closer to him, she said, "Joe, I'm worried about you."

He hesitated. "You know, you had some kind of strange dream last night, too," he told her.

"I did?"

He nodded.

"I don't remember," she said.

"That's good," he told her, thinking of the way she'd been sitting bolt upright, as if she were looking at something, watching someone.

Great. They should both head straight to therapy.

Except that she didn't know that there was anything wrong. She didn't remember what she'd been dreaming. She didn't know...

That he heard dead people speak.

"Joe, are you sure you're all right?" she asked, sounding anxious. "I don't mean to pressure you. I'm awfully glad you're with me, but—"

"Shh, I'm fine," he assured her.

"Joe," she said. "Joe...you kept saying..."

"Saying what?"

"'No, don't die. You can't die.'"

He winced. Which would be worse? Lying and telling her that he had been dreaming about Leslie, or admitting that he was dreaming about someone murdering her?

"I know what you're thinking, but I wasn't dreaming about Leslie," he said softly.

She swallowed, looking at him, her eyes so caring, so concerned.

"Joe, you were saying something else, too."

"What?"

"'I don't talk to the dead. I don't.'"

"Wow, I'm having some major-league nightmares, huh?" he asked lightly.

"Joe, have you been having these dreams for a long time?" she asked.

"I don't think so," he said.

"Is it...me?" she asked, sounding a little ill.

"Good Lord, no!" he protested.

"I would never want to hurt you, Joe," she said.

"It's exactly the opposite," he told her. "I would never hurt *you*. I would kill someone before I let them hurt you in any way."

She touched his face in that special way of hers. He felt as if he were melting.

"Joe," she said, "I'm so glad you're here with me. I've wanted you here for...for a while, I admit."

"You are a dream, do you understand?" he asked passionately. "You are the best dream, and never a nightmare," he told her.

She seemed uncertain for a moment. Then she offered him a dry half smile. "I know I have to be careful because of that big head of yours, but...you really are incredible."

"Aw, shucks, ma'am."

He ran a hand down the length of her back. Sleek. Arousing. Then he turned toward her. Kissed her.

Made love to her.

They slept again, and he had no more dreams that night.

There was something wrong with Joe. She was sure of it, no matter how hard he tried to deny it.

Over coffee the next morning, Genevieve sat in her den at her desk and mulled over the fact that something was seriously troubling him.

Something?

Oh, yeah. Something.

"I don't talk to dead people. I don't."

She started to pick up the phone, hesitated, then set the receiver down again.

She really was worried.

Joe cared about her, she was certain. He was still protective, of course, but there was more to it than that. He made love to her with undeniable passion. He teased her, and when she teased him back, he responded with heartfelt laughter.

But he was having terrible nightmares. The kind that made him tense up like a coiled rattler in the middle of the night. The kind that seemed to grip him in a brutal vise.

And he hadn't been having them for long. No, only since he'd been sleeping with her.

That certainly didn't bode well for a lasting relationship.

She opened a desk drawer that she had closed a long time ago and hadn't opened since. It contained the newspaper articles from when she had been kidnapped.

And rescued.

There, in one of the pictures, was a man named Adam Harrison. He had come because he had been a friend of Leslie's. And Leslie had been a psychic. A real psychic.

She remembered Adam and his firm, Harrison Investigations, from that difficult time. Soft-spoken, reassuring and kind, he had never made her feel fragile, as if people had to walk on eggshells and whisper around her. Her mother also knew Adam, but differently. He, too, had been born wealthy, and they had met in the course of their various philanthropies.

She logged on to the Internet and started searching. She found a number of articles about bizarre events that came to an end when Harrison Investigations got involved. There were even hints that the government had called in the company on occasion.

She found the official Web page for Harrison Investigations, but it made no claims for the group's ability to communicate with the occult. In fact, it made no claims at all.

It was simply a page with a "contact us" form.

She hesitated. Then she began to type in who she was...

And what was happening to Joe in his sleep.

Joe had made a lunch date with Larry Levine. They met at a sandwich shop within sight of St. Paul's.

"I read your article on the service this morning," Joe told Larry.

Larry smiled, deeply pleased. "It was good, huh?" he asked.

"Excellent. A fine tribute," Joe said.

"Have you found anything out? Is there anything I can help you with?" Larry asked him anxiously.

"That day...the day he died, you were working, right?"

"Yeah, I was in the newspaper office all day."

"Why?" Joe asked.

All of a sudden, Larry didn't appear to be so eager to help. "Because I'm not rich, and I have to work my ass off to make a living."

Joe grinned without humor. "You work every day of the week, then?"

"If I need to," Larry said grimly. "I'm always looking for a hot story. That's what a reporter does."

"What about a book? Have you ever wanted to write a book yourself? Like the kind of tribute to Poe and his life that Thorne wrote?"

Larry hesitated, staring at him. He reached for the sugar and stirred some into his coffee. "I was the one who suggested to Thorne that he write the book, using a lot of the information we'd discussed at our meetings. You've got to understand. We all have real lives—we're not totally focused on the memory of a doomed poet. But Poe is an arresting subject. He was brilliant, but also sad. His own worst enemy. And did you know that the first reading of 'The Raven' was in Greenwich Village? Anyway...sure, one day I'd like to write a book, maybe about Poe, maybe not. But that doesn't take away from the fact that Thorne wrote a damn good biography of the man. I envied him his talent, sure. But I was at work the entire afternoon he was killed. I was going to attend the same dinner, and that's why I was at work. I'd screwed around with some friends in from Buffalo on Friday, when I should have been finishing up a few routine articles, so I worked Saturday, instead. And you can check it out."

Larry certainly sounded sincere.

"What's your take on the other folks on the board?" Joe asked him.

Larry laughed. "They're supposed to be my friends, but...you want it honestly?"

"Of course."

"Let's see. Lila's place in society and her inheritance allow her to be a blowhard. On top of that, she's opinionated, and I think she had a crush on Thorne. Thorne, of course, would never have looked twice at her. With his kind of money, he got pretty young things hanging on him all the time. Lou, well, it's just not in her nature. Barbara is a mouse, but at least she's a mouse who loves Poe. Eileen? She's pure class. Mary Vincenzo was only around because of Thorne and Jared. Jared? Rich kid. Brat. Don Tracy likes to hear himself talk and hangs around with the literati so he can get his name in the papers. Brook Avery wants to be a literary giant, but he's got a long way to go. Nat Halloway is a money man who wants to hang with a more artistic crowd, and because of his connection with Thorne, he was able to do so. Sam Latham? Good man, and I hope he gets out of the hospital soon."

"So who killed Thorne, in your opinion?" Joe asked.

"Lila," Larry assured him knowingly.

When Joe left Larry, he had a notebook filled with the names and numbers of people Larry was convinced could assure Joe that he'd been working all day when Thorne had been murdered. And he had a gut feeling—which admittedly didn't prove anything—that Larry was telling him the truth, at least about his own whereabouts. He wasn't convinced that Lila had killed Thorne, though. She was far too vocal about accusing Larry, making far too much of a fuss. Guilty people had a tendency to lie low. Lila was doing anything but.

It was growing late, and Joe found himself wandering the neighborhood. He loved Lower Manhattan, but he hated it, too, for everything he had lost here. Eventually he found himself standing on the sidewalk across the street from one of the area's prime historic landmarks, Hastings House. Matt had died in an explosion there, and Leslie had almost died at the same time. But she had lived to return to the city, and to Hastings House.

And then she had died after all, saving Genevieve.

He stared at the house. It was open to the public, but the last tour of the day was long over. As he stood there, though, the front door opened. To the best of his knowledge, Leslie had been the last one to stay at the restored colonial manor. The tunnels that had led from the house to the old subway line where Genevieve had been held prisoner had been closed. Blasted shut.

No one should have been there, and in fact, no one was in sight, yet the door had opened.

He instinctively felt for the concealed gun at his hip and walked across the street.

The gate to the front walk opened to his touch, though it should have been locked.

One of the staff could still be there. One of the costumed historians who welcomed tourists could still be working, and the unlocked door could simply have blown open.

He felt responsible for the house, though God knew why. Perhaps he felt he owed it to Leslie, he thought. Her appreciation for the past was something that had stayed with him.

And she had loved this house, even after Matt had died here.

He walked through the gate and headed up the steps.

The only light inside the house was the red glow of the security lights. He stepped through the doorway and paused. "Is anyone here?" he called out. He walked into the parlor and looked up the stairway. Darkness loomed above him.

"Hey, is anyone here?" he said again.

He felt as if something brushed his cheek.

Joe.

It was just a whisper, so faint that he might almost have imagined it.

He was crazy. He *had* imagined it. He was tempted to go running from the house, screaming.

Hardly a macho thing to do.

Did he think of himself as macho?

No, but he'd never thought of himself as an overimaginative coward, either.

"Who the hell is in here?" he called out angrily.

Joe, it's all right. Just learn to listen.

There was a scurrying sound from the kitchen. He forced himself to walk toward it, though every instinct in him was screaming to get away. "Who the hell are you? Show yourself now," he demanded.

He heard the sound again.

Great. What the hell was he going to find? A ghostly figure, draped in white, floating above the ground?

He felt a brush of air again. It wasn't a cold breath but something warm, almost alive. Almost…tender. *Joe, go easy. Please, Joe.*

He kept himself under tight control and strode into the kitchen. While the rest of the house was furnished according to the period, the kitchen featured every modern convenience. He heard the scurrying sound again, and his hand tightened on the butt of his gun.

No, Joe…it's all right, the voice said.

But the voice and the scurrying weren't coming from the same place.

Something started to move. A shadow rising.

Joe, it's just a kid.

Then the shadow itself cried out, it's voice clearly young. "Don't hurt me!"

CHAPTER 10

"Show yourself!" Joe demanded.

The shadow stood up by the refrigerator, and in the red security light he saw that it was a teenaged girl. She had tousled blond hair and a face that was pinched with hunger.

"Don't shoot me! Please don't shoot me."

He let out the breath he hadn't realized he was holding. He'd never been so relieved in his life. She was real. She was flesh and blood.

Except that...

She wasn't the one who'd been whispering to him.

"Who are you, and what are you doing in here?" he asked her.

He didn't expect the response he got. The girl burst into tears and came running toward him, then threw herself against him. "I'm so scared!" she told him.

"Hey, hey, it's all right," he said awkwardly. He drew away from her and realized that she must be a runaway.

"What's your name?"

"Debbie," she said.

"Debbie what?" he pursued.

"Smith," she said.

He almost laughed out loud. She was making it up.

"All right, Debbie…Smith, why are you so scared? And what are you doing in this house?" he asked gently.

"I…slipped in before they locked up."

"And you left the door open," he told her.

She looked at him, shaking her head. "No, I didn't," she said firmly.

"All right, hang on," he said, and pulled out his phone, thinking he should call the police. But he didn't. He hesitated, and then he called Genevieve, instead.

"Joe?" She sounded relieved to hear from him, but also uneasy. He wondered why, but there wasn't time now to ask her. "Gen, I, uh, I think I have need of your prowess as a social worker," he told her.

"Oh?" she said, clearly curious. "Joe, where are you?"

"Hastings House," he admitted.

"Hastings House?" She sounded worried.

"The door was open," he explained, leaving out the how of it. "And I found a young…lady named Debbie Smith hiding inside, and now I'm not sure what to do with her."

"How old is she?" Genevieve asked.

"I don't know."

"I'll come down there right away."

"No!" He didn't want her going out alone, especially at night. In fact, he didn't want her going out alone at all, he realized, an opinion she would not appreciate.

"Fine. Come by and pick me up, then. You can bring her with you. I'll stand right by the doorman until you get here."

"Okay," he said. "Ten minutes." Then he hung up and looked at the girl, who looked eerie in the strange red light.

"You…you won't call the police on me, will you?" she begged.

"Not yet. But let's get out of here and go see a friend of mine. I'll have to call someone to come lock this place up for the night," he told her.

He didn't close the door as they left, but it closed behind him, and he heard a lock slide into place.

"Shit!" the girl said, jumping.

"It must lock automatically," Joe said, glad not to have to call someone and try to explain what the hell he had been doing there. He led her down the front walk, and when they stepped out onto the sidewalk, the gate closed behind them, as well.

"You're not going to leave me here, are you?" Debbie asked, panic in her tone.

"No, I told you, we're going to see a friend of mine. She'll know what to do," Joe said.

The traffic was bad once they picked up his car, and Joe chafed at the thought of Genevieve standing out on the street, even with her doorman. He knew he was being paranoid, but he couldn't escape his dreams.

Nor the fear that his own sense of insanity seemed to be growing worse.

The girl at his side was silent. He realized that he wasn't helping matters, but he wasn't sure what to say. "So, Debbie…where are you from?" he asked at last.

She stared at him as if he had just threatened her with torture. "Here," she said. Like "Smith," he knew it was a lie.

"Whatever," he muttered. "Let me try this one. What's your favorite food?"

She'd been staring straight ahead, but she looked at him then. "At this moment? Anything not out of a Dumpster," she told him, and he knew that, at least, was honest.

His nerves felt totally stretched by the time he finally pulled up in front of Genevieve's apartment, and then he was afraid he would snap like a bowstring from the tremendous sense of relief he felt when he saw her there, chatting with Mac, the doorman. She ran up to the car and hopped into the backseat.

"Hey," she said cheerfully to Debbie. "I'm Genevieve."

"Debbie," the girl said.

"Where should we go?" Joe asked, looking at Genevieve in the rearview mirror.

She shrugged. "O'Malley's, of course."

He nodded, and a few minutes later he let the two of them off in front of the pub and went in search of a parking space. Luckily, he found a place in a lot a block or so away. He made his way back as quickly as he could and found that Genevieve and Debbie were playing darts with his two favorite old timers, Angus MacHenry and Paddy O'Leary, and had claimed a nearby booth as their own.

"Joseph Connolly, that took ye long enough," Paddy told him.

"Hey, I'm not as young as I used to be," Joe said.

"Well, this young 'un is a pip at darts," Angus said. "And she's a Douglas. A nice Scottish lass."

He looked at Genevieve, who shrugged and gave him a little grin. "A Douglas from Philadelphia," she said softly.

To his surprise, Debbie walked over to him and gave him a quick hug, then looked at him with embarrassment.

He smiled at her, trying not to look as awkward as he felt. "Philly, hmm?" he said.

She nodded, then threw her next dart.

"Good shot," Genevieve said encouragingly.

Joe watched as Angus challenged Debbie to a head-to-head match, and she replied with a laugh and a promise to best him.

"Runaway?" he whispered to Genevieve.

"Yes. But we've called her parents. They're on their way." She turned to him, speaking softly. "She came up here with some older friends, who wound up leaving her on her own a few days ago when they decided to get warm and cuddly with a couple of druggies. There were some toughs on the street, and she got scared, so she ran into Hastings House. Luckily, they weren't able to follow her."

"Weren't able to?" he asked.

Genevieve shrugged. "Strange, huh?" she said, staring at him.

"What's so strange?" he asked, feeling as if he were choking.

"When she was running, the gate and the door both opened. But as soon as she was inside, they both closed. And locked."

He frowned, staring at Genevieve. "No. They must have just decided to let her go. When I was on the street, both the gate and the door were open."

"Right," Genevieve said, looking into his eyes.

"The security system must be going haywire," he heard himself say.

"Haywire," she echoed, but it didn't really sound as if she were agreeing with him.

"Was everything all right with you today?" he asked her.

She nodded and smiled. "Great. How did it go with Larry Levine?"

He shrugged. "I believe him," he told her.

"So…we're not getting anywhere," she said.

"Gen, you know as well as I do that finding out the truth can take a long time," he said.

She nodded, biting her lower lip.

"Hamburgers coming up!" Bridget, their waitress of a few nights back, called as she made her way through the crowd milling near the bar. Debbie all but clapped her hands.

"Oh, thank you," she said fervently.

Angus punched Joe lightly on the arm. "Thank ye kindly, Joe. Gen said you'd be buying tonight."

"My pleasure," Joe said, and laughed, then watched as Angus, Paddy and Debbie made themselves comfortable in the booth and started reaching for the ketchup and mustard.

"You did a good thing tonight, Joe," Gen told him.

"I did?"

"Debbie just got in with a wrong crowd. She's been here five days. Her parents reported her missing, but…well, you know how that goes. Anyway, if you'd called the police, it might have gotten complicated."

"Well, then…I'm glad I called you."

"Me, too. So, do you want a hamburger, too?"

"Sure. I'll just go with the flow," he said.

She grinned and started toward the bar to find Bridget and put in his food order. He slid in beside Angus on the banquette.

"Did ye hear about the way the old house welcomed the girl?" Paddy asked him.

"What?"

Debbie looked at him. She was a pretty kid, with warm brown eyes. "That house saved me tonight," she told him softly. "Well, you did, too, of course. But it was really weird, the way the house just let me in when I needed to get away from those guys."

"Security system," he said, but he didn't even believe that himself.

Because he'd heard *her*.

That night, he'd heard Leslie whisper to him, trying to make sure he knew Debbie wasn't a criminal, that he didn't shoot her.

But he couldn't escape the sense that she'd been trying to tell him something else, as well.

He gritted his teeth. Hard. "Security system," he repeated.

Debbie looked at him. "The house saved me," she said somberly. "It really did."

Hastings House, he thought. The place where Matt had died. The entry to the tunnel and the room where Leslie had died, where Genevieve had been kept prisoner.

The place was damned, he decided.

But not, he insisted to himself, haunted.

A moment later Genevieve came back and slipped into the booth next to him.

"Just how old is she?" Joe asked, indicating Debbie, who had finished her burger and gotten up to play darts again.

"Fifteen."

"Such a kid," he said.

Genevieve arched a brow at him. "You've had to look for enough missing kids. Debbie is lucky, and you know it. Most of the time, a kid of fifteen, she's already on drugs. Then she's hooking."

"Then she's Candy Cane," Joe said.

"Yeah." Genevieve said, studying him. "Have you heard from her yet?"

He shook his head. "I'll go back over tomorrow," he told her.

A few hours later, Debbie's parents walked in. There were a lot of tears as they embraced their daughter, then thanked Joe and Genevieve.

A few minutes later, when it was time to leave, Debbie gave Genevieve a long hug. After that, she walked over to Joe and looked at him solemnly. "Thank you," she said simply.

"Stick with the folks, huh?" he said. "They seem like nice people."

"I guess." She hesitated, then whispered, "He's not my father. He married my mom. They have a new baby."

"They still love you."

She squared her shoulders. "Look, I know I was a jerk. I just thought it would be cool to see New York. And...I know this is gonna sound weird, but I think that house used me to get to you."

He shook his head. "Debbie, it's just a house."

She stared back at him gravely. "No. It's not just a house. That house...it *breathes*. It's like it has a heartbeat. Honest. It's not evil, though. I'm telling you, it saved *me*. But it wanted *you*."

He felt a slight tremor shoot through him. There was a kid in front of him—a kid—telling him that Hastings House was...*alive*.

Ridiculous.

She had been scared, traumatized, that was all, and she was seeing things as spooky and chilling, when there was undoubtedly a perfectly logical explanation.

As soon Debbie had left with her parents, Joe decided that he needed a beer.

Later, he drove back to Genevieve's.

He pretended exhaustion. He couldn't help it. There was a whisper in his ear, and that whisper was Leslie.

But when he fell asleep, he dreamed again. And in his dream, Genevieve was walking toward him. They were on a beach, or maybe they were in the clouds. She was wearing something light that trailed behind her in the breeze. She was smiling, her expression radiant. Her hair whipped behind her like auburn silk.

And her eyes...

Her eyes were that endless blue.

She smiled, excited, as if she were expecting something... something good.

Then the bruises began to appear on her throat, and her eyes widened and began to bulge as she stared at him, choking, gasping for breath.

He heard her whisper, *Help me. Please, help me,* and he woke with a start, bolting upright in the bed.

He didn't wake her, though. Genevieve was asleep at his side in a soft yellow tank top and ladies' boxers, breathing easily. The light filtering in from beyond the drawn curtains played brilliant fire tricks with her hair.

He lay back down, convinced he really was losing his mind, then jerked into a sitting position again.

Debbie had claimed that Hastings House seemed to breathe. That it had a heartbeat. That it had tried to save her.

And the house—or someone in it—had whispered to him.

Dead people whispered to him.

He stared up at the ceiling, teeth clenched. No. He didn't want to talk to ghosts. He didn't want to listen to dead people and he damned well didn't want to believe that a house could be haunted, much less alive.

Suddenly he was afraid, but not for himself. For Genevieve.

Afraid that his dreams meant something, that she was in danger.

He perched on one elbow and watched her sleep, wanting to touch her, not wanting to awaken her.

But her eyelids fluttered suddenly, as if she sensed him, sensed his concern, even in the depths of her sleep.

Her eyes opened, and she caught him studying her.

"What?" she asked, and started to sit up.

"Nothing," he said softly.

"Then…?"

"I was just watching you," he said, knowing it was both a lie and the truth.

She reached up and touched his face in that special way of hers. Then her knuckles brushed down over his chest, and the next thing he knew, she was pushing him down against the mattress and straddling him. When he would have touched her in return, she whispered a soft but commanding, "No."

She bent and quickly brushed her lips against his.

Then she teased his chest with her kiss and the silky caress of her hair.

Finally she moved lower, but not until he was so aroused that he couldn't stand it did she allow him to reach for her, lift her and bring her back down on his erection. He felt as if the world exploded along with him as he entered her.

Later she slept again, and he lay beside her knowing that he had kept the truth from her. That she didn't know he was crazy. That he had gone to Hastings House and heard the whisper of the woman with whom he'd once been falling in love.

Leslie.

A dead woman.

And Gen didn't know that he kept seeing her eyes as the life was choked out of her.

She didn't know that the man she was depending on was slowly losing his mind.

In the morning, he left before she woke up.

He was suddenly anxious, because Lori Star had never contacted him.

At Lori's apartment, he once again got no response to his knocking. Before he could move on to Susie's place, her door opened and she came out to speak to him. She was clearly distressed. "I was going to call you today. I don't know what to do. I don't think Lori ever came home."

He frowned. "You haven't seen her since Sunday?"

"No. And I don't know what to do. I mean, I'm not her next of kin or anything. And I always heard that a person had to be missing for forty-eight hours before anyone could fill out a missing-persons report, but I don't even know if she *is* a missing person. Oh, God, I'm so upset. I just don't know what to do."

"It's all right. But it's definitely time to fill out a missing-persons report. I'll go down to the police station with you."

"Police station?" she said, and cleared her throat. "Um, Mr. Connolly, you should know…I've been arrested before."

"It doesn't matter," he assured her.

But she wasn't going to go down to the station with him, he quickly realized, so he put through a call to Raif.

"That's Missing Persons," Raif told him.

"Raif, this is the woman who was on television after that pileup on the FDR, saying she was psychic."

"Then talk to Traffic," Raif said.

"Raif, dammit, Sam Latham was in that accident. It might be connected."

"And it might not!"

Exasperated, Joe held his temper. "So do you have any answers on the Thorne Bigelow murder yet?" he demanded.

"No," Raif admitted after a moment, then sighed. "All right, I'll get someone from Missing Persons and come over."

"We've got to get into the apartment," Joe added.

"Ask her friend if she has a key," Raif told him. "Maybe she's supposed to water the plants or something like that."

Raif turned to Susie. "Do you have a key to the apartment?" he asked.

She shook her head, and Joe went back to his call.

"She's a missing person, Raif. Can't we get a warrant on probable cause to find out if she happens to be lying dead inside?"

"Yeah, yeah," Raif said. "All right, I'll be there as soon as I can."

Eventually Raif showed up with, as promised, an officer from Missing Persons. Susie did her best to answer all the necessary questions, but it was difficult. If Lori had living parents or other family, Susie had never met them. She didn't even know if Lori Star was her real name.

While the officer worked with Susie, Raif, who had the warrant in his pocket, entered the apartment. Joe followed him in without asking permission.

"There's nothing out of order," Raif said. He sighed, turning to Joe. "Look, I know you thought there was something believable about her, but...the woman is a prostitute. Who knows? She wasn't bad-looking. Maybe she found someone she could, um, 'work' for a while. Maybe she's shacked up in a motel somewhere."

"She didn't leave with any of her belongings, not according to what Susie told us," Joe said. "She went 'to see a man about a horse.' It sounds to me like she went out to meet someone, and that it didn't go very well."

"Either that," Raif argued, "or she went to meet someone and it went *very* well. Didn't you see *Pretty Woman*?"

"Raif, are you serious?" Joe demanded.

"No, but...I don't know what to tell you."

Frustrated, Joe looked through Lori Star's apartment, but try as he might, he couldn't see anything out of order, either. Nor had she left a note of her destination scribbled down on her phone pad.

"Can you trace her phone records, at least?" Joe asked Raif.

"I'll get someone on it," Raif promised.

At last, with nothing else to do, Joe left, still entirely frustrated.

But as he left Lori's apartment, he thought of the first time Genevieve had come to him about Thorne Bigelow's murder.

Quoth the raven: die.

New York City hadn't been especially good to Poe. The man had been self-destructive, true, but he had come to New York to make his fortune. In the end, the city hadn't afforded him the fame he had craved, much less any riches. Down and out, he had left the city to take a job in Philadelphia.

After he had left the city, a murder had occurred, that of Mary Rogers, known in the papers of the day as the beautiful cigar girl. She had disappeared on a Sunday.

Just like Lori Star.

Mary had left her home of her own free will.

Just like Lori Star.

Suddenly a sense of panic seized him, and he was desperate to see Genevieve, to make sure she was all right. He raced to her building, gave his name to the security guard and was cleared to go up. She met him at her door, an anxious look on her face.

"Joe, what is it?" she asked.

"Lori Star never came home," he told her.

He barely noticed that she returned to the phone on the counter and told someone, "I'll call you back later, okay?"

"Did you call the police about her?" she asked.

"Yes, of course." He met her eyes. "I'd like to go to my apartment," he told her.

"All right."

"And I want you to come with me."

"Sure," she agreed.

He felt some of the tension easing out of him.

Genevieve was fine. There was no reason for him to keep feeling this awful sense of panic.

"Joe, what's going on with you? What's wrong?" she asked him.

"Nothing. It's just...an uneasy time," he said, trying to sound nonchalant. "I'm not going to be happy until we find Thorne Bigelow's killer."

She looked at him and nodded, but she knew there was more to what was bothering him than that. But arguing with him wasn't going to get her anywhere.

He tried to keep things light as they drove out to Brooklyn. He asked her about Eileen, making sure she was keeping in regular touch with her mother.

"Of course," she told him.

"What are we doing here?" Genevieve asked him when they got to his place.

"I live here," he said as lightly as he could.

"No, I meant what are we going to do while we're here? What are we looking for?"

He hesitated. "This may be really farfetched and stupid," he told her.

"I'm listening."

"All right, let's suppose that someone really is reenacting Poe's work with real victims. Thorne was the first victim. And Sam... maybe that was intentional, too, or maybe the killer just saw a convenient chance and took it. But if the two *are* connected, the murderer must have been scared shi—alarmed when Lori Star started getting attention from the media."

"Even if they're not connected, Lori Star's certainty that she knew what happened on the highway might have disturbed someone," Genevieve pointed out.

"True."

"You think she's dead, don't you?" Genevieve asked him.

He started to deny it, but then he met her eyes and tried not to turn away. Tried not to imagine her being strangled, even though the vision haunted him night after night.

"Yes," he said.

"And...you think all three deaths are connected, don't you? Even though you're the one who told me that Poe's characters never committed vehicular homicide?"

He stared back at her. "Yes," he admitted flatly.

"Okay, so what are we doing here?"

"Research."

"On...?"

"'The Mystery of Marie Roget.' You take the story itself. I'll look up what really happened."

She looked skeptical, but she accepted his collection of Poe stories, while he turned to his computer. They worked in companionable silence for a while.

The Internet was full of leads, but also sent him from page to page following them up. He made notes as he went.

"There's a forword to the story in your book, you know," Genevieve said. She had curled into the extra chair in his office.

"Yes?"

"It was originally published in three segments. Poe probably knew the real girl, but he was living in Philadelphia when she was killed. He thought the story would put him on the literary map. He was convinced that the girl's first disappearance—she had disappeared for several days a few years before her murder, then reappeared—had something to do with her death. He had planned on making the murderer a Navy man, but then they discovered that she might have gone for an abortion, and that she might have died in a house in New Jersey, a small inn of sorts, owned by a woman named Loss who had three sons. They thought the sons might have tried to dispose of Mary's body. No one ever went to trial and, according to this preface, no one ever discovered the truth of her death. Poe altered his story before the final segment was published so it would agree with the latest facts in the investigation."

"When her body was first found," Joe said, studying his monitor, "the coroner noted that she'd been strangled. That there were bruises around her throat, and a piece of her torn dress was so tightly tied around her neck that it was embedded in the flesh."

He looked at Genevieve. "I don't believe Mary Rogers died because of a botched abortion, though that might have been what sent her to New Jersey. I believe the coroner's initial report was right and she was strangled. But what *I* believe isn't important. What matters is that I think the *murderer* also believes that she was strangled. And that he acted on that."

"Joe, we don't even know for sure that Lori's dead, much less how she died," she said.

"Let's take a ride over to New Jersey," he suggested.

"We're going to find her in New Jersey?" she asked doubtfully.

"Her body will turn up in New Jersey," he said with complete certainty.

Just then his cell phone started to ring. He answered it with a brief, "Connolly."

"Joe, it's Raif."

His friend sounded strange, Joe thought, and asked, "What is it? Have you found something?"

He could hear the deep breath Raif took before answering.

"Yes."

"What?"

"We've found her body."

Genevieve was staring at him, frowning intently.

"Lori Star?" Joe asked, though he didn't really need to. He knew that it was her. And he could make an educated guess as to what condition they'd found her in, too.

"Yeah, or so it seems. It's in pretty bad shape."

"You found it in the river on the New Jersey side, right?" Joe said.

"How did you know?" Raif demanded.

"I've read 'The Mystery of Marie Roget,'" Joe told him.

"What? Oh, hell, a Poe story, right? Shit. I'm going to have to brush up on my reading."

"There was a real murder, too."

"Great," Raif said. "Just what we need." Joe could see Raif in his mind's eye, sitting in the passenger seat and talking on the phone while Tom drove.

To Jersey?

"So this murder winds up in the hands of the New Jersey police, huh?" Joe said.

"Yeah, but the lead detective isn't a bad guy. I told him I had an interest, which he understood. I explained that we're all looking at a connection between Lori Star and our other vics. Folks can be territorial in law enforcement, but not usually stupid, so we're welcome to be in on it."

Joe winced, running his fingers through his hair. "Can I tag along?" he asked.

"That's why I called you," Raif said. "We're on our way over to Jersey now."

Bingo, Joe thought. "Tell me where I'm going and I'll meet you there," he said.

INTERLUDE

It's so damned hard, being a ghost. Trying to communicate.

It's just human nature, I suppose. We so badly want to know what lies beyond the world in which we live and breathe, but we're also terrified of that knowledge. It's so much easier to opt for denial, to pretend that we're immortal. That other people die, not us.

Even people with tremendous courage, the ones who will fight to the death for a cause, who will run into burning buildings to rescue others in danger, find something frightening about examining what lies beyond the veil.

What the living don't know is that sometimes, when you're very lucky, there is someone waiting there on the other side to help.

Matt says it's wrong to bring anyone into Hastings House, where I'm at my best. And he keeps trying to help me leave. But the two of them came by, and I had to help. The thing is, both of them *knew*.

Well, at least I was able to help that girl. And that's what it's all about. Helping.

I'm worried about Genevieve, though. I don't want to see her die, but I think someone else *does*.

We know what's happening in the world, Matt and I. He's figured out how to turn on the TV, and sometimes I can do it, too.

A lot of the time we don't need to make that effort—and trust me, it really is an effort—though. The docents have it on a lot during the day anyway, and they leave newspapers lying around all the time, so we keep up with what's going on.

That's why Matt decided we had to try to get out beyond Hastings House and try to touch others. To help them.

It was exhausting. I seem to be able to move easily enough through the subway tunnels. I can even connect to the PATH train and get over to New Jersey. But outside of the tunnels…

It had to be done, though. We followed the tunnel under the Hudson, and then we went outside and started looking for her. I kept feeling myself fading, but Matt held on to me, and somehow kept me going. Kept me, well, *alive,* for lack of a better word.

It wasn't easy, but we did it. We found her.

We found Lori Star, and she was still so scared, so lost. And what she had to tell us…

Well, it helped. And then again…

It didn't.

# CHAPTER 11

Genevieve was more disturbed than she had expected to find out for certain that Lori Star was dead.

The victim of a murderer.

Possibly—no, *probably*—the victim of the same killer who had murdered Thorne Bigelow.

She was certain that no one other than Joe and herself would instantly make that assumption. But Joe had *known*. He had known, before Lori was found, that she had been killed. And he had seemed to know that she would be found in New Jersey, as well.

She knew that he wasn't going to take her with him to meet with the police. His own position was going to be tenuous enough; he was just lucky that Raif was on his side, and Raif was lucky that the New Jersey homicide officers were willing to accept that there might be a connection to Thorne Bigelow's death and let the New York cops in on the case.

She was actually glad that she wouldn't have to come up with an excuse to get away from him that afternoon. She hadn't known how she was going to manage the feat, since he had been getting more and more adamant that she not go anywhere without him.

She didn't mind that Joe was so determined to be with her, but she *did* mind that he continually seemed not just preoccupied but so...

Haunted.

She was worried about him. He had been so strange last night.

"Make sure you keep in touch with me," she told him when he brought her back to her apartment. "Please."

"And you stay here. Promise?"

"I'll be around," she swore.

And she would be. Just not exactly at home.

Shortly after he left, she got the call she'd been expecting from Adam Harrison. He had gotten her message, he said, and had arrived in town, where he would be happy to meet with her at her convenience. She asked him to come right over.

She felt that she knew him fairly well. He had been there when she was brought back into the light of day. And he had been at Leslie's funeral. She knew that Joe had also gotten to know him when Adam had come to New York City to help Leslie deal with her ghostly communications when Genevieve had still been a prisoner far beneath the ground in the abandoned subway tunnel.

Adam Harrison was regal and dignified, despite his advancing age. He was a tall man, slender, with snow-white hair and kind eyes that looked out on the world without judgment. Probably the best thing about him was his ability to listen without distraction.

He greeted her like a distant uncle, with warmth, but without presumption. He held her at arm's length for long seconds, studying her with discerning eyes before commending her on how well she looked.

She made tea and asked him about the weather in Virginia, and then about Brent and Nikki Blackhawk, the employees who had been with him in New York.

He asked about her mother.

And then they were seated together at the table and she couldn't quite start speaking.

He laid his hand gently over hers and looked at her encouragingly.

She inhaled deeply, then plunged in. "Have you ever heard of a man named Thorne Bigelow?"

He frowned. "Yes, actually. He wrote an excellent book about Poe," he responded. "And he was murdered recently."

She nodded, and he waited patiently for her to speak.

"There was a society. The New York Poe Society—it still exists—and the members are known as Ravens. He and my mother are both on the board."

"Ah," Adam murmured, and leaned back in his chair. "I'm going to take it that you hired Joe to work the case. Because your mother is a Raven and you're worried about her."

"Exactly."

"So tell me what else has happened that has you so worried," he said.

She told him all she knew about Thorne Bigelow's murder, the accident on the highway, the disappearance of Lori Star—and the very recent discovery of her body. He listened gravely.

"Do the police seem competent?" he asked at last.

"The lead detectives on the case are friends of Joe," she said, then shrugged. "And he seems to think they're more than competent."

"Genevieve, I'm sure you're aware that my agency deals with the occult."

"Yes," she said.

"Do you believe that you've seen a ghost?"

"No," she said, then frowned, remembering the night she had dreamed she was someone else. When she had awakened and found that Joe had also had a strange dream.

"Genevieve, I can't help you if don't talk to me," he told her.

She smiled wistfully. "You know, Adam, I *wanted* to see a ghost. I even made myself think I saw one, at the cemetery, a year ago. I wanted to believe I saw Matt and Leslie, arm in arm, disappearing over a rise together. I wanted to believe that it was okay. I mean, don't you think that happens a lot of the time? We see and hear what we want to? We believe what we want to?"

"I'll put it this way," he answered. "I know that our energy goes somewhere when we die, and that some people can see that energy. But you called me for a reason. Would you like to tell me what it is?"

"It's Joe," she said.

"I see."

"I think something's wrong with him."

"What has he said to you?"

"Nothing."

"Then...?"

"I can see it."

"What is it that you see?"

"He's...strange. It's as if... I don't know. I don't know how to explain any of it. But it all started..." She hesitated, thinking back. "It all started when he was supposed to meet me at the museum. It was a fund-raiser in Leslie's honor, actually," she told him.

He nodded, and she went on.

"He didn't show up. When I called him, he was down at O'Malley's. He said that he hadn't been able to get to the museum because of the traffic. There was this really bad accident on the FDR. He pulled a little girl out of a car. And Sam Latham, another Raven—another member of the board—was hurt."

"Was anyone killed in the accident?"

"Yes. The little girl's uncle."

"Hmm," Adam said thoughtfully.

"Then...last night he was at Hastings House."

"Oh?" Adam said, his attention sharpening.

"He said he was just in the area and the house was open. So he went in and found a teenage girl hiding inside."

"Living, I hope?" Adam said.

"Yes, but she was strange, too. She said the house saved her. She was being chased by some thugs, and she said the house...let her in. That it saved her. And then Joe was so strange after that. I kept thinking he must have been remembering Leslie. I tried to leave him alone, even later, when— Even later."

A slight smile played across his lips. "So...you and Joe are together?"

She was surprised at how easily she blushed. "For now, anyway," she said. "I'm afraid that maybe he just feels overly protective of me."

"When you're overly protective," Adam said gently, "you sleep on a sofa. And that wasn't a sleeping-on-the-sofa blush."

"Well..." she mumbled.

"You're afraid that he's in love with a ghost, aren't you?" Adam asked her.

She wasn't ready to accept that there really were ghosts, so she said, "I think a man can easily be in love with a memory."

"Memories tend to be golden," he pointed out.

"Adam, Joe isn't the type to admit he sees ghosts," she said. "But from the way he reacted to what that girl said, I think maybe that's what's happening. Or what he thinks is happening, anyway."

"He doesn't know that you've called me, does he?"

She flushed again, shaking her head.

He drummed his fingers on the table. "Well, I think he'll see me anyway. Out of respect, if nothing else. I was a close friend of Leslie's, and he knows it."

"Can you...can you help, do you think?"

She was surprised when he was quiet for a long moment.

"I think that if Joe is seeing ghosts, one of them—maybe Leslie— is trying to tell him something," he said.

She was surprised at the misery she felt. They needed all the help they could get, so this was hardly the time to be jealous.

Especially of a ghost.

"Is, um, that the way it usually works?" she asked, and she could tell that her voice sounded distant.

"Look, you hired Joe because you were worried, right?"

"Yes," she said.

"And," he continued, "you also hired him because you wanted him around."

She lowered her head.

He touched her hand again. "That's a good thing. I'm pretty sure Joe wanted to be around."

"Thanks," she said, and looked at Adam curiously. "So how does it usually work? Do you...just walk down the street and see ghosts?"

"Actually, no," he told her. "I don't have a gift of any kind."

"But...you're the Harrison in Harrison Investigations," she said.

He stood, hands behind his back, and wandered to the window to look down at the street. "I had a son...who is gone now."

"I'm so sorry," she murmured.

"It's fine. He's been gone a long time. But before he died, he *did* have a gift. He knew what was going to happen. And he knew he wasn't long for this world. He actually told me when he would die, what would happen."

"I'm so sorry," she repeated.

"He didn't really leave," he told her softly.

She kept smiling, but Adam Harrison could see right through her.

"The souls of those we love do linger sometimes. When they need to," he told her.

"When they need to?" she repeated questioningly.

"Sometimes they just need to understand what happened to them. Sometimes they're lost. And other times it's as if they have a mission, something they have to do, someone they have to save." He paused, looking at her. "Leslie MacIntyre had an exceptional gift. She helped so many of them."

"So many of the dead?" Genevieve asked. She had always liked to believe that her mind was open. She had even liked to believe that the souls of the departed were real, that in giving up her own life, Leslie MacIntyre had found eternity with her beloved Matt.

But now...

She just felt crazy. And a little scared.

What the hell was Joe going to say? She had called in the ghost hunters to save him.

"Sometimes," Adam said lightly, "the gift seems to pass from one person to the next. After death," he added very softly.

Chills shot down her spine.

"Then Joe might have...inherited Leslie's gift, is that what you're saying?"

He shrugged and sat down again, looking at her. "Maybe Joe. Maybe you. Maybe both of you. I don't really know. There are no real rules that I know of, and there's certainly no manual."

Another chill shot through her. She shouldn't have called this man. Everything he said was just upsetting her more, not to mention how upset Joe was going to be with her.

As if he'd read her mind, Adam said, "Don't worry, please. I really am friendly with Joe Connolly. He's not going to think it's all that strange to see me. I'll have to call in a few more people, though."

"Ghost hunters?" she asked, almost afraid to hear the answer.

"Don't worry. Joe is already acquainted with a few my 'ghost hunters,' as you call them. He likes Brent and Nikki, and so will you."

"I met them. He's Native American, right?"

"Half." He laughed. "The other half is Irish. He'll fit right in at O'Malley's."

She didn't know if he was teasing or not. "I don't think Joe is going to like any of this at all," she said.

"I hope you're wrong, but either way, he needs it," Adam said firmly.

Her stomach had been fluttering, but now, as he looked at her, she was satisfied that she had done the only thing she could have. And that it was the right thing.

"We do have to get to the bottom of this," he said.

His expression was grave, and she suddenly wondered if she was in any personal danger.

Maybe she should have just stayed the hell out of it.

No. She couldn't have. She cared too much about Joe for that. But she was afraid, she realized.

She wasn't a Raven, though, so shouldn't that mean she was safe, if they were right and the Poe Killer really was going after members of the society, not just trying to cover his tracks? But Lori Star hadn't been a Raven, either. She had simply been a young woman who had connected herself to the case because she'd experienced some-thing strange and told her story.

Of course, Gen thought, as a shudder rippled through her, much the same could be said of her. She'd chosen to connect herself to the case, too.

There were certainly no obvious similarities between Marie Rogers' death in the eighteen-forties and the situation Joe found when he reached New Jersey.

He met Raif and Tom first, and they briefed him as they arrived at the mortuary, where the body had already been taken.

"The corpse was dragged out of the river about an hour and a half before I spoke to you," Raif said.

"She's been in the water some time," Tom told him.

"From what I've heard, she isn't very pretty," Raif said.

"Water really does a number on a body. Even after only a few days," Tom said.

Joe knew that already. "Cause of death?" he asked.

"Looks like strangulation," Raif told him. "Though they won't know for sure until they finish the autopsy. We should be just in time for it to start. They're rushing it, just in case there's a connection to the Bigelow case," he explained.

"Thanks for letting me in on this," Joe said. "Any trouble with the Jersey boys? Over me, I mean?"

"No. Vic says you've worked with him before," Joe told him.

Vic? It had to be Victor Nelson. He would be about fifty now, and he had apparently moved from Vice to Murder. Years ago, Joe had been hired to find a missing teenager. She'd been living in a crack house in Jersey City. When he'd found the girl, he'd helped the cops—including Victor Nelson—close down the house, and as a bonus, they'd broken up a gun ring that had been based there, too.

Victor Nelson greeted Joe and the others civilly inside one of the autopsy rooms. The doctor on duty was a man named Ben Sears. He nodded in acknowledgment as they came in, then got started.

Lori Star's skin was mottled, discolored, and her flesh gnawed. Fish and river creatures had already been busy, mostly on her extremities.

"You couldn't see the bruises on her throat when she was wet," Victor said. He was a gruff man, a good, steady cop. His looked a little green around the gills, though, and Joe thought it was good to see that, even after all these years, the autopsy of a murder victim still bothered him.

The coroner explained that the bruises had appeared as the skin had dried out.

They were deep blue and black, forming a horrible necklace around the woman's throat, just like in Joe's dreams. Except that in his dreams...

They had been around Genevieve's throat.

He swallowed hard as he felt bile rise in the back of his throat. He'd been to too many autopsies to get sick at one now. But if he were ever going to...

This would be the one.

Or was he only queasy because he had looked at the corpse's face and seen another? A face he knew intimately. Stared not into Lori's eyes but into Gen's. Eyes that he couldn't help thinking were staring back at him accusingly.

He found himself thinking back to a passage he had read online that morning.

July 28th, 1841. A group of young men out for a casual walk along the shoreline of the Hudson River, on the New Jersey side, in an area of Hoboken known as Sybil's Cave, a place where people often come to escape the busy, hectic crowding of New York City, came across what appeared to be a mass of clothing in the water. When the young men hurriedly took a boat from a nearby dock and went to investigate, they discovered that what they had taken for clothing was really the body of a young woman. Her face seemed to have been severely battered. She was a terrible spectacle to behold.

They would never have associated the decomposing corpse drawn from the river with the missing girl who had been regaled by an entire city for her sheer loveliness.

Joe swallowed hard and forced himself to stare at Lori's ravaged face.

No one would readily associate this corpse with someone who had once been young and pretty.

There was no way that Lori Star was looking at him. It was difficult even to see where her eyes should be.

Ben Sears spoke in a clear, emotionless voice, directing his words to the microphone that hung down above the body as he worked on it. The corpse had already been photographed, washed and laid out for him. Additional pictures were being taken by a police photographer as Sears pointed out injuries done to the flesh, asking for close-ups.

"Marks at the neck suggest manual strangulation. There is also a strip of lace, apparently from the young woman's blouse, that was tied around the neck so tightly that it sank into the flesh, even before postmortem swelling due to immersion. The pattern of bruising suggests that the killer is right-handed."

His voice droned on as he commented on the fact that the physical damage inflicted by her assailant appeared to be mainly to her face and head. The decomposition and damage done elsewhere on the body appeared to have been from her days in the river.

Joe stood by silently while the chest was opened and Sears stated firmly that strangulation was the cause of death, not drowning.

Organs were weighed.

Specimens were taken.

In the back of his mind, Joe was aware of the constant gurgle of running water washing away the fluids that leaked from the body as the medical examiner went about his work.

Scrapings taken from under the nails suggested that the victim had lacked the chance to fight back against her attacker, and ligature marks on the wrists suggested that her hands had been bound. Damage to the sexual organs was postmortem and possibly due to the depradations of the river creatures.

Sears ended the autopsy by asking his assistants to sew the body back up, and telling the microphone above the corpse that further comments on the death would come after he received the lab work on various samples he had taken.

Joe realized, looking at the cops assembled around the stainless-steel autopsy table, that the procedure had seemed to affect them all the same way it had affected him.

Every man there seemed frozen.

Finally they all roused themselves to walk out. There was no goodbye to the man at the front desk, nothing.

"Jesus," Vic said when they got outside, looking up at the sky and taking a huge gulp of fresh air.

"That was a bad one," Tom Dooley said.

"So do you think this murder's related to your guy?" Vic asked the New York detectives.

"I think we have to operate on that assumption," Raif said.

That assumption became fact a moment later, when one of the coroner's assistants came running out after them, holding a sealed evidence bag containing a torn piece of typing paper.

"Detective Nelson?"

Vic turned around.

"Doctor Sears thought you should take this to the lab right away. It was in her pocket. We're sending the clothes over for analysis ourselves, but he thought you'd want this first."

Vic held the bag up to the sun, so they could all see the contents.

It was just a ripped piece of what appeared to be run-of-the-mill printer paper, but there was something written on it that had all but faded away. Joe read the typed words aloud.

Quoth the raven: die.

There was a media frenzy.

Dr. Sears denied mentioning the scrap of paper to anyone, so maybe it had been one of his assistants. But it didn't really matter how word got out, only that it *was* out.

By the time the evening news aired, every station in the Tri-State Area was carrying the story, and linking the murder of Lori Star—born Lori Spielberg, one of the stations discovered—to that of Thorne Bigelow.

Someone had come up with a picture of Lori at her prettiest, and some enterprising reporter had made the Mary Rogers-Marie Roget connection, so she was now being compared to the beautiful cigar girl who had once worked at Anderson's Tobacco. The girl who had been given eternal life in her pathetic death by the great American author Edgar Allan Poe.

Lori was more famous than she ever could have imagined.

Her somewhat questionable past had been forgiven. She was the medium who had witnessed the accident through some spectral magic, connecting Sam Latham's injuries to Thorne Bigelow's death, a connection the police were now avidly following up on.

Joe had watched the news at a bar, sharing a beer with Vic, Raif and Tom. Then, disgusted with the over-the-top coverage, he excused himself and headed out. On the way to his car, he decided to follow the trail of the murder that had taken place in the eighteen-forties. He walked the Hoboken shoreline, but since he couldn't really go back in time over a hundred and fifty years, he could only close his eyes and try to imagine.

Of course, the contemporary killer couldn't possibly have gone back in time, either. And Joe didn't think the killer had done a particularly impressive job of murdering Thorne Bigelow à la Poe, anyway. The man had died via his love of wine, true, but he hadn't been walled up to die slowly, gasping for air, thirsting, known that the end was coming. He had been poisoned, a somewhat less drawn-out method.

Poisoning the unsuspecting was easy, while strangling an eager and unsuspecting young woman, though not impossibly difficult, would taken a certain amount of strength.

Did that eliminate the women as suspects?

He walked the shoreline, and realized after a while that he'd been waiting for something.

And then he knew what.

Dead people were talking to him.

He was hearing whispers in his ear when he shouldn't have been.

He spoke aloud to the breeze. "If I'm going to go crazy, you might want to give me some useful information."

Luckily there was no one around to hear him and think right along with him that he was going nuts.

He felt like a fool anyway.

When it seemed as if the voices weren't going to tell him anything, he gave up and walked back to his car, ready to return to Manhattan.

This murder had changed everything. There couldn't possibly be a Raven who wasn't frightened now. Not that Lori Star had been a Raven, but she had connected Bigelow's death with Latham's accident, and that had been enough to paint a target on her back.

He put a call through to Genevieve's apartment, his irrational sense of fear for her growing again. She answered on the first ring, and he was glad to hear her voice.

"You saw the news?" he asked.

"You can't miss it. It's on every network," she told him.

"Right."

"Are you all right?" she asked.

"Fine."

Yeah, right. He thought of his last visit to a morgue, when the corpse had turned to him. Thank God Lori hadn't spoken to him through that broken face.

He asked after Eileen, who Gen assured him was safe at home, then told her that he would see her soon.

His thoughts turned to Sam Latham, who was still in the hospital—and quite possibly in danger.

When Joe reached the city, his first order of business was going to be to visit Sam, and to make sure that his wife, Dorothy, had indeed hired private security to watch over him. There was no longer any doubt. Whether Sam had been a target that day on the highway or not, there was a serial killer on the move, and Sam was certainly a sitting duck now.

When Joe arrived at the hospital, he was relieved to see that there was an imposing uniformed guard in a chair outside the door to Sam's room. The guard asked him who he was, and Joe showed his credentials.

"Hey, I've heard of you. I should have recognized you."

"Why would you have recognized me?" Joe asked.

"Your face was just on the news," the man said, nodding toward the TV visible just inside the door to Sam's room.

"Why?" Joe demanded.

"The Lori Star murder. They linked it back to some literary group and a bunch of wealthy people, and one of them has a daughter, that Genevieve O'Something who was kidnapped last year. And that led to you," he finished.

Joe stared at the man, who'd sounded as calm as if he were reciting a chorus of "The hip bone's connected to the leg bone."

Damn it all, he cursed silently. He didn't want the city recognizing his face again, knowing him.

"Mr. Latham is sleeping, but his wife's in with him. I'll tell her you're here," the man said.

Joe nodded, still cursing fate.

When the guard ushered him into the room a moment later, Sam was sleeping, and Dorothy was sitting in a chair at his side, watching the small television with the sound turned down low.

"Mr. Connolly, so nice to see you," she said, and stood.

"Mrs. Latham," he acknowledged. "I'm very glad you've hired security for Sam's room."

She nodded, studying him. "Sam really was targeted by some madman, wasn't he?" she asked, worry evident in both her tone and her eyes.

"We don't know that for sure, but it's best to assume the worst and take precautions."

"I admit I'm terrified now."

"Just be careful and smart, Mrs. Latham."

She smiled warmly. "Dorothy, please."

"Dorothy," he repeated. "And I'm just Joe."

"Thank you, Joe," she said.

Even as she spoke, the machine monitoring Sam's vital signs began to beep shrilly.

"Oh, my God!" Dorothy gasped.

Joe frowned, staring at the IV leading into Sam's arm. "Who's been in here?" he demanded.

"No one but one of the nurses a few minutes ago," she said.

He didn't hesitate. Maybe he should have. But he didn't.

He strode toward the man in the bed and ripped the IV from his arm.

CHAPTER 12

In Jared Bigelow's penthouse on Park Avenue, Mary Vincenzo watched the news as it unfolded.

She had just come in, and this was the first time she was seeing everything that was being plastered all over the news.

And plastered it was.

She was watching coverage of an interview with a police spokesman on one of the major networks, but she could see reporters for the other networks and at least half a dozen cable channels in the background.

On the channel she had randomly chosen, a handsome man with a lean build and silver-white hair was solemnly comparing Lori Star's murder to the one it had clearly been intended to emulate, that of Mary Rogers, so many years ago.

Mary Rogers. A woman with her own name. She couldn't help finding something creepy about the coincidence. The newsman kept using the name as he spoke, and it gave her the shivers.

She wondered why it bothered her so much. After all, the girl who had just died was named Lori.

Watching, she shook her head. She could visualize the girl who had been killed, remembering her from when she had been on the news after the accident on the FDR. What an idiot she'd been to talk so publicly about what she knew. Of course, that was in retrospect. When Lori Star had gone to the news stations, she had surely never imagined herself as the next victim.

Mary watched, drawn like a moth to a flame. Had Lori's death been the work of the same killer who'd murdered Thorne? True, there had been an identical note, but the police weren't saying whether they were convinced that the same perpetrator was responsible. Someone might have had it in for Lori and then decided to blame it on the Poe Killer to throw off suspicion.

Behind her, Jared Bigelow sniffed. "Psychic actress, my ass," he said.

"Jared!" she snapped.

"What?"

"The girl is dead."

"So? That doesn't automatically turn her into a saint."

"Have some respect. She was murdered."

"And now she's dead and at peace—which she didn't need to be. She talked a ton of trash, hogging the limelight, after that accident," Jared said.

Mary turned to him, troubled. "Jared, that's horrible. It sounds like you're saying she asked for what happened to her."

"Your words, not mine," he said.

She shivered, hugging her arms around her.

"Oh, my dear Miss Mary," he said, using the nickname he had long ago given her. He walked over and sat down at her side, slipping his arms around her. "She was trash, Mary. Pure trash."

"But, Jared…"

"You're with me. You'll always be safe," he promised her.

She looked at him. He was the only child and sole heir of a wealthy man. He was intelligent, courteous and extremely handsome in his slightly long-haired, artistic way. He'd been given every earthly possession he had ever wanted. And despite all his advantages, he could be petulant, with a tendency to pout like a two-year-old.

She was just five years his senior.

She had started to fall in love with him when he'd been just seventeen. But her husband had been alive then, a man who had demanded all her attention. He'd been quite a bit older than she was, and rich. Very rich. A man with a family fortune and no children.

She hadn't been a bad wife. She'd been a faithful while he'd been alive, grateful for all the doors the Bigelow money had opened for her. She'd never had to work, unlike her sister back home in Iowa, who had grown old fast, serving hash and hamburgers at a roadside diner.

She had been grateful for her marriage, and if she'd dreamed of younger men and attending trendier clubs, well, she had limited herself to dreaming. She had made herself be a good wife.

Then he died of a heart attack. And the ironic thing—a truth somehow kept out of the papers—was that he had died in the arms of a younger woman. She'd almost found it amusing. She'd been as true as the pure white snow, while he had gone after a younger lover.

He'd been close to his brother and nephew, though.

So was she.

After all, she was family, and she remained family. And she had fallen more and more in love—or maybe just lust—with her nephew, who was, after all, only a nephew by marriage.

There was just something about him.

He could make her do anything, even when she knew he was behaving like a spoiled brat.

She looked at him now, though, and swallowed hard. "I would think you, of all people, could be sympathetic. She died a terrible death."

"What death isn't terrible?" he asked lightly. Then he wrapped his arms around her. His fingers teased suggestively against her breasts. She felt an instant surge of excitement sweep through her. He was young and handsome.

And rich.

She couldn't help be afraid that he would lose interest in her. She needed to go on acting a little bit forbidden, to keep herself exciting and erotic.

She rose and lifted her skirt so she could straddle him, where he sat on the couch. She knew that he liked it when things seemed a little taboo. Dirty. He liked to sneak in quickies in places where they shouldn't be exposing themselves. He liked to do it when she was dressed, just lifting her skirt for access. Like this.

She moved her hand, playing with his trousers, pretending to struggle with his belt buckle and zipper. As if she were desperate.

He was actually so easy.

And he had a real thing for her. He lusted after her. Maybe he even loved her.

They made swift, frantic love there on the couch, and she relaxed against him.

She had forgotten the television while they were in the throes of passion, but now she could hear the anchorman again as he suggested that Lori had been sexually assaulted by her killer, that she had probably been killed soon after she had last been seen, somewhere between four and nine o'clock on Sunday afternoon, and that several days in the water had accelerated the decomposition of her body.

Mary leaned against Jared and stared in his eyes. She could feel him growing hard again inside her.

"Jared?"

"What?"

Where were you on Sunday evening?

But the words wouldn't form on her lips. She shook her head, closed her eyes and leaned against him again. Afraid.

Afraid that he might realize what she had been about to say.

"Never mind," she said, and started to move above him.

At O'Malley's, Don Tracy, Brook Avery and Larry Levine were sharing a table.

"It's all so horrible," Brook said, shuddering.

"Nevermore, indeed," Don said, lifting his beer.

"Shit," Larry swore.

Brook set a hand on his shoulder. "Larry, we'll be all right."

Larry frowned. "Of course we'll be all right. That's not why I'm pissed."

"Then…?" Don asked.

"I should have fucking been there!" Larry said. "Can you believe it? I'm a Raven, and this is the story of the year, and I should be covering it."

Eileen Brideswell and the rest of the board members walked into the bar at that point, staring at the television as they walked over to join the others, who pulled over an empty table to make room for them.

Over in a corner, Paddy pulled out his phone. He hated feeling like a tattletale, but he couldn't help worrying about Eileen. In his opinion, Genevieve needed to know where her mother was.

In his robe, in his own room, Albee Bennet watched the evening news and lifted his teacup to the television.

"Quoth the raven," he said sadly. "Ah, Thorne, you would have loved the irony."

Then he set his teacup down and looked around.

The night had somehow become ominous.

He rose and locked the door to his room, even though the house had an excellent security system, and these days it was always set.

He wasn't about to end up like Thorne. He wouldn't trust anyone. He would be safe.

Even so, when he went to bed, early, he couldn't help feeling afraid.

She had hired Joe Connolly because he was good at his job, Genevieve told herself, even if she had to admit that other reasons might have lurked in the back corners of her mind. He was good, and she was living proof of that.

Adam owned a place up by Central Park, so he had headed up there a while ago and was making arrangements for his employees to join him. Brent Blackhawk, who was coming with his wife, was a sheriff in Virginia. A lawman. That should mollify Joe, once he found out what she had done, she thought.

With Adam out of the house, she tried to think as Joe would think, to reason. The possibility remained that the killer had nothing to do with the New York Poe Society and was using the connection as a smoke screen. She started with simple deduction. Had the murders been carried out in a manner that definitely spoke of someone emulating Poe's writings?

No.

Poisoned wine didn't connect directly with any of Poe's stories, nor was it terribly unique.

Sam Latham had been hurt in a car accident, and there was certainly no vehicular homicide in any of Poe's stories. Nor had a note been found at the scene.

Lori's murder was the only one that really lined up with Poe's work, and even then, the parallels weren't definitive.

Was the killer trying to slay every member of the society, or at least the board? There was no way to know, but certainly the killer wasn't limiting himself to that group, though Lori Star *had* connected herself to the case.

Okay, she told herself. Time to try eliminating some possibilities.

She made a list of the members of the board, then looked down it, considering each one as a suspect. She eliminated three names right off the bat: Thorne, because he was dead; Sam, because he was in the hospital; her mother…

Because she was her mother.

That left Jared Bigelow and Mary Vincenzo, whom she suspected were sleeping together. Both stood to gain from Thorne Bigelow's death—Jared directly, and Mary through her relationship with Jared. Lila Hawkins, unlikely, but not impossible. Lou Sayles? God, she hoped not. The woman had worked with the city's children for years, and the thought of a murderer having that kind of access… She shuddered. Barbara Hirshorn, such a timid little bird, but you never knew… Still waters and all that.

It took ingenuity, not strength, to administer poison, but what had been done to Lori Star had taken strength.

Four men remained as possible suspects. Five, if she counted Albee Bennet, and she knew Joe would. After all, he had admitted being in the house when Thorne was murdered. So she added him to the list that still included Larry Levine, Brook Avery, Don Tracy and Nat Halloway.

She was anxious to talk to Joe now, but she was afraid, as well, given that she had called in the ghostbusters. But something was disturbing him deeply, and she couldn't help feeling that Adam Harrison was the man who could help.

Her phone rang, and she picked it up absently.

She could hear noise and Irish music in the background, and frowned. Someone was calling her from O'Malley's, she thought.

"Hello?"

"Is that you, lovely Genevieve?"

The slight Irish lilt was a giveaway.

"Paddy? What's up? Why are you calling me?"

"I just thought you should know. Your mum is here. And all her bird society people."

"You mean, the Poe Society? Thanks for letting me know, Paddy," she said, then hung up a moment later and leapt to her feet. What was Eileen doing going out without protection, and with that group, of all people? Disturbed, she grabbed her purse and headed out.

Joe had been shoved out of the way when the doctors and nurses rushed in, but he was quick to warn them that they needed to find out what had been in Sam's IV.

He'd actually been afraid he was going to be tackled by the security guard, but Dorothy had jumped to his defense, and then, thank God, a nurse had shouted that she didn't like the look of the IV fluid, and taken the bag of fluids away for testing. One of the doctors suspected a morphine overdose, but final word would have to wait for the lab results.

Once the medical personnel got Sam stabilized—though he was still unconscious—inserted a fresh IV and left, Dorothy broke into sobs, and Joe tried to calm her.

"I hired security and everything," she said. "Why does someone want to kill Sam?"

Why indeed? Joe asked himself.

Two police officers arrived a few minutes later, men Joe didn't know. They started by interviewing the security guard, then Dorothy, then him, followed by all the medical personnel on duty on the floor, none of whom had been in to change Sam's IV.

The shift change had been at seven, about fifteen minutes before Joe had arrived, and Dorothy's best recollection was that someone had come in right in the middle of it to adjust the IV. It had been the perfect opportunity for someone to slip into hospital scrubs during the busy changeover, then casually walk in and inject something that shouldn't have been there into Sam's IV.

Dorothy wasn't certain she could identify whoever who had come in. She had dozed off and still been half asleep when the last person came in to adjust the IV.

The guard in the hallway swore up and down that no one who wasn't in proper hospital attire had gotten past him.

It seemed forever before things began to calm down. By then, Raif and Tom Dooley, looking seriously worse for wear, had arrived.

Another round of questioning began.

The police ordered official round-the-clock surveillance. Other than Dorothy and anyone she approved, no one wearing a surgical mask or without hospital ID was to be allowed into Sam's room, which was immediately changed. Records were altered so he was no longer listed under his own name.

A team of crime-scene investigators came in to examine the room, although everyone thought that it was a losing proposition. The would-be killer had been wearing scrubs, including latex gloves, so fingerprints were unlikely.

Around ten, Sam woke up, none the worse for an ordeal he'd been totally unaware of, but he could add nothing to what the police had already found out, since he'd slept through the IV change. After he heard the full story, he was simply grateful to be alive.

Genevieve was disturbed that her mother hadn't told her about her plans to go out with the Ravens, and she felt a keen sense of unease as she headed down to the garage to get her car. The garage wasn't ablaze with light, but it wasn't dark, either, though there were shadows. Still, it could only be accessed—whether from the street or from the building itself—with a resident's keycard.

Even so, the door had barely closed behind her before she felt a strange sensation sweep over her. It wasn't exactly fear. Not at first. It was more the sense that someone else was out there.

Then she felt the chill.

It was as if the shadows themselves were moving, as if darkness itself was snaking around her.

Touching her.

She started walking more quickly, looking around. She couldn't see anyone.

She almost raced back to the door to the building, actually pictured herself fumbling with the key, desperate to get inside as quickly as she could.

At that point her car was closer, so she started to run for it. And even though she had just *seen* that there was no one around, she *felt* that someone was there. Someone who was trying to stop her.

She reached her car, but her fingers were trembling, and she had trouble opening the door.

Darkness, like a living thing, seemed to be rising behind her. She could almost feel the whisper of its breath.

She got the door open at last and jumped inside, then slammed and locked the door behind her. She swallowed hard as paranoia seized her again, and turned around. She actually expected to see someone sitting in the backseat, someone who'd hidden there, waiting, and who was now ready to pounce....

But no one was there. Of course.

Then...

She could have sworn she heard a whisper.

Help me!

She swallowed a scream and swung her head around, from side to side, in panic. She was ready to abandon the car and even opened the door.

Then she saw someone walking through the garage and plainly heard a cheerful whistle. Her blood seemed to freeze in her veins.

"Evening, Miss O'Brien."

She sagged against the back of the seat and stared blankly at Tim Rindle, one of the night watchmen. Tim was a handsome twenty-something, clean cut, always cheerful. He had just gotten out of the service and was working nights to put himself through college.

"Are you all right?" he asked, as he got closer and saw her face, which she knew must have been as pale as a ghost.

She swallowed hard. Straightened. Felt like a complete fool.

"I'm fine, Tim."

"Are you sure? Do you need me to help you up to your apartment or anything?" he asked anxiously.

Fear was slipping away like a cast-off shawl. There was so obviously no one but the two of them in the garage.

She almost laughed aloud at herself. But then Tim's smile faded. "Miss O'Brien, you've got to be careful out there, okay?"

"Of course. I'm always careful."

"There's nothing on the news except about that poor girl who was murdered."

"I'll be careful, Tim."

He was still looking at her, worried and frowning. "I wish I was off duty—I'd go with you to make sure you get wherever you're going."

"I'm just going to O'Malley's. I know everyone there, and they all know me. My mother is waiting for me there," she fibbed, "and a bunch of other friends."

She gave him a wave and started the engine. Then she paused and rolled down the window. "Tim?"

"Yes?"

"There are two of you on duty tonight, right?"

"Always," he assured her.

"You haven't seen anyone walking around down here, have you?"

"Well, I gave Mrs. Larson—you know, in 10-D—her cat back a few minutes ago."

She laughed. "Pussy Galore?"

"Yeah," he said, and shook his head. "She's got to keep that cat inside. He's going to get run over one of these days if he doesn't stop sneaking through the door whenever anyone goes in or out."

She smiled and waved again. "Good night. And thanks."

As she merged with the traffic, she decided that she was going a little bit crazy. It was all Joe's fault, she told herself, then admitted that maybe it was at least partly her own, too. After all, she was the one who had just called in Harrison Investigations.

She had to stop her mind from playing games, that was all. All she needed was to be careful, make sure she stuck to safe places, and that she didn't take chances.

And she needed to see to it that her mother did the same.

With that thought in mind, she searched the street for parking and found a place in a busy area not far from the pub. But when she stepped out of her car to put money in the meter, she once again felt as if someone eerie and not quite real was nearby. For a split second, she felt the sense of shadows and darkness and fear closing in around her.

She told herself that she was on a busy New York street, a stone's throw from the pub itself, not to mention that she had great lung capacity and could scream like a banshee, if need be.

She turned around and realized that there *was* someone near her.

A bum.

"Lady, got some change?" he whined.

She felt ridiculously relieved and handed him a dollar.

He offered her a toothless grin and walked off.

Shaking her head, she hurried on to the pub.

CHAPTER 13

Everyone in the place seemed to be talking when she walked in, and the music playing in the background only added to the din.

Paddy, over by the dartboard, was the first to see her. "Gen!" he called out, and made his way through a throng of people to reach her.

"Hey, Paddy," she said, and gave him a kiss on the cheek.

"You're all right, lass?"

"Of course, Paddy, thanks."

He nodded gravely. "Eileen is at the table over yonder."

"Thanks," she said.

"Oh, aye, there's a group of them tonight, there be."

"I guess everyone is shaken up."

He lowered his voice to a whisper, though he could have shouted and no one would have noticed. "She shouldn't be alone with those folks right now, and that's a fact," he said.

Her heart seemed to skip a beat. "I agree," she whispered conspiratorially in return, then smiled and patted his shoulder. "But when she's here, I know she's fine. I know you and Angus will keep an eye on her."

He nodded gravely. "And on you, Gen," he swore.

"Thank you," she told him. "You always make me feel like

I'm…home. And safe. Give Angus a hug for me, huh? I'm going to go see what's up with my mom, okay?"

"Sure thing. You ever need me, young lady, you call."

"I will."

He started to turn away, then paused. "Adam Harrison is here, too," he said.

"Adam?" That did startle her.

He pointed. Adam was alone at the end of the bar, leaning against the wall, watching the room. He lifted his beer to her, and his eyes seemed to speak volumes.

In fact, they chided her. It was as if she could hear him saying, *You shouldn't have come out on your own.*

She smiled. Okay, first she would go over to see Adam, since a quick glance told her that her mother was fine and hadn't even noticed she was there.

"Adam," she said, reaching him. "I'm so glad you're here."

"Right. Now you won't have to call to tell me you're on your way," he said.

She flushed. "I guess I should have called someone, huh?"

"Yes. You should have."

"But honestly, Adam, this isn't about me. It's about Eileen."

He leaned low. "Shall we accost her together?" he teased.

"Why not?"

He finished his beer and set down the glass. "Genevieve?"

"Yes?"

"Murder can happen anywhere at any time. And whether you like it or not, this Poe Killer thing is personal. Because of who you are, you have to be careful all the time, but now you need to be even more vigilant."

She inhaled. Exhaled. Remembered how terrified she had been in her own garage.

"I don't want to turn into a little old lady who's afraid to leave her own apartment," she told him. "And I really am careful," she assured him.

"You drove down here alone, right?"

"Because my mother was here."

"But that's not being careful," he said gently.

"How did you know to come here?" she asked, looking him in the eye.

He stared back at her. "Hunch," he said. "Now, before we go over to see your mother, tell me who all those people with her are. A few of them look familiar, but a refresher course won't hurt."

She told him quickly who was whom, and then he took her hand and led her through the crowd.

When Eileen saw Genevieve's face, her own went a little white. It was guilt.

She hadn't called Genevieve, and she was with the Ravens. Brook had called and asked her to join them for a drink at the pub, and she had agreed without really thinking.

But she had never thought she was in danger from any of them anyway—or, to be honest, from anyone else. She spent her time worrying about Genevieve.

Then she saw Adam, and her face was suffused with color again, and she smiled delightedly. "Adam!" she called, interrupting the conversation around the table.

"Eileen," he replied, with a smile of his own.

She was sitting between Larry and Lila, but she quickly excused herself and got to her feet, hugging Adam, offering a kiss to Genevieve, then turning to introduce him to the others. He had indeed met several of them at various charity functions, and greetings went around the table.

With Eileen on her feet, talking to Adam, Larry and Lila, who had so vigorously pointed fingers at each other regarding Thorne's murder, were now next to one another—and pointedly ignoring each other, Gen noticed. Suddenly Lila jumped up and demanded, "So, Adam Harrison, what are you doing in town?"

"You're not up here because of this dreadful business, are you?" Lou asked.

"Just came up on business," Adam said lightly.

"Well, you managed to arrive just when the city is going insane," Larry said.

Meanwhile, Brook dragged over some extra chairs, and in a minute they were all seated.

"Honestly, that murder is all that anyone is talking about," Larry said. "Everyone's forgotten about war in the Middle East and global warming."

"This girl…" Brook said. "I can see why everyone's so interested in her. She was a lost child of New York."

"A lost child of New York. I like that. Can I steal it?" Larry asked. "It'll make a great headline."

"Go right ahead. I'll be looking for something deeper, something that gets into the psychology of the phenomenon, for the magazine," Brook said with a shrug.

"You're both awful!" Barbara exploded.

They all fell silent, staring at her. She flushed. "One minute you're complaining because people are treating this like the most devastating news in the world, and the next you're talking about the spin you're going to give the story yourselves."

"Bravo," Don Tracy said, and applauded, causing Barbara to turn an even deeper shade of crimson.

"Not to mention that we're all forgetting what it means to us personally," Lou said quietly.

"Just what *does* it mean to us?" Nat Halloway asked.

"My dear money man, so sweet and accommodating—and unimaginative," Lou said, but not unkindly. "It means there really is a psycho out there with a Poe fixation. And that no one in the city is safe—especially us."

"Just how did you all end up here tonight?" Adam asked pleasantly.

"Well…we get together here all the time," Don said. Then he laughed. "Hell, I'm here because I needed a drink."

"I called Eileen," Lou said. "And she said we should call Lila, and Lila called Barbara."

"It's where we hang out," Larry said a little lamely.

"Just like *Cheers*," Don said, lifting his glass. "Everybody knows our names."

"We needed comfort, if you ask me," Nat said, and they all fell silent, because unimaginative or not, he had hit on the truth.

The table was still quiet when Genevieve noticed, from the corner of her eye, that the front door had opened and someone else was coming into the crowded bar.

Joe.

She knew she should have tried to get hold of him, at least to let him know she was on her way here, even to invite him to join them. Then again, he had gone off on a trip she certainly hadn't been invited to share.

She certainly hadn't expected to see him here now, though.

He saw them and made his way through the crowd and directly toward their table.

"Hello," Joe said, as if he were greeting everyone at the table all at once. And he was. But his eyes were on Adam, and he wasn't pretending he wasn't surprised to see him.

Adam had risen, his hand out to greet Joe warmly, and apparently Joe wasn't going to be churlish enough to reject his greeting. They clasped hands, then joined in a quick embrace before drawing back to study each other in the way of two men who hadn't seen each other in a while.

"You look good, Joe," Adam said.

"So do you. So what the hell brings you to town?" Joe asked pleasantly, only his eyes betraying his suspicion.

They had an audience, Genevieve knew. And Joe was playing the scene well. But when he looked at her, she stiffened. A shaft of cold air seemed to blast straight at her, his eyes were so cold.

He knew. Somehow he knew that she had called Adam.

"I have some business here in the city," Adam said. "Naturally I gave Genevieve a call."

"Naturally," Joe echoed dryly. "And you just happened to show up here?" he asked Genevieve, his tone still pleasant.

"We were just talking about the way we all gravitate to this place," Eileen said, giving Joe her most radiant smile.

If Joe admired anyone, Gen thought, it was Eileen. And in fact, his eyes did soften as he turned to her.

"Joe, what's your take on this murder?" Brook asked.

"I don't know who killed her, if that's what you're asking," Joe said.

"She disappeared on Sunday," Barbara said, her gaze focused straight ahead, her eyes unseeing, as the words left her lips. "Mary Rogers. Eighteen forty-one. She left her home on a Sunday. She was found on a Wednesday. In the water. Just the same."

"He's getting better," Don Tracy said darkly.

"Better?" Joe asked.

Don grimaced. "First Thorne, a murder that had similarities to several of Poe's stories but didn't really parallel any of them. But this…this was on the money. She was found by the river. Relatively near the spot where Mary Rogers was found. Found in pretty much the same…state of decomposition."

"But this investigation will be very different," Eileen said firmly.

"And how is that, Eileen?" Nat asked her.

"Science," Eileen said. "The police have so much more to work with these days. What is it, Joe? At every crime scene, the killer inadvertently takes something away or leaves something behind. Isn't that true?"

"Yes," he said.

"Maybe not a really clever killer," Barbara said, shuddering and turning to look at Joe with wide, frightened eyes.

"They'll catch this guy, I'm certain," Joe said firmly.

Barbara nodded, as if she trusted his words.

"Let's hope they catch him before— Well, soon," Lou said.

"She was a slut," Lila pointed out.

"Oh, Lila!" Nat Halloway protested. "No one deserves to die like that."

"I didn't say she deserved to die like that," Lila said irritably. "It's just that…we reap what we sow."

"The killer will be caught," Joe said again, and his words were followed by an uncomfortable silence around the table.

"Well, I, for one, should be calling it a night," Larry said. "The presses wait for no man."

"We should probably all get moving," Lou suggested. "It was good to see everyone, though."

Goodbyes were said, and eventually only Eileen, Adam, Joe and Genevieve were left. Eileen slid back into her seat and patted the chair beside her. "Adam, it's so nice to see you. Have a seat."

Joe was staring at Genevieve, who sat down across from her mother. She was dying to ask him about the afternoon, but this didn't feel like the right time.

Without waiting for an invitation, Joe sat down next to her and stared intently across the table at Adam. "So. Which one of them called you?" he asked. "Eileen or Genevieve?"

Lie, Genevieve silently begged Adam.

He didn't. "Genevieve," he said evenly.

Joe nodded. "Right. Well, this is a dangerous situation."

"Maybe I can help," Adam told him.

"Maybe Genevieve and Eileen should leave town for a while," Joe said.

"Joe," Gen began, ready to argue.

But Eileen laid her hand on her daughter's arm to silence her and looked at Joe. "We could. But, Joe, if someone out there is determined that Genevieve or I should die, that someone will find us wherever we go. I believe it would be best to stay here and get to the bottom of this."

"What did you discover today?" Adam asked Joe.

"Don was right. The killer did a much better job of imitating Poe this time," Joe said.

His voice was cold and hard. Gen could only imagine what he had seen today. "You were in New Jersey all this time?" she asked him.

He shook his head. "I've been at the hospital. To see Sam," he said. He looked around the table, meeting their eyes as his gaze went to each of them in turn. "There was another attempt on his life."

Gen told herself that it was natural for Joe to want some time alone, given everything he'd seen and done that day. But inside, she knew that his decision not to be with her tonight had nothing to do with the day he'd had and everything to do with the fact that she had called Adam—and he was too smart not to suspect why.

The good thing was that at least Joe seemed to trust the older man. Of course. He'd met Adam Harrison through Leslie. And at least Adam didn't correct Joe's apparent assumption that the three of them had all come to O'Malley's together.

And so Joe left alone, after suggesting that Gen stay at her mother's house that night.

Genevieve would have protested, but Eileen said, "Please, dear. Just tonight."

So, an hour later, she was in the den, speaking with Adam,

who had gone back with the women, ostensibly to make sure they were safe.

"He's really angry that I called you," she said.

"He had a bad day."

"That's not it," she said.

"Have you ever been to an autopsy?" he asked her.

"No. But that's still not it."

"Genevieve…he just needs time alone."

"Right. Because he thinks I've betrayed him somehow."

"Give him time. Let's talk about you."

"Me? I had a nightmare," she admitted.

"What was it about?"

She hesitated then, feeling as if someone had taken a cube of ice and run it straight down her spine. "It was about being strangled," she said. "Oh, God."

"Oh, God…what?"

"It was as if I…"

"Keep talking, Genevieve."

"It was as if I were Lori Star. It was Sunday night. The night she disappeared. Oh, God, Adam, I might have been having that nightmare right when…right when she was actually being killed." She gasped. "I saw her on the news, and that's what she was saying. That it was like she was the driver of the car on the FDR. She felt anger and…intent. Malice." She stopped speaking. Her skin was crawling, and she wanted to go back, to pretend that she hadn't said what she had, that the horror would just go away.

"That's good," Adam said gently.

"Good?" she protested, horrified.

He smiled sadly. "You may be able to tap into the victim."

"Tap into the victim?" she repeated.

He nodded. "Anything else?"

"What the hell else do you want?" she demanded.

"Anything else?" he repeated firmly.

"No." She realized that she was lying, that she didn't want to go any further, but she knew she had to. She groaned. "Yes."

"Talk to me, please," he said.

She inhaled. "Earlier…when I was leaving tonight, I kept feeling as if there were someone in the garage…someone in the shadows. Or more…as if the shadows themselves were someone. Does that make any sense?" she asked.

"Oddly enough, in a way it does," he told her, then rose. "Well, I'm going to get some sleep."

"What?"

"I'm not exactly a spring chicken, you know. I need to get some sleep," he said. "And your mother has been kind enough to have a room made up for me here."

"Just like that?" she demanded. "You drop these…bombshells on me, and then you go to sleep?"

"Tomorrow will be a long day."

"Oh, so you can *see* that it will be a long day?" She wondered why she sounded so resentful. *She* was the one who had called *him,* after all.

She was frightened, that was why.

"Adam…"

"Joe will need help tomorrow," he said, and left the room.

Admittedly, he was angry.

What the hell had he done to cause Genevieve to call Adam Harrison? About him.

He'd never told a soul about speaking to a dead man on the highway—except for the med tech who had assured him that the man was dead, and he wouldn't have said a thing then, either, if he'd known. He sure as hell had never told anyone about the corpse on the Gurney at the morgue.

When he left O'Malley's, he didn't head for his car. He had too much on his mind to go home right away, so he walked. He loved walking, and New York was the city for it. And as he walked, he tried to be rational.

Okay, rationally, he hated the fact that Genevieve had called Adam. Regarding him. There were far more serious matters at hand—tonight's attempt on Sam's life, for one thing. The police had suggested that the news not be shared with the news media or anyone else, except for on a need-to-know basis. There was no escaping the fact that there was a serial killer out there, one with either a real or feigned Poe fetish, and holding some information back would help them separate the real killer from the pretenders who were bound to come forward.

The killer was real and needed his concentration. So think about that, he told himself. He'd tried to eliminate at least some members of the New York Poe Society board by examining their alibis for the afternoon and evening when Thorne had been killed. Now the process of elimination would be easier, because he could find out where each of them had been this evening around seven, the night of the car crash and the night Lori went missing, then cross reference everything and eliminate more of them from his suspect pool.

They'd all been at O'Malley's tonight, but where they had they been beforehand?

He would find out, he thought grimly. Of course, that didn't mean he would have the killer in his sights. It was still possible that the killer was someone else, and there were millions of people out there in New York to choose from.

But not a million people that Thorne Bigelow would trust.

Joe suddenly realized that his steps had led him back to Hastings House.

Once again, it was closed, since it was only open at night for special functions, as it had been the night Matt was killed at the gala held to celebrate the house's rebirth as a museum. That night Matt had died and Leslie had touched the other side, but she had returned....

For a year.

Enough time in which to capture his...what? His heart? Or his soul?

As he stood there on the sidewalk, he noticed that the gate was ajar. "No," he said aloud.

But he couldn't stop himself. The compulsion was too great. He told himself it was his own determination to prove that nothing was going on that science couldn't explain, but...

But he knew he was looking for something more.

He let himself in through the open gate and slowly walked up the path to the steps. He looked up at the house and told himself that it was just that. A house. Brick, mortar, wood. A house. It didn't live and breathe. No matter what Debbie thought, the house hadn't saved her. Brick, mortar and wood would not—*could* not—reach out to help people.

But Leslie would.

Great. Now he was going to force himself to walk into the house, where he would no doubt imagine that he could hear her voice. That she was still there.

No, he told himself. He was going to step into the house, discover that the wiring was shot and the security system was going haywire.

He walked up the steps to the porch.

The front door opened.

He walked in.

It looked just the same as it had the other night. He looked up the stairway, lit by the pale red security lights. He examined the furnishings there in the entry, checked out the runner that protected the hardwood floor. There was an oil painting on the wall, a rider in a tricorn hat. Candles in sconces.

There were no sounds this time, though. None at all.

Strangely, the house felt warm. It was a museum, he reminded himself. It had to be kept at a certain temperature to protect the antique furnishings. But it wasn't good, and it wasn't evil. It was simply a house.

Joe...

The sense of warmth increased, as if he were being comforted, beckoned. He felt something brush against his cheek, the touch almost tender.

"I want you to be here," he said aloud, feeling like a fool but unable to stop himself.

His cell phone started to ring. He answered it. "Connolly."

There was no one there. "Dammit," he muttered aloud, and closed the phone.

Well, what the hell had he expected? That he was going to walk in and Leslie would be there, waiting for him in jeans and a T-shirt, hair loose and manner easy? That in her casual yet somehow intense manner, she would invite him in for tea?

"I'm an idiot."

He turned back toward the door.

Then he felt the hand. A hand, dammit. On his shoulder.

Joe...

He heard his name again, but it wasn't Leslie's voice.

It was Matt's!

Oh, hell, he really was crazy. Leslie wasn't here, welcoming him in. She was here with Matt. They had taken up residence in Hastings House, or maybe just within the tortured confines of his mind.

It's all right. Please, we can help.

He muttered a curt expletive and turned, staring intently into the shadows.

There! Had that shadow moved? Was there something misty taking shape in front of him? Would he be shaking hands with his cousin in a matter of moments?

He swore again. Maybe it really was time for that psycho-therapy now.

He winced. "If...if you're there, leave me the hell alone, will you, please?" he whispered.

Crazy. He had gone completely crazy.

He turned around and left the house, hardly noticing when the lock clicked into place as the door shut behind him.

CHAPTER 14

Lori Star made all the morning shows.

It was sad, Gen thought, that she would have been glad to know she was, even in such a horrible way, immortalized.

Genevieve had gotten up early and headed home. Now, watching television in her own apartment, she decided to call her mother and reinforce the need for her to stay home, where she would be safe. She was turning into a nagging parent, she realized. Too bad.

"I don't want you going anywhere alone," she told her mother. "Or with Lou or Lila or any of them," she added firmly.

"Genevieve, seriously. It can't be any of them," Eileen said.

"I mean it. I can't believe you went out last night."

"So did you."

"I don't trust that group, and I don't want you trusting them, either."

"You trust Adam. And Joe," Eileen said.

"Don't turn this around. Just don't go anywhere today. Promise?"

A sigh. "I promise," Eileen said. "Speaking of which…I'm curious. About Adam. You called him? You asked him to come?" she said.

"Yes."

"Leslie believed in him, you know. He was very dear to her."

"I know. I take it he's a friend of yours, too?"

"Well, the families, you know. I've met him at various functions over the years. And then, last year, when I hired Joe and everyone was looking for you…well, yes, I saw quite a lot of him then."

Genevieve waited for her mother to elaborate further. When she didn't, Gen asked, "Did you…?"

"Did I ever need help with anything paranormal? No," Eileen said. "But Adam is a very good man." She hesitated. "Joe knows that. I hope he'll trust him with…whatever."

"I hope so, too. I…um, I love you, Mother."

"I love you, too. More than I can ever say," Eileen said softly.

At ten, Adam called Genevieve. "My friends have arrived," he told her. "Brent and Nikki Blackhawk."

"You saw how Joe was last night. I don't think he'll want to meet with them."

"Yes, he will. Brent has some information for him."

"Information?"

"Yes, he's not just a ghost hunter, you know," Adam said, and she couldn't tell if his voice was teasing or not. "He's a great investigator, and I think he can help Joe on this. Anyway, don't worry about it. I'll call Joe and set up lunch."

Great, she thought. Joe was going to be just thrilled. But all she said was, "Let me know."

She hung up and walked back into her living room, where Lori Star's face was still front and center on the television. She turned away, then heard someone say, *Help me.*

She swung back to the television. For a moment Lori seemed to be staring straight at her, but then she realized that the video was from the night Lori had been on television claiming to have "seen" the accident. And that there was nothing unusual about it.

Even so, she had the strangest urge to escape her own apartment. All she wanted was to run.

But she couldn't run away from herself, and she knew it. She remembered the strange sensation of being the other woman in the dream, remembered how she had seen the shadows come alive in the parking garage. And now she thought that a dead woman on television was looking at her, asking for help.

She thought about how strangely Joe was behaving. Perhaps he was running, as well.

Maybe they were both going crazy.

She turned off the television off, and as she did, she heard her cell phone ringing. It was Adam.

"I made a reservation for one o'clock. I've got a car, so I'll be in front of your place at a quarter of."

"Joe is fine with this?"

"He'll be there," Adam told her.

She hung up, reflecting on the vast difference between "He'll be there" and "Yes, he's fine with it."

Doctor Frank Arbitter was a homebody. It was just that his home seemed to be the morgue, Joe thought. The man could eat, drink, chat and read the comics, all with a corpse awaiting his attention, and apparently be no more worried about it than he was about the phone on his desk.

An elderly white woman lay beneath a sheet that morning, only her head visible, so Joe wasn't sure what stage her autopsy was at. As Frank welcomed him and indicated a chair by his desk, Joe paused. The other man watched but didn't comment when Joe gently pulled the sheet up to cover the woman's face.

"She was murdered?" Joe asked.

"No, she was just alone. It was a heart attack, I'm fairly certain, but since no one was there, we have to do the autopsy. Hey, do you want a cat?"

"What?"

"She came in with her cat. They didn't know it was hiding in the blanket she had around her when she died."

"Frank, I'm the last person in the world who should own a pet. I'm never home."

Frank lifted his shoulders and let them fall, shaking his head. "It's a beautiful cat. Rag doll or something. Furry."

"Maybe she died trying to brush it," Joe suggested.

"And I always thought you were a nice guy."

"I'll ask around. Raif Green has kids. Maybe they'll want it."

"You should reconsider, Joe. You have a place, not a home. A pet would make it a home. Let me take that back. A wife would make it a home. Hell, even just a live-in lover."

"Frank, give me a break. Can we move on?"

"Sure. Sit."

Joe took the offered chair. "Have you talked to the guy over in Jersey?"

"By 'the guy over in Jersey,' I'm going to assume you mean the medical examiner in charge of Miss Star, Dr. Benjamin Sears?"

"Yes, that guy," Joe agreed.

"He sent me a copy of his initial report," Frank said. "But why are you asking? You were at the autopsy. I wasn't."

"Sears said the bulk of the injuries were postmortem, including those to the genital region. What does that mean to you?"

Frank frowned, looking at him. "Hey, I'm basically a mechanic. I look at the pieces. I'm not a psychologist."

"All right, I guess I want collaboration. Do you think the killer could have been imitating a crime, rather than committing one out of personal passion?"

Frank looked steadily at Joe. "I watch the news. You want to know if he was mimicking a real crime, or maybe the literary version of it. Mary Rogers. Marie Roget. Did you know that a number of researchers have bemoaned the fact that there were two autopsies done on Mary Rogers, the original in New Jersey and one later, in New York? No one ever definitively answered the question of whether she died as the result of a botched abortion, or if she was assaulted and killed by a gang. Back then, the Five Points area was overrun by gangs. Most people wanted to think it was gang members, wanted to use that as ammunition to get the police to clean up the streets."

Joe stared at him, surprised.

Frank grinned. "Hey, I live in New York. I may not be an expert on Poe, but I know my share of local history."

"Okay, what's your take on this theory?" Joe asked, leaning forward. "The killer is an opportunist. Thorne Bigelow needed to die. The killer didn't want the finger of truth pointing back at him, so it had to look as if Thorne died for some reason other than the real one, so the killer left the note referencing Poe, even though he hadn't done a very good job of making the murder fit any of Poe's works. And maybe, almost by accident, Bigelow became the first in a series of killings. The killer happened to see Sam Latham on the FDR and figured if he took him out, it would really give credence to the Poe connection. He only landed Sam in the hospital, but it was still good enough for his purposes. Maybe too good. Lori Star sealed her own fate when she went on television, purporting to be a psychic and saying she knew what happened. He couldn't have that, but luckily for him—or her—Lori was easy to get rid of. All he had to do was convince her that he was a reporter or a writer or something, and that he was ready to make her really famous. He demanded to meet her alone, and you know the rest. This time, though, he had time to make a big deal of the Poe connection. With Lori dead, he should have felt safe, but then he started thinking about Sam and whether he might start remembering more of what happened on the highway, so he took steps."

"Someone tried to kill Sam? I didn't see anything about that in the news."

"You won't. The police are hoping that keeping something secret will give them an edge in finding the killer."

"What was the method?" Frank asked, his brow creasing.

"They're pretty sure it was an overdose of morphine, administered by someone in hospital scrubs and a mask. And if he'd succeeded, I bet a note would have shown up, too. So what do you think about my theory?"

"It sounds pretty convincing, but at this point it's only a theory, right? The police haven't actually figured anything out, have they?"

"Not yet, no," Joe admitted.

"And it could have started out as a random killing that escalated."

"It can't be random," Joe said. "Thorne Bigelow let his killer in. That wasn't random."

"No." Frank was quiet for a long moment. "You know, Joe, back then...the killer was never identified. There were theories, plenty of them. But no one ever went to trial."

"I know. But this can't end this way."

"Why not?"

"Because I'm afraid it won't end at all if this guy isn't stopped." Joe stood up suddenly. "Thanks Frank."

"For what? I didn't do anything."

"Yes, you did. You just made me focus on a really important question."

"What's that?"

"Exactly why did Thorne have to die?"

Genevieve paced in her apartment, feeling like a caged tiger.

She'd spent her life being active, taking steps to make the world a better place, not just attending charity functions and luncheons. She'd majored in social sciences, received a degree in psychology and another in social service. She'd worked the streets convincing hookers to quit working for two-bit pimps, and she'd gotten a lot of women real jobs. She knew how to keep herself safe on the streets. She'd only been kidnapped because she'd been taken unaware by someone she knew and had thought she could trust.

Just like Thorne Bigelow.

Who hadn't survived.

She thought about Lori Star and suddenly felt the urge to know her better.

It was a bit too late to get to know the woman herself, but there were other ways to find out more about her. Of course, Joe would be furious if she went out, investigating on her own.

Screw Joe. He certainly wasn't consulting her about his plans.

She grabbed her keys and hurried out, but she didn't take her car. Downstairs, she greeted the doorman, and asked him to hail her a cab. At Lori Star's building, she exited and walked up the three flights of steps.

There was crime-scene tape on Lori's door, but she hadn't come to see the apartment. She strode over to Susie's door.

Before she could knock, it opened and Susie, her face swollen, peered out, looked around warily, then quickly drew Gen inside.

"Sorry for acting so hush-hush. The press keep coming around, even though they're not supposed to be able to get into the building," Susie said.

"Oh? No one stopped me," Genevieve said.

"I guess most of the cops have cleared away. And maybe whoever is down there decided you didn't look like a reporter."

"I guess."

Gen didn't think the police were actually watching the building at all anymore. She didn't tell Susie so, but she suspected the reporters probably thought they'd gotten all they could from the neighbors.

Susie had evidently been through the wringer. She looked as if she had cried a lot and might start crying again at any moment. Genevieve's heart went out to her.

"Some guy down there offered me a bunch of money if I had any sexy shots of Lori, or if I could tell him any sordid stories," she said, and sniffed contemptuously. "And they called her a whore! They're just a pack of pimps themselves. I'd never sell out a friend."

"I'm sure Lori would have appreciated that," Genevieve said, touching her arm consolingly.

Susie sniffed again, and wiped her cheeks, then tried to smile. "You're different, you and that guy, Joe. He wanted to help. I know he did."

"Yeah. He's a good guy," Genevieve said.

Susie frowned. "So, uh, why are you here?"

"I came to see you."

"Why?" Susie asked, her tone slightly apprehensive.

"I'm not even sure," Genevieve admitted. "I guess…I guess I just wanted to get to know Lori now, even if it's too late. I feel that… knowing more about her might somehow help."

Susie indicated her couch. It was worn, but the apartment was neat and tidy. "Sit. I'll tell you what I can. She really did want to be an actress, you know. She worked a lot as an extra, and she went to auditions…even got some callbacks. But she didn't get that one break she really needed."

Genevieve nodded encouragingly and waited for Susie to go on.

"She was…she was just real, I guess you could say." Susie hesitated. "Did she turn tricks? Well, yes, but she was discreet. She went with guys she liked and accepted what she could get. But she really worked at being an actress, and I think she would have made it."

"So why did she go by Candy Cane? Why did she give that name when she was arrested?" Genevieve asked.

Susie laughed with dry humor. "I'm Peppermint Patsy. We all use names when we go clubbing. You don't always want to be known. Hell, if I'm out for a good time and need a little sustenance from a guy, I don't want him knowing who I really am."

Genevieve asked, "Do you think she realized, when she went to the press, that they would check her out and discover her arrest record?"

"Maybe she thought it was worth the risk. The thing is, when she talked about what she saw, she was telling the truth. She believed it with her whole heart. She wouldn't have lied to me." Another big tear fell on Susie's cheek. "Life's a bitch and then you die. Sucks, huh?"

Genevieve felt her old life suddenly wrapping around her. "Susie, I can't help Lori now. But if *you* want to get a real job—where you have to work hard, but you'll make good money—I can manage that for you."

Susie grimaced. "I work hard now. I just don't seem to get anywhere. I flipped hamburgers for a while, but I couldn't pay the rent."

"I'll get back to you. I know of a place where you can work out front and make good tips."

"Is there a pole involved?" Susie asked skeptically.

Genevieve laughed. "No. It's an old Irish pub. They're always busy, so they're always looking for waitresses, and I swear, you'll like it."

"And you can get me a job there?" Susie was clearly still doubtful. "Where is it? I couldn't keep one job because even with the subway, it still meant a mile walk, and I was always either late or nearly getting mugged."

"It's walking distance from here."

"Downtown?" Susie asked.

Gen nodded. To her distress, Susie suddenly burst into tears.

"What? I'm sorry," Genevieve said quickly.

"No, no, it's just that Lori loved downtown so much. You know what she always told me she would have been, if she'd ever made it through school?"

"What?"

"An archeologist. She loved all the old buildings downtown. Trinity Church, St. Paul's, City Hall…Fraunces Tavern, even though it's pretty much a made-up restoration. She spent her life hanging out in old places. She even liked cemeteries."

Susie started crying so hard at that point that she couldn't talk anymore, but Genevieve couldn't find the words to stop her. She was too busy thinking that Leslie MacIntyre would probably have loved to know Lori Star, no matter what she'd done for a living. From what she'd learned about Leslie, she hadn't been the kind of person to judge others.

She suddenly felt as if she really had gotten to know Lori Star. She rose quickly and extended her hand. "I'll find out about that job for you."

"I guess you really do wield a lot of power," Susie said.

"I don't, but I know people who do."

Susie was silent for another moment, then asked, "Do you think you can find a way to keep Lori out of a pauper's grave?"

"I can do that," Genevieve promised.

At the door to the apartment, Susie impulsively hugged her.

She hugged Susie in return, and thought back to the days before the kidnapping. She had known her way around then. She had changed things with indignation and by insisting that people do their jobs. Right now, though, she was just grateful that she had come from money, because there were promises that enabled her to make.

"I'll call you, and don't worry, that's not hot air. I'll see to it," Genevieve promised.

Susie thanked her, managing to regain her composure as she wiped her cheeks.

Genevieve noticed the time when she was out on the street. She had stayed longer than she intended. It was already midday, and finding a taxi to take her back to her apartment shouldn't have been hard. But short of throwing herself on top of one, she didn't seem to be able to get anyone to stop.

Cursing beneath her breath, she simply started to walk.

Move fast. He's behind you.

She jumped, stopped and spun around, staring.

A man with a Yorkie on a leash was to her left. A priest nodded politely as he passed. Two black-clad goths, laughing together, were ambling along in her direction, and a woman in high heels, carrying a briefcase, was talking on her phone as she wove through the others.

Gritting her teeth, telling herself that she must have imagined the voice, she started walking again.

Hurry. Please hurry.

It was broad daylight, and the streets were bustling. She couldn't possibly be in any danger.

But just as that thought went through her mind, she passed a narrow alley that seemed to contain nothing but dirt and shadows, even at high noon. An attacker could simply push someone into it and…

She quickened her pace, noticing what she seldom did: that there were numerous little alcoves along the way—between buildings, at construction sites—where someone could suddenly take a step—and then disappear.

And suddenly she knew with complete certainty that she *was* being stalked.

She hurried out to the street, her arm raised to attract a taxi, determined not to budge from the spot until she caught one.

Maybe the driver of the next taxi sensed her intense determination. Maybe she had managed to develop new powers of mind control. Who the hell knew?

The important thing was that he stopped, and she immediately slid into the backseat and gave him her address, then looked anxiously back at the sidewalk.

There were so many people there, but there was one man. His back was to her, and he was wearing a hat and a trench coat. She couldn't have said whether he was young or old, light or dark. But she got the strongest feeling that he had stopped and turned away because he knew she was looking back.

The taxi moved, and she told herself she was crazy. But she couldn't stop wondering why he'd been staring so intently into the window of a women's shoe store.

When she got out of the cab in front of her building, she felt ridiculously grateful to see her longtime doorman, and she gave him a huge smile as she went over to chat. Adam was due in ten minutes, so she would just stay close to safety until he showed up, and worry about her sanity later.

Joe still couldn't quite believe that he was meeting what boiled down to a pack of psychics for lunch. He respected Adam Harrison, and he knew Leslie had loved the man, who had been her salvation after the explosion at Hastings House.

Joe had argued that he simply didn't believe in any of it. He'd known even then that he had been lying, but it was almost as if by refusing to acknowledge what was going on, he could make it go away.

Adam Harrison, however, had a way of making believing in things simple.

"If my colleagues and I can help in any way, why not let us try?" Adam had asked calmly. "You want to catch this guy sooner rather than later, right?"

And Joe had pictured the body of Lori Star, lying on the autopsy table, then thought of the way she had died, and how he kept seeing Genevieve being throttled in his nightmares.

"Yeah, sure, what the hell."

But as one o'clock loomed closer, he grew impatient. That morning, he had felt as if he were on to something at last, and what he was thinking required legwork. He wanted to know where every single member of the Ravens had been, not just at the time of Thorne Bigelow's death, but during every related incident. He had called Raif, who had assured him that he and Tom would be on it, and Joe knew they could check out alibis just as accurately as he could himself and probably a lot more easily. But...

But he preferred things he heard for himself. He believed them. Or, more important, sometimes he *didn't* believe them. Body language, tone of voice...those were things that were often far more honest than words.

But he had agreed to meet with Adam, so he found himself downtown at a quiet restaurant, one of the old steak houses that had been around forever. He gave his name at the door and was led to a table for five, where he saw that Brent Blackhawk was already waiting.

Blackhawk was an intriguing man, with the very strong features associated with Native Americans, but with light-colored eyes that made his face instantly arresting. He had the look of a natural athlete.

He was alone at the table, reading the menu. But when he saw Brent, the man rose, and his smile was natural and welcoming. "Hi, Joe. Good to see you again."

The two men hadn't seen each other since shortly after Leslie's funeral. Leslie had liked and trusted Brent, just as she had his wife, Nikki.

Blackhawk was a decent guy, Joe knew. He was smart, assertive without being aggressive, and he liked sports. He was a man's man. What the hell was not to like about him?

How about that he believed in a world around them that most

people didn't see? And Joe had no intention of becoming someone like that.

"It's good to see you, too, Brent," Joe said, but words were stiff, even though he tried hard to hide his wariness. "How's Nikki?" he asked.

"Very well. She'll be right here—she just stopped off in the ladies' room."

"Oh." Joe sat, wondering what the hell he was supposed to say now.

"How have you been doing?" Brent asked, picking up the slack.

"You're here because Adam called you, so I'm sure you know what I'm doing."

"I didn't ask *what* you were doing. I asked *how* you were doing."

"You mean, do I see Leslie in my dreams at night? No," he said. He didn't add that he did hear her whisper at strange times, that he even thought his cousin, gone two years now, had talked to him.

He knew he was being offensive, but Brent didn't seem to be bothered. His shrug was easy.

At that moment Nikki walked over to the table. She was a beautiful woman, with light breezy hair, fine features and, like her husband, a natural ease of movement.

Both men rose.

"How are you, Joe?" Nikki had a radiant smile. She was so light and delicate. Brent was so dark and solid. They made a beautiful couple, Joe decided, and he couldn't help liking them. There was simply nothing about them to dislike, even if they did believe in ghosts.

"Great," Joe said. "But the circumstances in which we meet don't get any better, do they?" There was that damned hostility in his tone again, he thought.

"The point is that we have to make the current circumstances better," Brent said.

"We didn't do so well last time, did we?" Joe asked, then winced. "God, I'm sorry. We all tried. So hard."

"It's all right," Nikki said, laying her hand gently over his.

He looked into her eyes. They were large and filled with empathy. Not pity, empathy. "Yeah, well… So are we going to try some kind of hocus-pocus? Is that what this is all about?"

A look flashed from Brent to Nikki, and Joe thought the other man's normal equanimity was about to break. Brent looked as if he were about to say something pointed, but apparently his wife kicked him beneath the table.

"Brent's great with intuition—and a computer," she said.

"Nikki, it's all right," Brent said. "We all know where you and I…come from. But at the moment, I gather Joe's been having some *different* experiences of his own."

There was an edge to Brent's final words, and Joe had to admit, he deserved it. But as for his own "different" experiences…he would be damned if he was going to admit to them.

"Have you shown him the articles yet?" Nikki asked her husband.

"What articles?" Joe asked sharply.

Brent reached down for a briefcase beside his chair, pulled out a folder and pushed it toward Joe, who opened it to see several photocopied pages.

"What are these?"

"Read them."

Joe looked down. The first article was from a Richmond paper, dated three years earlier. The headline read, "Poe Scholar Found Dead in Own Basement."

Joe glanced up. Brent's face was impassive, so he went back to reading. According to the article, a literature professor named William Morton had been found dead inside his brick-walled wine cellar. He had been strangled. There was no mention of a note being found with his body, but given the Poe angle, a connection to the murders of Thorne Bigelow and Lori Star had to be considered.

"Did the killer leave anything?" Joe asked the other two. "Was there a note found with the body?"

"I know the cops who worked the case," Brent said. "It's gone cold, but it's still open. And no, there was no note found with the body."

"Did you, um, *work* the case yourself?" Joe asked.

"I just happen to know the cops who landed it," Brent said. "Check out the next article."

It was from a Baltimore paper, and it was dated a year ago. This headline read, "Professor Found in Family Tomb. Noted Poe Scholar Dead of Heart Attack."

Joe read quickly through the article. Bradley Hicks, fifty, had been found lying on the floor of his family's mausoleum. The door had been unlocked, but the coroner's supposition was that the man had thought he was trapped, and that his terror had brought on the heart attack that killed him.

Joe looked up at Brent Blackhawk and his wife, who looked back at him without saying anything, allowing him to reach his own conclusions.

Joe skimmed both articles again.

The second mentioned the professor's scholarly monographs, and the first touted William Morton's acclaimed fictional account of Edgar Allan Poe's life.

"No note found at the second scene, either?" Joe asked.

"To be honest, I didn't know about the Baltimore death until Adam called and I started doing research. In fact, Hicks's death isn't even on the books as a murder. It's listed as accidental. The investigators concluded that he went into the family mausoleum for whatever reason, thought he'd locked himself in, then panicked, had a heart attack and died. As far as William Morton goes, I don't think anyone ever thought his murder had anything to do with Poe. And maybe it didn't."

Joe stared thoughtfully into space. Maybe this wouldn't be so bad after all. Blackhawk had presented him with some really solid research, the type that could give him what he needed to crack the case.

"We'll need to find out if any of the New York board members were in either city at the relevant times," he said.

"None of them," Brent said. "At least, none of them was living in either place."

Joe frowned. "You've already checked?"

"Of course," Brent said.

"But either one is easily reachable from here," Nikki put in. "By air or driving."

"Do we know if any of the board members were on vacation in either area at the time?" Joe asked.

"I haven't had time to pull their credit-card records. We're looking at three different cities and three different states, but we'll get there," Brent said. He tapped on the paper. "I know William Morton's widow," he said.

Joe looked up at him. "You do?"

"Yes. I happened to meet her when I was in Richmond, doing some…some work at Hollywood Cemetery there. She had brought flowers. We talked. I'd say she considers me a friend."

"Can we interview her?" Joe asked.

"Yes. And here's something interesting. Her husband knew Thorne Bigelow."

"Not surprising, given that they were both interested in Poe. Still, the police in both jurisdictions should start coordinating their investigations. In fact, the FBI should be involved," Joe said.

"I'm sure they will be," Brent said, leaning back. "But we're still talking law-enforcement agencies, and lots of legal hurdles they can't circumvent."

Joe felt as if he were listening to Raif Green. Cops couldn't always do what he did. They were public servants.

He wasn't.

Just then Brent looked past him and rose. Turning, Joe saw that Adam and Genevieve had arrived. Adam was wearing a suit and looked as if he belonged on Wall Street. And Genevieve…

He winced inwardly. Her eyes were on his, and they were full of hurt.

He didn't look away. He wondered if she could read his own feeling of betrayal in *his* eyes.

But despite that, he also felt an instant surge of appreciation for the fact that she was there. He realized, seeing her, the luster of her hair, the easy grace of her movements, even that look in her eyes, that, whether he liked it or not, she had come to mean so much to him. No, not so much. Everything.

Still…

He turned away. He couldn't help it. He was still angry. She had asked for his help, and he had given her his best. And she? She had betrayed him.

She had called in Adam Harrison.

And then she was there, exchanging hugs and hellos.

"Brent, Nikki, it's wonderful to see you again. Thanks so much for coming." Her greeting was enthusiastic.

"Joe," she said, after greeting the others.

Little enthusiasm there.

"Hey, Gen," he replied, and gave her an awkward kiss on the cheek.

"Shall we order drinks?" Adam said.

"There are some loose ends I'd like to tie up here," Joe told Brent, getting back to business—and trying hard not to look at Gen—once they'd ordered iced tea all around. "But then I'd like to stop by the Baltimore police station, and get down to Richmond and interview your cop friends. And the dead man's widow, as well."

"What's going on?" Genevieve asked.

"Brent found some similar deaths that just might be related to your murders up here—and might bring us closer to the truth," Adam explained.

"Really?" Genevieve asked. "So when are we leaving?"

"I need the afternoon for those loose ends I mentioned," Joe said. "I want to bring Raif Green and Tom Dooley up to speed on what I've just learned, for one thing."

"There's something else I think we need to take care of," Brent told him.

Why the hell was the man looking at him that way? Joe wondered.

"I think you and I need take a trip together first," Blackhawk said.

"A trip together? What are you talking about?" Joe asked impatiently.

"Hastings House," Blackhawk said.

CHAPTER 15

Genevieve saw Joe's expression darken and knew he wasn't pleased, to say the least.

And yet, though she had enlisted Adam's help because of Joe, she was tempted to say, "Hey, what about me? I need some help, too."

But she had never mentioned her own strange experiences to Joe, any more than he had confided in her about what was preying on *his* mind and making him act so strangely. Maybe she was like him, determined not to acknowledge the reality of certain things. At the same time, the very fact that she had called Adam in meant she was at least a little bit more receptive than Joe was.

They hadn't eaten yet, but suddenly Joe stood and said, "We'll see. But you'll have to excuse me. I just remembered something I have to do. Enjoy your lunch," he added. Then he turned and left.

And that was it. Everyone else at the table was left staring after him.

"Hmm, that went well," Nikki said, after a moment.

And Genevieve had to laugh, even if there was just a hint of a sob in it.

"No, I'm serious, that went well," Nikki repeated.

"How can you say that?" Genevieve asked.

"He didn't tell us all to go fuck ourselves, for one thing," Brent said, offering her an encouraging smile.

"Brent..." Adam said.

"Sorry."

Then Adam waved the waiter over, and Gen realized they were still going to have lunch, though she was sure she wouldn't be able to eat a thing.

"How about you? How are you doing?" Nikki asked her, once they'd placed their orders.

Genevieve looked at the other woman, her senior by only a few years. She suddenly envied her tremendously. She was fully comfortable with her "gift," whether other people believed in it or not, and she was also head over heels in love with her husband, who had an ever greater "gift" and who completely understood her.

"I'm sure it's just the stress getting to me, because I thought... well, I mean, it's not like anyone was really even there," she said, then bit her lip. She hadn't really intended to say that out loud, had she?

"What?" Brent asked, and flashed a glance at Nikki.

Genevieve winced. "I'm sorry. Like I said, it's just the stress of worrying about my mother and the whole Poe thing."

"I heard," Nikki mused, obviously sensing Gen's discomfort and willing to let her off the hook, at least for now, "there are Poe tours here in New York."

"Are you suggesting we take one?" Adam asked.

"Why not?"

Genevieve was surprised to discover that the offer of the diversion was a welcome one, even for her.

While they waited for their meals, Adam made a call and set everything up, and as soon as they finished their meal, they were on their way. Their guide was knowledgeable, taking them around the city by minivan, pointing out Poe's familiar haunts in Greenwich

Village, and describing what the Five Points area would have been like in the eighteen-forties so well that they could practically see gangs like the Forty-Thieves and the Plug-Uglies running rampant. Then he took them up to Fordham, in the Bronx, where they visited the Poe Cottage, where his beloved wife—and cousin— Virginia had died, finally succumbing to tuberculosis.

Brent didn't spend much time in the cottage. Genevieve came across him standing outside. It was a beautiful day, and his head was lifted up to the sunshine and the blue sky.

"You're not enjoying the tour?" she asked.

"Not the cottage," he said.

She hesitated. "Did, um, anyone in there…talk to you?"

He smiled at her, amused by her reticence to talk about something he considered totally normal, but he didn't answer directly. "There's just such an aura of sadness there." He didn't say anything else, but she felt that as if she could read his thoughts, and she knew that being inside the cottage was actually painful for him.

She almost told him then about her feeling that someone had whispered in her ear, asking for help, but she couldn't quite bring herself to say anything.

The tour ended at the cottage, and as they headed back into Manhattan, Adam suggested that they call Eileen and arrange to pick her up to have dinner.

"At O'Malley's?" Genevieve teased.

Adam shrugged. "Why not?"

Still, when they returned to the Village and his driver picked them up, Adam leaned forward and gave him the address for Hastings House, rather than Eileen's apartment.

"I…thought we were picking up my mother?" Gen said.

"I'll call and tell her we'll be a few minutes late," Adam said.

By the time they reached the street where the historic house sat, the workday was at an end, darkness was falling and the neighborhood seemed almost eerily quiet. Adam's driver parked and waited, while the rest of them got out and stood on the sidewalk, staring up at the house.

"It's closed by now," Genevieve said to Adam. "If you want to get in after hours, you can call tomorrow, and I'm sure the powers that be will give you a key."

"I don't think we'll need a key," he said, and started across the street.

Gen looked at Brent and Nikki, hoping that they would linger behind, but they didn't. They followed Adam without hesitation.

As Adam approached the gate, it opened. Genevieve swallowed hard. She was afraid. She didn't want to be, but she was. A locked gate shouldn't have opened that way, without even being touched.

To add to her discomfort, it seemed that the sky went from dusk to full dark as she hurried across the street and followed the others up the path to the porch.

Joe had been here the other night and found Debbie, who had insisted that the house had opened up and saved her.

Genevieve wanted to run and almost did, but Nikki slipped an arm around her shoulder. "There's nothing evil waiting for you here, I promise you," she said softly.

Gen was embarrassed, not wanting to appear cowardly. "Of course not," she agreed.

It was too hard to explain to Nikki that just because something wasn't evil, it could still be terrifying.

Gen followed the rest of them to the door.

Which opened.

Gen shuddered and told herself that Hastings House was good, It had saved Debbie. It was *good*.

It was also scary as hell.

But she walked in anyway.

"Leslie?" Nikki asked softly at her side. "Matt?"

Genevieve froze, not knowing what to expect, much less what she wanted to happen. She closed her eyes, terrified that when she opened them she would see a white mist turning into the woman she had known so briefly.

The woman who had died in her stead.

But nothing materialized. When she opened her eyes, there was no giant cloud of white mist. She could *feel* the air, though, and it wasn't cold or unpleasant. It felt as if it were moving around her with a comforting warmth. Almost as if it were holding her, trying to reassure her.

"They're here?" Adam asked very softly.

"Yes," Brent told him.

"Did they say why?" the older man asked.

"Because of Joe and Genevieve," Brent said.

"They're in danger?" Adam said.

"Yes, because Joe didn't mean to, but he opened a door," Brent said.

"So why is Genevieve feeling things, hearing them?" Adam asked. "Please ask them."

Brent turned to the older man, grinning. "They can hear you, Adam."

Genevieve felt ready to scream. They were acting so…normal, and she could feel her hair standing on end, despite the warmth swirling around her.

"Well?" Adam persisted.

But Brent didn't answer, walking away from them and seeming to tense up at something Gen could neither see nor hear.

"Brent?" Adam asked worriedly.

Brent turned to face them, his eyes reflecting the red security lights with an eerie glow. "Genevieve was the intended target," he said.

"What?" Gen gasped.

"The killer wanted *you,*" Brent said flatly. "Lori Star had to die because of what she saw, but in the killer's mind, you would have been the perfect victim. You're the beauty who held the city spell-bound when you disappeared, and…"

"And what?" Adam urged.

"And she's still on his list," Nikki said. "The killer still wants Genevieve."

Irish whiskey was not her favorite drink, but Gen managed to down quite a bit of it anyway. Beer just wouldn't have been strong enough.

Adam had called Eileen to explain that they would be a bit later than expected, only to have her tell him that she'd realized she had to finish up some paperwork for one of her charities before she went out, so she would arrange for car service to drive her to the pub and meet them there.

"Gen, you've got to calm down," Nikki told her, taking her hand from across the table.

"Calm down? The man who killed Lori Star really wanted to kill *me*." She felt hysteria rising. "Not to mention that we went to a house I *know* was locked that unlocked itself for us, and you and Brent talked to ghosts, who told me that I'm still on the killer's list. And you want me to calm down?"

"When you put it that way…" Brent said.

Adam put his hand on her chin, turning her to face him. "Look, Genevieve, I know this is all a lot to take. But *I* know that *you* already *know* spirits can linger behind. And you're tough—hell, you already survived one maniac."

"Yes, and being taken by a maniac should be like being struck by lightning, shouldn't it? I mean, the whole world is not peopled by maniacs, and lightning isn't supposed to strike twice in the same place," she told him.

"I know it's scary, but you needed to know," Nikki said. "Because you can't be too careful."

Brent leaned forward, taking both her hands and holding them until she looked at him. "Genevieve, you have to stay with one of us at all times, or with Joe. Do you understand?"

She nodded. "I—I've taken a lot of self-defense classes."

Right, she thought. Like that really helped right now. She tried to get a grip on her emotions. Safe. She would be safe with this group.

Who the hell was ever *really* safe?

She closed her eyes for a moment and listened to the band. They were singing "Danny Boy," and it was beautiful.

It was also about death.

She swallowed another gulp of straight whiskey. She had to get a grip on herself, and she knew it. She took a deep breath and felt alcohol send pure heat streaming into her blood and bones. "If…if Matt and Leslie are really still in that house—in their spiritual forms, at least—and they know so much, why don't they just tell us who the killer is?" she challenged, disbelief strong in her voice.

"Because they can only report on what's out there," Brent said.

"Now you've lost me," Genevieve told him.

"Ghosts aren't all-seeing and all-knowing." He smiled. "They know things because they hear people talking."

"And they read the newspaper," Nikki offered.

Genevieve stared at her blankly. "They read the newspaper?" she repeated. *"They read the newspaper?"*

"The people who work there bring in the papers or a magazine, and then Leslie and Matt read them," Nikki explained. "Actually, that's one of the biggest clues that you have a spirit in your house. You come home, and you'd swear you left a magazine by your favorite chair, but you find it on the kitchen counter."

Genevieve couldn't help it. She lifted a hand in a casual wave. "Well, of course. How the hell could I have missed that? Of course spirits exist. I believe you now."

"You *do* believe, Genevieve. You called me," Adam reminded her. "You called me about Joe."

"Yes, and…"

"And about yourself," he finished for her.

She shook her head. "Not at first, but…"

"But time to 'fess up," Nikki said. "What's been going on with you?"

And so she told them. Told them about the nightmare, and then the whispers.

"It has to be Lori," Nikki said. "Matt was right."

"Matt was right?" Gen echoed skeptically. "And what was Leslie's guess? Elvis?"

Brent leaned forward. "I know this all sounds really weird to you, but you have to understand…Matt is better at being a ghost than Leslie. He's been a ghost longer, and once you die, you have to learn everything all over again. You become pure energy, and you have to learn to do things by focusing that energy."

"That's why some places that are haunted have more obvious manifestations than others," Nikki explained. "The ghosts there have been around a while, and they've learned to manifest more strongly and to affect the physical realm, even to leave 'their' place and go out into the world. Leslie isn't able to get out much yet," she added.

"And Matt hates to leave her," Brent put in.

"So Matt *can* go out?" Genevieve asked. She couldn't believe they were having this conversation.

Nikki nodded. "And he spoke to the spirit of Lori Star."

"Of course," Genevieve said, feeling her skepticism disappearing in the face of their matter-of-fact belief. "So why doesn't she tell him who killed her?" she asked.

"She doesn't know."

"How the hell can she not know?" Genevieve demanded.

"Because he was disguised."

"What? Did he dress up like a dragon or a giant turkey or something?"

"No," Nikki said, laughing.

Genevieve took a deep breath. "But we do know she was killed by a man, at least."

"She's almost certain. Because her killer was very strong," Nikki said.

"She's *almost* certain? How can she not know if it was a man or a woman? What was the killer dressed up as?"

Nikki and Brent exchanged a glance. "Edgar Allan Poe," he finally said.

After he'd walked out on lunch, Joe had pulled out his cell and given Raif a call and asked if the cops had come up with anything, but other than a stack of mostly anonymous and probably mistaken tips that Lori had been seen in various parts of the five boroughs, he had nothing.

"Shit, Joe. You know how it is," Raif said. "We have to check out every lead. Policework has to be thorough. And being thorough takes time."

Time.

Joe had a feeling he didn't have much of it.

Joe thanked Raif and hung up, knowing the detective was right. Legwork took time, and it was frequently tedious.

He went back to his apartment to be alone, to think, and to do some legwork of his own, including calling the Ravens, starting with the women. His plan was not to ask them about the Sunday night when Lori had disappeared but to start casually with the previous night, when what had now been confirmed as an extra dose of morphine had almost finished Sam Latham.

Barbara Hirshorn was first on his list. He tried her at the library where she worked, and after a few minutes the young man who had answered the phone found her.

"Mr. Connolly?" she said curiously.

"Hi, Barbara, how are you doing?"

"I'm terrified, to tell you the truth. I'm afraid to walk through the stacks. Last night I couldn't even stand to be at home after I left work. I was so glad everyone decided to go to the pub. Lila picked me up and saw me home, but I don't know what I'm going to do now. I can't afford to take the car service everywhere."

"I'm sorry. What were you up to on Sunday, by the way?"

"I didn't leave my apartment. I was too shaken up by Thorne's death. Honestly, I'm so scared."

He said something reassuring and hung up. According to what she'd volunteered, she'd gotten off work and gone straight home, but was there any proof of that? He was glad the police had decided to keep the attack on Sam a secret. Only the killer would know that anything had happened, so only he or she would think to come up with a lie, and lies could be found out.

He continued to make calls to see what the rest of the Ravens had to say. Last night Lila had gone straight from a fashion show to pick up her friends, and then she had gone to the pub. He could verify that, and he did. Lila Hawkins hadn't left the showing on Fifth Avenue until seven, and based on what Barbara had said, the rest of the timing fit, too. According to her, she'd spent the Sunday at her daughter's house on Long Island, and he would verify that, too, if need be.

Lou Sayles had picked up her kids, which he confirmed by calling the school. She'd spent Sunday with her family, at a Little League game, and the game checked out, though he would have to do more investigating to confirm that she had been there.

And Eileen… Maybe he shouldn't have told her about the attempt on Sam's life at the hospital, but it was too late to worry about that now.

He caught her at her desk. "Hi, Joe. I'll see you at dinner, right?"

"Dinner? Where?"

She laughed. "Well, I suppose we should all be getting a bit sick of it, but…O'Malley's."

"Sure, I guess. Later," he said. "So are you with Genevieve?" he asked, after satisfying himself as to her whereabouts at the times in question.

"No, she's out with Adam, and Nikki and Brent."

Joe winced. His own fault for walking out on the lunch, he supposed. "They would never leave her alone, would they?"

"Of course not," Eileen assured him. "I thought that you were with them, as well."

He heard the slight reproach in that, but thanked her and told her that he would see her later.

He called Mary Vincenzo next. Just as he was expecting to get her machine, she answered, sounding as if she had been sleeping. Or smoking dope. There was an odd mockery mixed with sensuality in her voice tone. "Why, Mr. Connolly, to what do I owe the pleasure of this call?"

"I was wondering where you were last night?" he asked after the usual pleasantries, opting to be direct with her.

"Jealous?" she drawled.

"If you don't mind answering…"

"You're not the cops."

"I'm just trying to help."

"Oh, yes, that's right. You're everyone's savior, aren't you, Mr. Connolly?"

"Mrs. Vincenzo, if you would just—"

"I prefer being called Mary," she said, interrupting him.

"Mary, if you don't mind…"

"I was at Jared's penthouse. If you must know, we were fucking."

"We?"

"Jared and I."

"What about Sunday?"

"Let me see…Sunday. Hmm. Oh, we were fucking then, too."

"He must be quite the Energizer Bunny," he told her pleasantly.

She was silent for a moment, and he realized with a flash of insight that she hadn't been sleeping or getting stoned. She'd been drinking.

"Can anyone verify that you were there all day?"

"Are you suggesting that we invite people in to watch us while we're fucking?" she drawled insinuatingly.

"Can anyone verify you were together at Jared's penthouse?"

"Maybe we *should* have people over," she mused. "I mean, they talk about us already. You talked about us. In fact, you *knew* about us. When others didn't. Maybe we should have *you* over. You could even join us, if you'd like. How big are you down there, Mr. Connolly?"

"Thanks for talking to me, Mary," he said, and hung up, then put her name right under Jared's in the "potentially guilty" column.

He didn't like her, so maybe that wasn't fair. If it came to that, he didn't like Jared, either. But the truth was that Jared was the major beneficiary of his father's death, and Mary benefitted through Jared.

He kept calling and making lists. He was certain the police were making the same lists and decided they ought to compare them.

Larry Levine had once again been at the newspaper, something Joe had no trouble verifying. The reporter couldn't remember what he'd done during the day on Sunday, but he'd been drinking at O'Malley's—of course—most of the evening, and a legitimate alibi for Sunday automatically made him a less likely suspect, so…scratch Larry.

Don Tracy had been at the theater until almost seven. He wouldn't have had much time to get to the hospital. Possible, but unlikely. Still… And on Sunday he'd had a matinee, but matinees were over by five or five-thirty.

Nat Halloway had been at his office until he left for the pub, in plain view of half a dozen people yesterday afternoon. Sunday he'd been home alone.

Finally Joe called the Bigelow mansion. Albee Bennet answered after the third ring.

"Hi, Albee. Joe Connolly here"

"Mr. Connolly, hello. Can I help you in some way?"

"Routine, Albee. Where were you on Sunday?"

"Here, Mr. Connolly. I don't seem to have the heart to do much else but stay home. Mr. Jared is still up in the air about what to do with the place."

"Well, I'm sure you'll be fine."

"Happily, I will be. I won't be rich, but I'm sure that Thorny saw to it that I'd be taken care of."

"So you stay home night and day, do you?" Joe asked.

"Pretty much so, Mr. Connolly."

"Joe."

"Pretty much so, Mr. Joe. Last night I raided the DVD library. I watched three old movies, made some popcorn."

"Very nice," Joe said. "Well, thank you."

He hesitated then, thinking about the information Brent had passed on about the other two deaths. "Albee?"

"Yes, Mr. Joe?"

"Did Thorny—Mr. Bigelow—like to travel a lot? When he was researching his book, perhaps?"

"Oh, certainly. We got around. We spent a lot of time in Philly."

"What about Richmond, say, or Baltimore?"

"I can't remember dates offhand, but, yes, we were down there."

"You and Mr. Bigelow?"

"Oh, yes. And Jared, of course. And Miss Mary."

Jared and Mary, too? Now things were really getting interesting, Joe thought.

 CHAPTER 16

Genevieve had to admit to being surprised when she saw Joe walk into the pub.

"Joe, hello," she slurred somewhat drunkenly as he pulled up a chair at the end of the table.

She saw him look questioningly at Adam, who shrugged.

"Long day," Brent said.

"Really? What did you do with your long day?" Joe asked him.

"We played tourist," Brent said.

"Great," Joe said. "Where's Eileen? Didn't she come with you?" he asked, looking worried.

"Eileen is fine. She called about five minutes ago and made her apologies. She's tired and decided to stay home," Adam explained.

"How was your day?" Adam asked Joe.

"Not bad," Joe said, and glanced at Genevieve.

She smiled pleasantly at him but kept silent and played with the condensation on her glass, knowing she was too far beyond tipsy to safely speak. She focused on the music, which was really quite good, she decided. And the whiskey wasn't half bad, either. In fact, the more she drank, the better it tasted.

Frowning, Joe returned his attention to Adam. "I talked to the Ravens, and also to Albee Bennet," he said.

"Poor old Albee," Genevieve put in, her words slurred.

"Is she all right?" Joe asked, looking at Nikki.

Trust a guy, Gen thought, to figure only a woman would have another woman figured out. Chauvinist. "I'm fine, and I can speak for myself white…quite well, thank you," she told him, her delivery giving the lie to her words.

He studied her for a long moment, then clearly made the decision to ignore her. "Albee said that Thorne had traveled to research his book. He'd been to Richmond, Baltimore and Philly."

"But…Thorne was the victim," Nikki said.

Joe nodded. "He didn't travel alone."

"Aha! The butler *did* do it!" Genevieve said triumphantly and much too loudly.

They all stared at her.

Joe said, "Jared and Mary accompanied him on all his trips, along with Albee."

Brent frowned. "The son and the sister-in-law. They would be at cross concerns, don't you think?"

"I spoke with Mary. And I think she'd lie in a second flat to give Jared an alibi," Joe said. "They're sleeping together."

"But she's his aunt," Nikki said.

"By marriage," Joe said.

"I don't care," Genevieve offered. "That's just…ewwww."

"So you think Jared did it?" Adam asked thoughtfully.

"I don't like him, so that probably adds to my conviction," Joe said. "And there's nothing to prove it. But he's the major beneficiary, and the person supporting him—saying that he gave his father CPR, even though the body was found at the desk—is Mary. It bothered me from the beginning, the position of the body. Everything could have an explanation, but it's all starting to add up."

"And Jared Bigelow could look like Poe," Genevieve announced happily.

Joe stared at her, frowning. "What the hell is she talking about?" he asked the table at large.

"Long story, better left for another day," Adam said.

Joe groaned.

"In fact, I think I'll get my driver and see Genevieve home," Adam said.

Joe stood. "I'll take her home," he said in a tone that dared anyone to contradict him.

"Wait, wait, wait," Genevieve said, and stared at Joe, trying to focus. It would have helped a lot if his head had stayed still. "Don't you want dinner? And what if I want to stay?"

Joe ignored her and turned to Brent. "Are we still heading out tomorrow?" When Brent nodded, Joe added, "Do you mind an early start?"

"No problem," Brent said. "How early?"

"Six. We'll make it on down to Richmond, stay there overnight, then hit Baltimore on the way back."

"I'll arrange for a larger car," Adam said.

"I'll drive," Joe said.

"Is your car big enough?" Adam asked.

Joe crossed his arms over his chest. "I thought just Brent, Nikki and I would go."

"Aren't you are just full of it?" Genevieve said angrily.

"Genevieve—"

"I do believe I'm your employer," she said, trying to sound dignified, but she heard her own voice, and knew she just sounded snotty.

"I quit, then," Joe told her.

"You can't quit. You…you owe my mother."

"Genevieve, you need to go home and get some sleep," Nikki said gently. "In the morning—"

"In the morning Adam and I will be going with you on that trip or I will be doing whatever the hell I want back here in New York," she said icily, then winced. Oh, God, she really did sound like a bitch.

"I think I'll take her home now," Joe said. "Adam, we won't need a car service. I'd like to drive, so we'll just rent something." He inhaled deeply as he clenched his teeth. "Something big enough that the five of us can be comfortable."

"Thank you," Genevieve said primly, though she was tempted to cry. "And now I need to go home," she said, standing and immediately starting to teeter as her head spun.

"I've got you," Joe said, and put his arms around her to steady her.

The world was still spinning, but one thought occurred to her very clearly. *Yes, you do have me. Too bad neither one of us can tell if you actually want me or not.*

"Good night," Joe said to the others. "See you at six o'clock at Gen's, all right?"

"Fine. And I'll arrange the rental," Adam said. "Just one thing…"

"Yes?" Joe replied.

"I'll explain everything tomorrow, but for now, Genevieve can't be left alone. Not for a minute, do you understand?"

"I understand," Joe said huskily.

No, he didn't, Gen thought. Not yet, anyway. How on earth were they going to explain to him that the killer had dressed up as Poe to abduct Lori, even though she herself would have been his preferred victim, and that they knew this because Lori's ghost had passed the message through Leslie and Matt, who were still hanging around at Hastings House? That was *so* not going to go over well.

As they walked toward Joe's car, his arm still around her to keep her upright, he suddenly stopped and stared into the night.

"What is it?" she asked.

"Nothing," he replied after a long moment.

"They're out there, you know," she said solemnly.

"Who?"

Ghosts, she thought, but decided not to say so.

"I heard footsteps. Real footsteps," he said, when she didn't answer his question.

She laughed softly. "That's because there are real people in this city, lots of them."

He looked down at her, and she could see him decide not to argue with her. It was scary, the way she was able to read his expressions, she thought, sure that if she hadn't been with him, he would have investigated further.

The sounds from the pub were distant, and the street was quiet. He stood still for a minute longer, then urged her on to his car.

He was quiet as they drove, and she concentrated on not being sick. She felt his eyes touch her now and then, but they reached her building in silence. He signed in so he could get a visitor's parking pass from Tim, who welcomed them both with a friendly smile.

As soon as Joe parked, she started to get out of the car on her own, certain she could accomplish the feat, but she fell back into the seat as she tried to stand, and the door swung back on her. By then Joe had rounded the car to help her, and he held the door open and helped her out, saying, "I'm not sure whether you're going to be up to traveling tomorrow morning or not, Miss O'Brien."

"I'm fine," she protested. "I'm just a bit...tired. I assure you, I can handle my whiskey. It was Irish whiskey, after all, and I *am* Irish," she said proudly.

"All right, Irish, let's get inside."

He grabbed his overnight bag from the trunk, then supported her into the building and up to her apartment, where she made a studied point of getting her door open. "Can I make you tea or something?" she asked politely. The words were clear, but she ruined the effect by staggering.

"No, thanks. Keep walking, straight to bed. Where are those

hangover pills you gave me the other morning? Might help if you took a few now."

She waved a hand in the direction of the bathroom. He led her to her bed, supporting her while pulling down the sheets, and left her sitting there on the edge of the mattress. A minute later he was back with the pills and a tumbler of water. As soon as she had taken the pills, he took off her shoes.

"I'm really all right," she said, but she was shielding her eyes from the light that seemed to radiate like fire from the bedside lamp.

He turned it off, helped her lie down and pulled the covers over her.

"Is the room spinning even with the light off?" he asked.

"No." She sighed. "Yes."

"Let's hope the pills kick in soon, then."

For a moment she was both floating in her own wavering world and simultaneously aware that he had undressed and climbed in beside her. She inched closer to him. After a minute, she heard him sigh. And then his arm came around her, and he pulled her closer.

"What the hell made you do this?" he asked softly.

"Ghosts," she said, before she could stop herself.

He tensed, and she thought he was going to pull away from her, but he didn't.

"You shouldn't have called Adam," he said. "Ghosts…can't help. All they can do is muddle your mind. Remnants of the past that tear at your soul."

"Because you were in love with her," she said.

"I *could* have been in love with her," he replied. "But she loved Matt."

"She's with him now, you know."

"Yeah, yeah, they're both dead," he said.

And despite the liquor sloshing around in her body and confusing her mind, she propped herself up on one elbow and stared down at him. It was now or never.

"You're wrong. They're together. Really together. And they can help us, if we let them. If you need everything to be flesh and blood, to be real and physical, go ahead and think it's all in your mind. Think of it as the memories pointing you in the right direction. Do whatever works for you, but just don't discount it. Don't be afraid, because you know I always had the feeling that Joe Connolly wasn't afraid of anything. And don't be angry with me about calling Adam. Leslie believed in ghosts, you know."

"And she's dead now," he interrupted harshly.

Because I'm alive, Genevieve almost said.

But she didn't.

And neither did he.

Despite that, the words hung in the air between them, as if they were ghosts themselves.

She was sure there was more she needed to say, as if this were an argument she needed to win. But then she sighed, exhaling all the air that was in her, and there was nowhere else left to go.

She lay back down, and the darkness continued to spin, weird little squiggles of light dancing behind her eyelids. No wonder she had spent so many years hating whiskey.

There was nothing but silence, and she thought he must have fallen asleep, so she was startled when his voice came out of the darkness, deep and tormented.

"Dammit, Genevieve, don't you see? I don't want that for you. You've already suffered more than anyone should. And if you keep going in this direction—whether it's in your mind, real… whatever—you'll just stay tortured. You'll always be trying to understand, searching for another clue… Oh, God, never mind. I can't explain, it's just that…that world is that world. The dead are dead and gone. Let them rest in peace."

She was stunned by the passion of his words, and she let several seconds go by. Then she felt the mattress shift and sensed him looking down at her. She stared back up at him in the shadows.

"What if they can't rest in peace? What if they're here because they're determined to help us, whether we're able to accept their help or not?" she whispered.

He groaned.

"Joe," she said softly, reaching up, delicately brushing her fingers over the rugged contours of his face. "Joe, something is haunting you, I know it," she told him. "It started…it started that night at O'Malley's when you were the one who got drunk."

He lay down on his back beside her again, shaking his head. "We've got to get some sleep," he said.

It was an argument she wasn't going to win, she thought. Not tonight, anyway. But maybe even an argument was better than the angry silence they'd shared before. Just then he reached for her and drew her to his side.

Protectively.

It felt good, she thought, to be exactly where she was, even if he was just there as her guardian, a sentinel determined to keep her safe.

"Take another couple of these."

Joe was standing above her. He'd already showered, and his hair was still damp, but he was already dressed to face the day.

"What…time is it?" She squinted against the painful light of early morning and sat up, accepting the pills. She felt disoriented, but not as sick as she knew she deserved to, after everything she'd had to drink. She just wanted to go back to sleep.

"Five-thirty," he said.

She swallowed the pills. "Ten more minutes," she told him.

Wasn't happening.

He jerked the covers back, caught her arms and dragged her up.

"Shower. Now. Unless you want to stay here, locked in this room, until we get back."

So she headed for the shower.

When she got out, she had about ten minutes left. Frantically, she began throwing things into an overnight case.

"If you forget something, we can buy it when we get there," he told her. "Here." He was back in front of her with a cup of coffee.

She took it from him and drank gratefully.

To her surprise, he smiled at her and touched her chin. "That hair of yours is a mess," he told her.

She turned, ready to look for her brush.

"Hey, leave it. It's sort of sexy, in a hungover kind of way," he told her.

She cast him a glance of ice, causing him to laugh softly again.

"There's your bell—they're here," he told her.

"I'm ready," she said, and quickly swallowed the rest of her coffee. He had added enough milk to keep it from scalding her throat, and it was good.

A road trip.

Joe couldn't believe he was on a road trip with four other people. He expected the usual question to come from the backseat: Are we there yet? But his passengers were quiet.

Brent had brought an audio collection of Edgar Allan Poe's work. As they drove, they listened to "The Black Cat" and then "The Pit and the Pendulum," moving on to the poems by the time they passed into Delaware.

Just over the Maryland line, Joe pulled over at a rest stop to get gas. Everybody decided to get something to eat at that point, and he was sure they would have to wake Genevieve, who had fallen asleep before they ever left Manhattan. She was awake, though, and he noticed with amusement that she'd brushed her hair back into its usual sleek cascade.

"What time do you think we'll get there?" Nikki asked, as they all sat down to have breakfast.

"With or without traffic?" Joe asked.

"We're doing well so far," Brent said, and glanced at Joe. "If we keep moving fairly quickly, we can make it by one-thirty or two."

"When we get there, you and I will interview the widow and stop by the police station," Joe said.

"Oh, really, and what about the rest of us?" Genevieve demanded, looking none the worse for wear. She'd apparently had a pretty decent sleep while he'd been driving, Joe thought.

"We should look into Poe's history in the city," Nikki suggested. "Maybe find another tour to take."

"Joe is right," Adam said. "He and Brent won't be able to get much out of the police or the widow if we all come in like a traveling circus."

"Another Poe tour," Genevieve mused, cradling her coffee cup. She looked up at Joe. He expected an argument, but got a smile instead. "Good. I keep thinking that..."

"That Edgar will make an appearance?" Joe asked dryly.

"I keep thinking that maybe one of the guides will say something to give us a real clue to what's going on," she said.

"Maybe," Joe agreed. He didn't believe it for a minute, though. The current killer had a modern agenda. Either he planned to accomplish it by the murders, or he was psychotic, and Joe didn't think it was the latter.

He was convinced that the killer was Jared. And that the agenda was greed.

Except that...

Was he behind the deaths in Richmond and Baltimore, as well? If so, the motive couldn't have been greed. Jealousy? That was the most logical second choice. But jealousy over what? Poe? Why? Thorne, not his son, had been the scholar.

Joe excused himself while they waited for their food and called
Raif Green. They'd talked the night before, as Joe was on his way
to the pub, and this seemed like as good a time as any to check on
what they'd talked about.

"Joe," Raif said, and it sounded like a groan.

"Were you able to get anyone assigned to follow Jared Bigelow?" Joe asked.

"I'm doing my best. This is a city of millions, you know. And
the police department is always understaffed. I've already got plain-
clothes people at the hospital."

"Someone has to watch Bigelow," Joe insisted.

"Easier said than done."

"Bull. You know how to work the system."

He heard Raif laugh. "Quit worrying. Yes, I've got someone
watching him. I'm working things from here, I swear. And as soon
as you can give me something solid from another state, we'll have
FBI access, as well. The chief's already called the bureau. Seems they'd
already been called by someone. Someone with clout," Raif said.

Adam Harrison, Joe thought, his first reaction irritation. Still,
did it matter, if it got them where they needed to be?

"Thanks," Joe told him.

"Joe, you, of all people, should know this may take time."

"I'm just afraid that we don't have a lot of time. Bigelow, Lori
Star…and now Sam. This guy's gone after three people in less than
two weeks."

"I know, I know, and we're working it."

Joe hesitated. "I've got one more thing for you. Just a hunch that
might prove interesting."

"What?"

"Pull all the phone records. Say, from a week before Bigelow's
murder until now."

"All the phone records?"

"For the Ravens. Let's find out who was calling in, as well as who they called."

"What will that prove?"

"I'm not sure. I told you, it's a hunch."

"You've got to be joking. Do you know how big a project that is? The D.A. will have a fit."

"I'll bet you know the right people to get it done," Joe argued.

Raif started swearing, and Joe moved the phone away from his ear.

Finally Raif said, "I'll see what I can do." He started swearing again, so Joe thanked him and hung up.

When Joe returned to the table, their food had arrived. He glanced at his watch and ate quickly, and then they were back on the road.

When they reached Richmond just before two, they checked into a bed-and-breakfast Adam had arranged for them. Then Joe and Brent headed back out on the road for the police station and an appointment with Nancy Morton, the widow of the man who had been found strangled in his own wine cellar.

Adam sat down and started setting up his notebook computer and portable printer, and Nikki got out a map and started planning a self-guided tour of Poe's onetime haunts.

"Stay safe," he warned them.

"Adam, stop worrying," Genevieve said. "We're here, and the murderer is back in New York."

Her logic was sound, but he frowned anyway. Then Nikki came to her defense. "We're going to be tourists, Adam. There will be plenty of people all around us."

Nikki got on the phone and arranged another rental car, and as soon as it was delivered they left for the Old Stone House, now a museum dedicated to all things Poe.

Poe had never lived in the Old Stone House, but he would have passed it in his early days as he walked to school. It had been built in seventeen-thirty-seven, and was the oldest house in Richmond. Inside, they studied the relics of Poe's everyday life. Furnishings from the home he had shared with his foster parents, clothing, documents, first editions of his work, even a lock of his hair. Genevieve found herself enjoying the museum, despite the stress of everything going on. It was fascinating, beginning to know someone who was long gone but had made such a deep and continuing impression on the literary world, and who continued to influence writers and moviemakers. Visiting sites dedicated to him, walking where he'd walked, made him flesh and blood.

As they walked outside, they heard the words *tortured genius* and realized that a docent was giving a speech, so they hurried closer to listen to her.

"Poe's pain began at an early age, when his father abandoned the family, and then he lost his mother before he was two years old. Scholars believe that many of his stories focus on this loss. So often he writes about a beautiful woman, taken far too soon. He felt himself caught between the very real world, in which he was constantly fighting a battle against poverty, and the ethereal world of the dead. John Allan, his foster father, was a stern man. A highly moral man. He never formally adopted Poe, and he meant to make of Poe a man in his own image, one who was responsible, stern and moral. As a result, they fought often.

"In contrast, Poe loved his foster mother, but he was barely an adult when he lost her, as well, another motivating factor in the omnipresence of the dead, dying and decaying in so many of his works. He fell in love with and married his cousin, Virginia, and she, too, was frail, and died at a young age. Perhaps it was only natural that Poe should be obsessed with death. We recognize Poe now as one of the great literary geniuses of American history, but in his time, he struggled. He longed to be respected by his peers, but that respect was never forthcoming. The ironic tragedy is that he was on the verge of achieving all that he craved at the time of his death, and in fact, his own death was shrouded in mystery.

"He was in love with Elmira Shelton, who had been a childhood sweetheart and was then a widow. She had accepted his marriage proposal, and might have had the age and wisdom to curb the drinking that was his ongoing downfall. He had written happily to his aunt and mother-in-law, Maria Clemm, to say, 'I hope that our troubles are nearly over.' Here in Richmond, he was becoming a fixture on the lecture circuit. He wasn't getting rich, but he was being well received. And then…he headed for Baltimore. He disappeared for several days, then was discovered in the street, delirious, wearing another man's clothing. He died on October seventh, eighteen-forty-nine, and his last words were, *'God help my poor soul.'* His life was a litany of depression, alcoholism, lost love and great sadness, his death a mystery as dark as any story he ever penned."

The docent nodded gravely, and her audience was spellbound as they followed her into the museum. All except for Gen and Nikki, who remained standing outside in the sunshine. Genevieve, frowning, kept watching the spot where the woman had stood.

"What is it?" Nikki asked.

"Something she said."

"That his death was a mystery?"

"No…no. I've heard all the theories on his disappearance. I have a feeling that it had to do with the voting scandal of the time." When Nikki looked at her curiously, she explained. "A candidate's supporters would find a man, keep changing his looks and send him out to vote over and over again. By giving him a lot to drink, they kept him docile and willing to do whatever they told him. And then, when they were done with him, they assumed he would be all right and sent him on his way. Unfortunately, Poe was an alcoholic and he *wasn't* all right."

"So what's bothering you?" Nikki asked.

"It's the whole tortured-genius concept," Genevieve said. "She said, 'he longed to be respected by his peers.' I don't know why, but that just keeps coming back to me. The whole tortured-genius thing. If we were only looking at the murder of Thorne Bigelow, Jared would be the prime suspect. Even Lori Star was probably only killed to cover up the first murder. But if the deaths here and in Baltimore are related, we need to look at the bigger picture, at different motives. So…Poe was a tortured genius. Maybe the killer sees himself as a tortured genius, too."

"You could be on to something," Nikki said. Then she grinned and said, "But don't *torture* yourself over it. We'll figure it out soon enough."

She sounded so certain, Gen thought, and asked, "Where to next?"

"Let's do the churches. Monumental Episcopal and St. John's."

Monumental had been built on the site where Elizabeth Poe, Edgar's mother, had once worked as an actress. They were able to sit in the same pew where Edgar Allan Poe had gone to services with his foster parents. From there, they moved on up East Broad Street to St. John's, the church where Patrick Henry had given his famous "Give me liberty or give me death" speech. There the historical marker at the churchyard entry claimed two very famous grave sites, one for the patriot George Wythe, and another for Elizabeth Arnold Poe. A local guidebook that Nikki had picked up at the museum explained that Elizabeth's grave was at the far eastern edge of the churchyard for a reason.

She'd been an actress. And that, in her day, had been scandalous. The congregation of the time had been appalled that she was allowed to be interred in their graveyard at all.

As they walked the grounds, Genevieve kept her eyes on Nikki. But if the other woman was seeing ghosts, she gave no sign.

Inside the church, they couldn't help being swept up in the building's revolutionary history. But because her mind was so heavily on the task at hand, eventually Genevieve found it wandering to her own mystery.

Then she noticed the memorial. "Nikki, look."

It was the kind of marker that usually noted the fact that a certain person had been laid to rest beneath the floor. But this one wasn't old, and it didn't refer to anyone buried in the church. It was just a memorial.

To William Morton.

According to the inscription, he had not only attended the church, he had helped to keep up the building and grounds, and he had given generously of his time and his earnings.

And he was buried in a nearby cemetery.

"Let's go," Nikki said.

They hurried back out to the car, where Nikki glanced at a map for a moment, then started the engine and pulled back onto the road.

Genevieve read from the guidebook as they drove. "This says there are three presidents buried there," she told Nikki. "James Monroe and John Tyler and Jefferson Davis, president of the Confederate States of America."

"It's a technicality as to whether that makes it two or three, then," Nikki said with a laugh. "Of course, some Southerners would say that the most important president ever is buried there."

"This book was written by an Englishman," Genevieve said, reading the cover blurb. "We'll assume that he really didn't take a side."

Nikki grinned, as they drove into the cemetery and parked. They went into the office, where they pretended to be relatives of William Morton so they could get directions to his grave.

As they started walking, Genevieve felt an odd sense of unease slipping over her, despite the beauty of the setting. "Nikki?" she said.

"Yeah?"

"Are we here because you're hoping to, uh, talk to William Morton?"

"Who knows? It's worth a try."

Genevieve found herself distracted when she saw a sign pointing to the grave of George Pickett, famous for Pickett's Charge at Gettysburg. She wandered over to the grave and studied it, saddened by thoughts of how much had been lost when the country had been torn in two by war.

"Nikki?" she said, then realized the other woman wasn't with her, so she started walking again in what she hoped was the direction of William Morton's grave.

Then she turned a corner and froze.

There were ghosts, and she knew they were ghosts, standing right in front of her. A man, tall, slender, gaunt even, and very stately, with graying hair and strong, tormented features. And a woman. Very tall, as well, in eighteen-fifties dress. She was of medium build, a very handsome woman, but looking as tormented as the man.

Genevieve's jaw locked, and she shook her head.

They were just there on the path, surrounded by stone angels.

As she stood transfixed, another man came up to the pair. He wore a gray uniform with butternut trim, a handsome officer's jacket and a cockade hat. The officer said something to the couple, then tipped his hat and turned to walk down the path.

Right toward Genevieve.

As he got closer, she realized that she could see right through him.

He was a handsome man, and as he passed her, he tipped his hat as if it were perfectly natural that she should see him.

She sensed someone behind her, and she couldn't help it. She screamed.

"Genevieve! What on earth is the matter?"

She turned to see Nikki standing there.

"You've seen someone," the other woman said.

All Genevieve could do at first was point.

"That's Jefferson Davis's grave. His wife is buried right next to him, and there are a number of Confederate officers nearby."

Genevieve stared at Nikki. "I—I can't do this." She gulped for air. "I just can't...."

"Just breathe and you'll be fine. And then I want you to come with me. I've found William Morton's grave. It's just over there, and I was thinking you might be able to sense something, because you have a connection to this case that I don't."

"Do you see these people all the time?" Genevieve asked, finally able to speak coherently again.

"Not all the time, but often enough. You really do get used to it," Nikki told her. "I swear to you, Genevieve. You'll be all right. You haven't passed out, and that's a good sign."

Why pass out when she was certifiably crazy? Gen thought.

Then she straightened her shoulders. It was still daylight. The cemetery wasn't shrouded in mist. In fact, it was beautiful, filled with monuments to the dead, to the persistence of love beyond the grave. She took a deep breath. "Show me the grave," she said to Nikki.

CHAPTER 17

At first the police weren't as cooperative as Joe had hoped for, but then Brent asked to see Detective Ryan Wilkins, and after several minutes the detective came out and greeted Brent warmly, suggesting they go around the corner to a coffee shop to talk.

The day was warm, so they sat at an outside table, and Wilkins produced a file. "I copied everything we have for you. Told the chief about your research down here maybe helping put an end to our cold case, and he was obliging."

"Thanks. This is terrific," Joe said, opening the file.

A lot of the information was dry. He started with the medical examiner's report, and the cause of death was simple: strangulation by a right-handed killer.

"We had no clues. Nothing to go on. To begin with, the Mortons were very neat and orderly people. There was no dust on the basement floor, so…no footprints."

"The house hadn't been broken into?" Joe asked.

Wilkins, a handsome black man of about forty, shook his head. "No. No sign of forced entry in any way. The house is out in the country. No close neighbors. Mrs. Morton was at a meeting of her garden club when it happened."

"She discovered the body?" Brent asked.

Wilkins nodded. "Yes. She went down to the basement looking for him and found him in the wine cellar. She tried to revive him, so he'd been moved when the paramedics, and then my partner at that time, Sharon Autry, and I arrived. We're pretty sure it was done by a friend of the family or someone smart enough to wear gloves, because we didn't find any fingerprints that didn't belong there. We talked to every single family friend, and everyone had an airtight alibi for when the murder occurred. We just ran out of clues and leads. Mrs. Morton still calls, and I tell her that I'll never really close the case while I'm alive, but…" He lifted his hand. "Crime goes on."

"What about any local Poe enthusiasts?" Joe asked. "There must be some kind of Poe society here, with this being where Poe grew up."

"You bet. And yes, we covered that angle, too. All our 'Poe people' were thoroughly checked out," Wilkins told them. "Thoroughly," he repeated for emphasis.

"How about a Poe researcher who was visiting from somewhere else?"

"I can make some calls for you today, find out if any of those folks remember anyone else being in town. But, you know, anyone's free to come here to research Poe without having to check in anywhere," Wilkins pointed out.

"We appreciate you seeing what you can find out. We're afraid we may have a serial killer on our hands who started off slowly but is building up speed," Joe said.

"Will do," Wilkins promised, then looked at Brent. "So you're off to see Nancy Morton, I hear."

"Yes, how did you know?" Brent asked him.

"She called me," Wilkins said. "She wanted me to know you were coming, in case maybe you can find an answer to things I couldn't."

"You okay with that?" Brent asked.

"Absolutely," Wilkins said easily. "I don't give a damn how things are solved, as long as the bad guys are stopped. Well, you know, so long as no one has to do anything *too* illegal."

Joe was certain that that *too* had been thrown in not just as a figure of speech, but with purpose.

A little while later, they all shook hands, and Wilkins headed back to the station. Back in the car, Brent directed while Joe drove, and in a little while they were on the outskirts of the city, where the houses became estates, and where neighbors could go months without seeing one another.

At last they drove up a long driveway to a porticoed house. It was new, but had the look of an old southern mansion. A maid in a cheery, flowered apron answered the door and led them in. Nancy Morton was waiting for them in the parlor, tea service at the ready on a silver tray. She was a slim woman of at least sixty. She looked younger, but had the slightly pinched look that came from plastic surgery, though it had been done well. Her hair was tinted an ash blond and was elegantly coifed.

She greeted Brent with a wide smile and rose up on tiptoe to plant a kiss on his cheek. Then she offered a hand to Joe.

"I'm Joe Connolly, Mrs. Morton," he said.

"Nancy, please," she said. "Why don't you two sit down? I'll tell you everything I can, but I'm afraid it's not much."

They accepted tea, despite the fact that they'd just had coffee. It seemed to be important to Nancy Morton that she provide them with something.

"This is a beautiful house," Joe commented, taking his cup.

"Thank you. William designed it," Nancy said, and sighed. "We never had children. We didn't plan it that way, but we...we just never had them. But we were very lucky. We had a good marriage, got along well, enjoyed the same things. Gardens, literature, music."

"I'm sorry for your loss," Joe said quietly.

She smiled and absently touched the pearl necklace she wore. "Thank you. He was a good man." She smiled wistfully. "Detective Wilkins is very sweet. I know he thinks I should move, but…this is my home. I still feel close to William here."

"We're sorry to dredge all this up again, Nancy," Brent said.

"Don't be. I don't mind. Especially if anything I say can help."

"Why don't you just tell us about that day? If it won't be too painful," Joe said.

She looked off into the distance, as if she could see into the past that way. "I had gone out around ten. I had a meeting of the garden club. We were planting flowers in one of the local parks. I had dirt all over me when I came home. I had to explain that to Detective Wilkins, because at first the detectives thought that was suspicious. It was Sophia's day off, so William had been alone. I got home around one and left the car in the driveway, right where yours is now, because I thought I'd hop into the shower, and then William and I could go to a late lunch. We'd talked about that over breakfast. But when I came in and called him, he didn't answer. He kept his office down in the basement, with all his books and his computer. And of course, the wine cellar is down there. We don't have a fancy refrigeration system, just the old brick walls and wooden racks. I assumed he had to be downstairs, so I went down, but he wasn't at his desk. I walked into the wine cellar and…and there he was." Tears dampened her eyes. "I tried mouth-to-mouth, but it didn't do any good. Then I called 9-1-1, and the paramedics came, and the police. I couldn't help thinking that if I had just gotten home sooner, I might have been able to save him, but the police said that he'd been…strangled, and that he was already dead when the murderer left him there. But I'll still always wonder…."

"And nothing was taken?" Joe asked.

"Nothing I was aware of. Nothing valuable, certainly."

"Your husband had all kinds of files on Poe, didn't he?" Joe asked.

She stared at him, clear-eyed and frowning. "Files on Poe? Of course. He wrote a book. It was fiction, of course, but his research was impeccable."

"Were any of his notes missing?" Joe asked.

She was briefly silent. "I'm afraid I wouldn't know. His desk appeared to be in order."

"Nancy, do you mind if we go downstairs and look around?" Brent asked.

"Of course not."

She led the way down a carpeted staircase. The basement was as she had described. There was a huge, polished desk with a computer in the center of the room. There were bookshelves lining two walls and a filing cabinet against a third wall.

The fourth wall was brick and held the door to the wine cellar.

They didn't need to ask her. She walked straight through the door and they followed. It wasn't a huge wine cellar, but it went beyond modest.

"He was lying over there," she said softly. "Right by his favorite merlot."

The floor was as dust-free as Wilkins had described it. Nancy obviously liked a clean house.

"Do you mind if I look through the filing cabinet?" Joe asked.

"Not at all," Nancy told him.

There were many files on many authors. William Morton had kept newspaper clippings and magazine articles, along with his own notes. There was, as expected, a folder dedicated to Edgar Allan Poe, containing a few articles and some pictures that had been taken at various sites. But it was curiously…small.

A man who had written a book on Poe should have had far more information, Joe thought. Admittedly, this was the age of the online investigation, but still, when compared with all the information

William had stored away regarding Thoreau, Emerson and others, his file on Poe seemed suspiciously slim.

"Did you ever help your husband with his research, or with his filing?" Joe asked.

Nancy played with her pearls again. "Good heavens, no. I wouldn't have dared interfere." Nancy led them back upstairs then, and paused by the fireplace to pick up a framed photo of a clean-shaven man with graying hair and a pleasant, dimpled face.

"William, right before he died," she said.

A few minutes later they thanked her for her time, and she asked them to notify her if they found out anything, or if she could do anything else for them.

As they drove away, Joe looked back at the house. He hadn't felt anything, hadn't seen or heard anything out of the ordinary. He looked at Brent and asked softly, "Well?"

Brent shook his head. "I've got nothing, except…you think his killer stole some of his files?"

"Yes."

"Will that help us any?"

"I don't know."

Brent was silent a moment. "Did you see anything?"

"Only in my mind's eye. A man, dead next to his favorite merlot. Poe, in a way, but badly."

"How's that?" Brent asked.

"He was behind a brick wall, but he hadn't been bricked in, much less bricked in alive."

"His killer wanted to be sure he was dead and to get away with murder."

"Yeah," Joe said darkly. "And so far, he has."

There was an old stone bench next to William Morton's family mausoleum. The Federal-style tomb held the mortal remains of the family from eighteen-fifty-five onward, the latest burial being William's.

His wife's name, with her date of birth and a blank expanse of marble where her date of death would one day be etched, was next to his.

Genevieve and Nikki sat on the bench together, and Gen tried to decide whether the world that had opened up to her was terrible or intriguing.

They were alone, yet the cemetery was crowded.

A child in knickers went running by, chasing a ball. A woman with a bustle went racing after him, calling out distractedly, *Ethan Taylor, you come back here right now!* She offered Genevieve and Nikki an apologetic smile as she passed.

She wasn't real, of course, and neither was her son.

After a while, Gen felt the softness of a breeze and looked toward the monument. A pleasant-looking man of sixtysomething was standing by the iron-gated doorway. He was wearing a suit and could have been out for a pleasant stroll in the historic cemetery, pausing momentarily to catch his breath.

Except that he wasn't going to catch his breath again. Ever.

"So sad," he said, looking at Genevieve.

She forced herself to speak. "Mr. Morton?"

"William," he said, smiling crookedly. "Not Will or Bill, much less Willie or Billy. I was always William. Don't know why."

She stood slowly, her hands clenched into fists at her sides. Nikki stood up with her, so at least she wasn't alone, but whether Nikki saw him or not, she didn't know.

He slammed a fist against the tomb, and Gen almost jumped back. But she realized he wasn't angry with her when he said emphatically, "I want to help."

She cleared her throat. "You were murdered."

"I know that," he said

"Who did it?" she asked.

He shook his head. "I don't know."

"You have to know!"

"Young lady, don't you think I would tell you the name of my killer if I knew it?"

"But…you must have let him into your house."

He crossed his arms over his chest and stared at her as if daring her to dispute his next words. "All right. Poe."

"What?"

"Edgar Allan Poe."

Apparently Nikki *did* see him, because she said, "Excuse me?"

"We were getting ready for Poe Fest," he said. "When the doorbell rang, I assumed it was Beau Headley. He was supposed to come by so we could discuss the lectures we'd be giving that Saturday night. I was busy, just finishing up on the computer, so I wasn't paying a great deal of attention when I opened the door. I said something like, 'Gee, Beau, great costume, let me just run down and turn off the computer.' But whoever it was followed me. I didn't realize it…until I was being throttled. I fought back, though. I gouged him pretty good on his chest."

"But his face," Genevieve protested. "Can't you at least describe his face?"

"He had on false whiskers and a wig. And his eyes were brown and the pupils seemed too big, so I'm thinking he had on some kind of contact lenses."

"Are you at least sure it was a man?" Nikki asked.

"Yes. I think so."

"You think so," Genevieve said. She was amazed at how frustrated she was feeling. Last night she had been terrified by the very concept of ghosts, and today she was angry with one.

"We think he's killing other people, so if you can come up with anything else, it would really help," she said.

He was thoughtful, leaning against the tomb. He rubbed his chin. "You see me pretty well, right?" he asked.

"Yes," both women said together.

"I can't quite get the hang of getting out of here," he said. "The cemetery, I mean."

"We can't really help you there," Nikki said. "I'm so sorry. From what I understand…you just keep trying. Others here may be able to help you."

He sighed. "Tell me, please…how is my wife? Do you know?"

Nikki glanced at Genevieve, then turned back to the ghost. "My husband is seeing her this afternoon," she said. "I believe she's doing well, though I'm certain she misses you."

"If you can, will you let her know that I love her?" he asked.

"Of course," Genevieve said.

"I'm sure she knows," Nikki told him softly.

"Is there anything else you can tell us that might help to solve your murder?" Genevieve asked.

"Do you think I'll be able to go then?" he asked wistfully, then shook his head. "I don't think so. I think…I think I'm waiting for Nancy. We did everything together. I can't take a major journey without her."

They both just looked at him, not knowing what to say.

And then William Morton was gone. He faded away, and then, there was nothing where he'd been but the air.

They all met up back at the bed-and-breakfast just before seven. Adam had been busy on the computer all afternoon, and he had information.

"Thorne Bigelow and his family *were* here when William Morton was killed. They had come to attend a series of lectures at something called Poe Fest. They got here the day before he was killed and didn't leave until five days after."

He produced several pictures he had found online and printed out. "These were taken during the festivities."

One shot was of a man giving a lecture, and he was dressed like Poe.

Another was of a group at what appeared to be a garden tea party. The women wore period gowns, and several of the men were dressed like Poe.

"Kind of like trying to find a clown at a circus," Nikki said.

"It had to be Jared," Joe said. "Because Thorne is dead, and Mary Vincenzo couldn't have carried it off—not alone, anyway. What we need now is proof."

"We're looking at a dozen would-be Poes here," Brent said.

"Would-be Poes? What does that have to do with it?" Joe asked.

Gen cleared her throat. "The killer dresses up like Poe."

"And how do you know that?" Joe demanded. He seemed tense. *"How do you know?"*

Genevieve braced herself, lifted her chin and met his eyes squarely. "William Morton told us. This afternoon, at the cemetery. And..." she paused, wincing "...Leslie and Matt talked to Lori, and she said the same thing, that her killer was dressed up like Poe."

Joe rose. She was sure he was about to tell them that they were all crazy, but he didn't. He just ran his fingers through his hair and asked, "Do you know what would happen if I were to call Raif Green and tell him that a ghost told me we're looking for a killer who dresses up like Edgar Allan Poe?" he asked.

"There might be another way to make the suggestion," Adam said.

Brent leaned forward. "Joe, we all know that the rest of the world doesn't see what we do. But you learn not to talk about what's obvious to you to other people. You go around it. You call the cops, and you leave an anonymous tip that someone might have dressed up like Poe to kill Lori. Then someone starts checking the costume shops."

Adam leaned back and sighed thoughtfully. "Trouble is, even if we can prove that Jared Bigelow rented a Poe costume, we still can't prove that he wore it to kill anyone."

Joe sat down again. "We have to come up with enough evidence for Raif to go to the D.A.'s office with at least a strong circumstantial case."

"Let's see what happens tomorrow," Nikki advised. "In Baltimore."

"For now, I think dinner's in order," Brent said. "I don't know about you guys, but I haven't eaten since breakfast."

They picked an Italian restaurant, on their innkeeper's recommendation, and headed out. As they drove down Monument Avenue, Genevieve looked out at the statues that gave it its name, then gasped suddenly. "Stop!" she cried.

Joe pulled off to the side of the road so quickly that the driver behind him blasted his horn as he passed by.

"I'm sorry. I just…do you mind if I hop out for a minute?"

Joe lifted his hands and let them fall, at last staring at her as if she were crazy.

She climbed out of the car, aware that Nikki was following her as she walked across the street to stare up at the equestrian statue that had caught her attention so dramatically. Then she read the plaque at the bottom, identifying it as General James Ewell Brown Stuart, C.S.A.

"It's him," Genevieve breathed.

"Who?" Even Nikki sounded worried.

"I saw him. I saw him today at the cemetery. He spoke with Jefferson Davis and his wife. He tipped his hat to me."

There was no denying it now, she thought as they walked back to the car. She really was seeing ghosts. She might have made up William Morton or somehow been influenced by Nikki's proximity, but there was no denying that she'd seen General Stuart.

"I'm sorry," Genevieve apologized when she got back in the car. "It's such a beautiful statue that I just had to get a closer look."

"Sure," Joe said, and pulled back into traffic.

Genevieve had been given a large bedroom with a queen bed and a garden view. She wondered if Joe would be sharing it with her tonight, since she wasn't sure of their footing at the moment. He had stayed with her last night, but that could have been simply because he was a good guy. He wouldn't have left her alone, not when she had barely been able to stand.

But she was glad when he took it for granted that they would be staying together and went with her to her room. "This place was really a nice choice," he told her, when she opened the door. "Leave it to Adam." When she looked at him questioningly, he grimaced. "I probably would have opted for a chain hotel."

She smiled. "Adam is good," she said simply, then headed into the bathroom to shower. She closed the door, but she didn't lock it. Then she turned the water on hot. And waited.

But he didn't come. She sighed and picked up the soap.

You can initiate things, you know, she told herself. But she had already done that, hadn't she?

She had already soaped herself when she heard the door open. And then he stepped in behind her. A swift sensation of gratitude was quickly replaced with simple physical pleasure as she felt the bulwark of his body behind her. He pulled her close, reaching for the soap, then running it up and down her body in sweet suggestion.

She turned to face him. As steam and water cascaded around them, she looked up into his eyes, somehow feeling guilty, feeling that she should tell him everything.

But before she could say anything, he kissed her. Long and deep. It felt as if his tongue dipped down into the heart of her, as if they were locked together in the mist and heat. When his mouth lifted from hers, she met his eyes and would have spoken, but he whispered a soft, "Shh," and she was lost.

His hands caressed a path down her back and encircled her buttocks, lifting her closer to him. Excitement drove through her like fire, and she pressed herself flat against his body.

They clung to one another, and his mouth found hers again, hot and sensual, no tenderness involved, just a need that seemed to fill her every cell with a soaring sensuality. She ran her finger over the wet skin of his shoulders, then down his spine. He reached past her, groping for the faucet, turning it off, and then he lifted her against him, stepping from the tub.

They didn't bother with towels. On the bed, his tongue coursed over her, as if he could lick her dry. She gasped and shuddered, and the headboard hit the wall as he shifted above her.

"Shh," he teased. "You don't want to wake the neighbors."

She nipped his shoulder, pushing him back, pushing him down. She moved with abandon against him, her body slick as she rubbed against him. She kissed and teased the muscled flat of his stomach, stroked his thighs, caught his erection in her hand. She heard his breathing deepen, catch, heard the growl that escaped him as she crawled atop him.

He wrapped his arms around her and swept her beneath him. She met his gaze, smiling, alive, feeling ridiculously vital and excited. She locked her thighs around him, and a soft moan escaped her as he thrust into her.

They began to move.

And whisper.

Words that inspired, that caressed, that soared alongside their passion.

The air was cool, his body was fire, and each thrust and parry seemed to drive her more insane. His lips found hers, broke away, found them again, and she heard the bed squeaking and didn't care. The world began and ended with him.

She climaxed violently, her body a vise around him, shudders tearing through her at volatile speed. She felt his power as he climaxed with her, jerking into her, once, again and then again. Her arms tightened around him, and she clasped him tighter, feeling the matching drumbeats of their hearts. He caressed her head, smoothing back her damp hair, cradling her tenderly to him.

There was a loud thunk from the other side of the wall. They stared at each other, startled, then laughed.

"Is that Brent and Nikki's room?" he whispered.

"Shush," she teased.

They didn't say anything else. He held her, they dozed and then they made love again.

As she finally drifted to sleep, she wished that she could really talk to him, that she dared to pour her heart out to him, to tell him about the fear and the wonder of what was happening to her.

They were so close, and yet, there were still such...ghosts... between them.

CHAPTER 18

The next day Brent called Ryan Wilkins and told him that they suspected a visitor to the Poe Fest might have been responsible for the Morton murder, then suggested that he might want to talk to the costume shops that had rented out Poe costumes at the time. He also told Wilkins that Joe was convinced something had been taken from the house: the bulk of William Morton's notes on Poe.

Brent took the wheel when they left for Baltimore, because Joe was on the phone with Raif.

"I got the phone records, but I'll be damned if I know what they prove," Raif said.

"Did you find any calls between anyone in the society and Lori Star?" Joe asked.

"No. Were you expecting me to?" Raif asked.

"No. I was just hoping. Anything unusual at all?" Joe asked.

"They all called each other a lot, that's for certain. Let's see, there are more from Lila Hawkins to Eileen Brideswell than to any of the other members. And Larry seemed to call Thorne and Don more than he did anyone else. A lot of calls went out from Thorne to both Lou Sayles and Barbara Hirshorn."

"Interesting," Joe said.

"Yeah? Well, the weather can be interesting, too," Raif said wearily. "I've traipsed all over New Jersey—with the blessing of the cops there—and I've still got nothing."

"Have you checked on boats?"

"She didn't take a ferry over, if that's what you're getting at," Raif said.

"No, what about rental boats?"

"Hey, what are you, my captain or something?"

"Is that a play on words, or are you just being pissy?" Joe asked him.

"Of course we're checking on boat rentals," Raif said. "Shit."

"You might want to check to see if anyone rented a Poe outfit anywhere," Joe said, wincing slightly.

"What?"

"And check around with the neighbors about it."

"You mean, Bigelow's neighbors? Or Lori's? Doesn't matter. We've talked to the neighbors."

"But you haven't asked them if they saw anyone dressed up like Poe walking around—" he said.

"They would have said so, don't you think? I mean, that would have been pretty weird."

"It's New York, Raif. Think about it. How much weird stuff do you walk by every day of your life?"

"All right," Raif said. "Why the hell not?"

They hung up, and Joe saw that Nikki and Genevieve were both looking back at him gravely.

"What?" he said.

Genevieve shook her head.

"We're just glad that you mentioned the Poe costume idea, that's all," Nikki said.

He turned away without replying. He wasn't admitting that ghosts were out there talking to people. He was simply…grabbing at any straw.

But he knew.

When they reached Baltimore, they went straight to the Poe house on Amity Street. Poe had gone to live there after one of his arguments with his foster father, and it was probably a place where he had found happiness. He had live there with his aunt, Maria Clemm, and his future wife, his cousin Virginia. He had done a lot of writing in the house, and though the house itself was the real attraction, it also held Poe's lap desk, which he used when traveling, his sextant, and a full-size color reproduction of the only known portrait of Virginia.

The house itself consisted of a living room and kitchen on the first floor, with two bedrooms above and an attic. It had been saved from demolition by the city's Poe society in nineteen-forty-one, and was reverently maintained.

They moved on to Church Hospital, where Poe had died.

It was originally called Washington College Hospital. Poe had arrived there in a carriage on October third, eighteen-forty-nine. He was attended by Dr. John J. Moran, who, later in life, made his living by telling the tale of Poe's death, which meant he had expanded on it so much that the truth was hard to discern from the fiction. But the facts seemed to be that Poe had arrived, after a disappearance of several days, in a state that appeared to be drunkenness. He was taken to a tower room, where alcoholics were usually kept to keep them from disturbing the other patients. Poe's cousin, Neilson Poe, tried to visit him on the sixth but was told that Poe was too excitable, so he left. Neither he nor any member of the family would ever see Edgar Allan Poe again, at least not alive.

His cause of death was listed as "congestion of the brain."

Because it was still a working hospital, they simply stood outside and looked at the building.

Genevieve realized that Joe was watching her, and she looked at him and smiled. "It was so sad, the way he died. His whole life was so sad."

"The grave site?" Adam suggested, and they moved on.

Even in death, poverty had followed Poe. He had originally been buried with no headstone. Later, Maria Clemm had written to the same cousin who had tried to visit Poe as he lay dying, and Neilson had commissioned a monument.

It would have been a nice one, Joe thought. Neilson had asked that the Latin for "Here, at last, he is happy" be inscribed on one side, while the other side would have read, "Spare these remains." But the monument had been built near the train tracks, and a train wreck had destroyed it, and Neilson hadn't had the money to pay for another.

Poe's stone did not go up until eighteen-seventy-five. By then, Poe had at last received tribute from his fellow writers. Letters from Longfellow and Tennyson, among others, were read at the ceremony. Eventually Maria Clemm was buried beside him, and the remains of his beloved Virginia were brought from New York to rest with him, as well. Somehow, his birthday was mistakenly written as January twentieth instead of January nineteenth, an error that remained.

There was a crowd of tourists around the grave, listening to a guide, and Joe couldn't help wondering if ghosts would appear to his friends when there were so many people in the area. Then he wondered if they would give any indication of what they saw even if they did see something.

What the hell was the point of all this, anyway? It was fine to acknowledge the sad life of a great writer, but he didn't see how that would be helpful in solving a series of modern murders.

When the guide, a lean man of about twenty-five who was dressed as the poet, was finished, Joe stepped forward and asked him if he knew anything about Bradley Hicks.

"Poor Bradley."

"You knew him?"

"Yes. And what a terrible way to die, frightened to death in his own family vault."

"Was he easily frightened?" Joe asked.

The man frowned, clearly curious as to Joe's line of questioning, so Joe showed him his license. "My friends and I are looking into the recent murders in New York," he said.

The man's eyes widened. "You think…?"

"We don't know."

"Look, I'm done here, so I can show you Bradley's grave, if you want. Poor guy. He died there, and now he's buried there. I'm James Boer, by the way. Nice to meet you."

Joe made the introductions to the rest of the group, and then they got back in their car and followed James.

Bradley Hicks had been buried in a very old cemetery, rich with funerary art, slightly overgrown, and melancholy. The Hicks family had been in Baltimore for a long time. The first interment had been in eighteen-ten, and there were literally dozens of names inscribed on the tomb.

"Can all of those people really fit in there?" Nikki asked doubtfully.

"I imagine some are cremations," Joe said in reply.

"They found him in there, though. There are shelves on three sides, and a couple of tombs on the ground where you go in," James told them. "Hey, you can see for yourselves. You can look through the grating."

Joe stepped up and looked in. Though shadows hid some things, the interior was just as James had described it.

"Here, use my flashlight," Adam volunteered, handing over his keychain, which had a small but powerful penlight attached. When Joe looked at him in surprise, the older man just shrugged. "I encounter more tombs than you do," he said lightly.

The beam showed Joe what he needed to know. On the other

side of the grating was a wooden door, now open. Inside, there were four stone coffins on the ground and a number of others filling the shelves.

"That's Bradley, over there," James said, moving up and pointing. Bradley Hicks was resting on the top shelf on the right-hand side.

"Who keeps the keys to the mausoleums?" Joe asked James.

"The families, of course, and the cemetery manager has one," James said.

"You want to get in?" Adam asked. Joe nodded, and Adam said, "I'll see what I can do."

"Take the car," Brent suggested, tossing him the keys. "It's a long walk back to the office."

Adam nodded, and Nikki decided to go with him.

"What are you trying to prove?" James asked.

"I'm just trying to see how he could have thought he'd locked himself in," Joe explained, then was startled by a choked-off scream. He turned quickly to see Genevieve and Brent standing together on the narrow path leading to the tomb. The scream had come from behind them, where a young woman of about twenty was standing, carrying a bouquet of flowers.

Genevieve hurried over to her, frowning.

"No," the young woman mouthed, wide-eyed.

"It's all right," Genevieve said, touching her shoulder gently.

The woman ignored her, raised a finger and pointed at James. "You were here!" she said accusingly. "You were here the day that man died."

"No, I wasn't," James protested. He looked at the others, shaking his head. "I swear, I was working." He turned back to the young woman. "I'm a tour guide," he said quickly. "I dress like this for work, but except for today, I've never come here in costume."

"Calm down, everyone," Joe said. "Miss, were you here when Mr. Hicks died?"

She nodded.

"Are you related to him?" When she shook her head, Joe went on, "So you were here because...?" he asked.

She pointed to another family mausoleum about fifty yards away. In bold letters it announced the name 'Adair.'

"Your family?" Genevieve asked, trying to draw her out.

Another nod, then, "I'm Sarah Adair."

"What happened?" Genevieve pursued.

"I...came to bring my grandmother flowers. I like to come. Our tomb is always open. It's like a little chapel," she said.

"Did you see Mr. Hicks that day?" Joe asked. "Before he died?"

She shook her head. "No, I only heard about it later. But I saw *him!*" She pointed at James.

"I'm telling you, I wasn't here," James said.

She studied his face. "Okay. I saw someone who looked like you."

"Someone who looked like Edgar Allan Poe, you mean?" Joe asked.

She shrugged. "I guess. Like Poe." She suddenly clamped her hand over her mouth. "The paper said the man who died loved Poe. He wrote an article about him or something."

"Miss Adair," Joe said, "can you tell me about the day Mr. Hicks died?"

"Like I said, I came to bring flowers to my grandmother. When I left, I saw a man who looked like him—like Poe—walking in front of me, and the way the path runs, he must have come from over here. I didn't think anything about it. But then I heard on the news that Mr. Hicks had a heart attack in his tomb, so I told the police that I had seen someone in the cemetery. But they told me lots of people had been here, and that there was nothing suspicious, that no one had locked Mr. Hicks in and both doors were unlocked when they found him."

Just then Adam and Nikki returned. When they stepped out of

the car, Adam was dangling a key triumphantly; then he frowned, noticing the addition to their party.

"This is Sarah Adair," Joe explained. "And she was just telling us that there was a man dressed as Edgar Allan Poe in the cemetery the day Bradley Hicks died."

"Oh?" Adam stared at her with renewed interest.

"Are you going in?" Sarah asked.

"Well…" Nikki said.

"You can go into any of the tombs. The keys are just hanging on the rack in the office."

"They just leave them there for…whoever?" Joe asked.

"Of course. People come from all over the country to visit relatives who are buried here," Sarah said.

Joe took the key from Adam, fitted it into the lock and found that the iron grate swung open easily. Unless it had been oiled since Hicks's death—something he would have to look into—there was no way it would have stuck and trapped anyone inside. With Adam's flashlight in hand, he stepped in and closed both the outer grate and the inner wooden door behind him. Both opened instantly to his touch.

He closed the doors again and turned off the flashlight, then tried to imagine being Bradley Hicks.

Trying to open the door…

Not being able to.

He might have tried banging on the walls, but they were brick, and very thick.

But could anyone have counted on him to have a heart attack so conveniently?

He must have had a weak heart, and his killer must have known it.

He opened the doors again.

It was almost amusing. They'd lined up in front of the tomb as if they were waiting for Lazarus to arise.

"The doors don't stick," Joe said briefly, then turned to James. "You said you knew him pretty well, right?"

"Yes."

"Did he have a heart condition?"

James nodded somberly. "That's why they figured he had the heart attack."

"Makes sense," Joe agreed. Then he turned back and locked both doors to the tomb. "I guess we're done here," he said. "James, thank you. And, Sarah, thank you, too." He handed her his card. "Just in case you remember anything else about that day."

Joe slipped an arm around Genevieve, and with the others behind them, they started walking back to the car.

They decided to have an early dinner in Baltimore, and just after they'd ordered, Joe's phone rang. He saw that it was Raif and excused himself to step outside.

"I found it," Raif said.

"What?"

"I heard from a fellow in the Richmond P.D. thirty minutes ago, said he wanted to let me know that an Edgar Allan Poe costume—complete with wig, mustache, shoes, the whole bit—was rented to a T. Bigelow the day William Morton was killed. And one of our cops here managed to find a shop here on Broadway that had rented another one just two days before Bigelow was murdered. It was rented to Thorne Bigelow, as well."

"Thorne is dead."

"Credit cards can get around, you know?"

"So who do you like for it?"

"Jared Bigelow. And I've got him in custody."

"You've arrested him for murder?"

"Don't be ridiculous. I still don't have any proof on that. Although we did find a lady who lives down the block from him who said she saw Edgar Allan Poe walking around the neighborhood."

"That's something," Joe said.

"I don't know. She also told me that Martians had landed and were living in the house next door."

"So what do you have Jared on?"

Raif chuckled softly. "Traffic."

"Traffic?"

"And attempted bribery. He seems to think he doesn't have to pay his parking tickets. He owes the city almost a thousand dollars, and the officer who stopped him wasn't impressed with his offer of a gratuity, so at this moment, he isn't getting out—no matter what kind of fancy lawyer he has—till the judge hears his case in the morning."

"Oh, hell, Raif, you know he'll make bail, so you don't really have him."

"I do if you can come up with something by tomorrow morning."

He didn't have a prayer, Joe thought. No, he didn't even have the ghost of a chance. Still…

"Thanks, Raif. I'm still down in Maryland, but we're heading back as soon as we finish eating." He looked at his watch. "Think you can fix it so I can talk to him tonight?"

"Sure. I can arrange that."

When Joe returned to the table, he quickly explained the situation.

"But he'll get out, won't he?" Genevieve said.

"As soon as we get back, I'm going to talk to him and try to get him to trip himself up. And if I don't, I'm going to write up all the circumstantial evidence we have, which hopefully will be enough for the D.A.'s office to get a search warrant for his place and maybe even hold him." Joe looked around the table. "They found out that one of the Bigelows, using Jared's credit card, rented a Poe costume in Richmond and again in New York."

Genevieve let out her breath softly. "So Jared did do it. Oh, God. He dressed up like Poe and met Lori Star, and then…"

She wondered if she looked as sick as she felt. Probably.

Their waitress arrived with their food. They ate quickly, then returned to the car and hit the road.

Adam promised that as soon as they got back he would get on the computer and start trying to place the Bigelows in Baltimore when Bradley Hicks had met his untimely demise, and also find out if Bigelow's credit card had been used to rent a Poe costume there, too.

When they reached the station and Joe got out, he paused and held Gen's eyes for a long moment. "Genevieve—"

"I know," she interrupted softly. "I'll be careful."

He nodded. "I have my cell," he said. "Call if you need me. For anything."

"I can't believe this might really be over," Genevieve breathed as Brent got behind the wheel and swung the car out into traffic.

"Maybe. We'll have to see," Brent said. He met her gaze in the rearview mirror. "Want to come back to Adam's place with us?"

She smiled. "Thank you, but no. I want to get home. Call my mom and talk for a bit. And no one has to babysit me, not tonight, anyway. Jared Bigelow is in jail."

Adam frowned. "We *think* we're on to the right man. We don't *know* it yet. Genevieve—"

"I know," she said firmly. "I'm just going to go home, talk to my mother and…reconcile myself, I guess."

"To?" Nikki asked.

"Life—and death," Genevieve told her.

Brent got the doorman to watch the car and carried her bag up, then went into the apartment with her, looked around to be sure it was safe, then smiled. "You going to be okay? I know it's got to be tough, getting used to seeing a different world."

"I'm going to be fine. But you and Nikki aren't leaving right away, are you?"

"No. We'll stay a few days." He sobered. "We still have to make sure the case against Jared will stand up in court."

"Right."

He kissed her cheek. "If you need anything, just give us a call."

"I'll do that."

A few minutes later, alone in her apartment, Genevieve made a cup of tea and then called Eileen. She didn't tell her mother that she had started seeing ghosts. She simply told her that they might have found some solid evidence against Jared Bigelow.

"Jared!" Eileen said. Genevieve could imagine her mother's stricken expression.

"Mom, you can't say it's a terrible shock, that he's such a nice guy."

"No, I suppose not. Does that mean I can go out with the other Ravens now? Maybe get a drink at O'Malley's?" Eileen asked.

Genevieve hesitated. "Mom, they may not be able to keep Jared in jail past tonight."

"All the more reason to head out now, then. Darling, I'm going stir-crazy."

"Oh, Mom, I don't know…."

"I'll call for a car and have Henry walk me straight to it, and I'll have it drop me off right at the door to O'Malley's. I'll even have it wait until I'm ready to go home, and get someone to walk me back to it, and I'll call Henry and have him meet me when I come back. How's that?"

"I suppose that will be all right."

"Why don't you join us?" Eileen asked.

"I don't know. I think I'll probably just hang out here."

"All right. But you're welcome to come if you change your mind."

"I'll keep it in mind," Genevieve promised.

They bade each other good-night, and Genevieve hung up the

phone and started unpacking. When the phone rang a few minutes later, she hurried to answer it, hoping it was Joe.

"Hello?"

"Genevieve?" It was a woman's voice, but not one she recognized.

"Yes?"

"You wretched bitch!"

Stunned, she stared at the receiver, then hurriedly put the phone down. When it rang again, she didn't answer it, just let her machine click on and waited.

"You stupid wretched bitch! You were jealous of me, and I know it. You made that friend of yours come after Jared."

She realized that the caller had been drinking.

She also realized it was Mary Vincenzo.

She listened as the woman continued to rant into the phone until the built-in timer stopped Mary midvent.

The phone rang again. Determined to put Mary in her place, she started to pick it up, but the machine came on immediately. "I'm going to tear your hair out and cut your uppity rich little heart into pieces. You're always flirting with him, now that you know who your mommy is. Well, you're still just a bastard. A bastard she threw away at birth. And you should die. You deserve to die. And you know what? I'm coming to get you. I am!"

She walked over to the phone to pick it up to tell Mary what she should do with herself, but the phone clicked off.

A minute later it rang again. She picked up the receiver. "Look, Mary—"

"Um, it's not Mary," a shy, tentative voice interrupted her. "It's Barbara. Barbara Hirshorn," she said, as if afraid Genevieve might not remember her.

"Oh, Barbara. Sorry," Genevieve said quickly.

"Lou and I are going to meet your mother at O'Malley's. We were thinking you might want to join us."

"I talked to my mother a little while ago and told her I thought I'd just stay home, but thanks for asking," Genevieve said.

"Are you sure? We could swing by for you."

Gen hesitated. She might as well go. Her mother wanted to see her, she wanted to see her mother, and she had no idea whether Joe would be coming by or not.

"You know, I think I will come. But you don't need to pick me up. I'll take my own car. I'll see you all there in a little while."

As soon as Barbara hung up, Gen dialed Joe's cell. She didn't expect to get him, and she didn't, so she left a message. "Hey, Joe. It's Gen. I'm going to be at O'Malley's with my mother. Meet us there when you can. If you want to, I mean."

That done, she brushed her hair, put on some lipstick and headed out. She took the elevator down to the garage, but she hadn't taken two steps before she got the strange feeling that she was being followed. A ghost again? The ghost of Lori Star trying to reach her?

She felt the strongest temptation to run back to her apartment. All of a sudden she wanted to be anywhere but in the garage.

She heard a shuffling sound, followed by a breeze, like a whisper.

"Hey, Tim!" she called loudly. Surely he was here somewhere. "Tim?"

There was no answer, and she could still feel the softness of the breeze against her face, warm and....

Urgent.

Almost imperceptibly at first, the air began to take shape, forming into something both there and not there. She could have sworn she was seeing Leslie MacIntyre, and she was speaking, desperately and in a whispered rush.

Go back, Genevieve. Go back to your apartment. Lock the door and call the police. Now! Quickly!

Without questioning why, Gen raced for the door, her key card out and ready.

And then she heard footsteps behind her. Real footsteps. Panicked, she turned…

And saw Edgar Allan Poe coming for her.

"Stop right there," she snapped, at a loss for any other option.

And for a moment, it worked. The would-be Poe seemed to trip, even though there was nothing in his path.

Genevieve thought she heard Leslie's voice again. *Hurry!*

She dropped her purse as she fumbled with the door. The damned thing wouldn't open. She realized too late that it had been jammed somehow. She hurriedly reached down for her purse, groping for the canister of Mace she always carried. She found it and turned, but she didn't get a chance to use it, because something hit her in the head so hard that she saw stars.

"Bitch!" she vaguely heard someone say.

She couldn't pass out, she told herself. If she did, she would be lost.

Who the hell was it? Mary Vincenzo? Had she come to make good on her threats?

She realized the canister was still in her hand, and she managed to aim it in the direction of her attacker and hit the spray button. She was rewarded with a howl of pain, but it was too late. Something came down on her head again, and she crashed to the garage floor.

CHAPTER 19

Jared groaned when he saw Joe enter the private visitors' room.

"Oh, great. The brilliant P.I. Okay, you got me. I didn't pay my parking tickets."

"But you did kill your father."

Jared stared at him angrily. "Don't be ridiculous. Of course I didn't kill my father."

"You killed your father, you killed William Morton and at the very least you contributed to the death of Bradley Hicks. You also murdered Lori Star and attempted to murder Sam Latham."

"No!" Jared cried.

His horror and his fierce frown of denial certainly seemed real, Joe thought.

"Jared, I just came from Virginia, where you rented a Poe costume."

"What?" Jared asked, sounding truly confused.

"Look," Joe told him. "I can get the cops in here now, and they'll take your confession and help you work out a deal with the D.A. to avoid the death penalty."

"The death—what are you talking about?" Jared said. "What does renting a Poe costume in Virginia have to do with *murder?*"

For once, he didn't look like a cocky rich kid, Joe thought. He looked genuinely frightened.

An act?

"Jared, we have proof," Joe said, knowing he was stretching the truth pretty much to the breaking point.

"Proof?"

"Proof that you used your father's card to rent a Poe costume, then drove out to William Morton's house and killed him."

Jared shook his head, staring wildly. "My father liked William Morton. He thought he was brilliant."

"Is that why you killed him? Because you were jealous that your father thought more of Morton than he did of you?"

He was stunned when Jared suddenly burst into tears. "Look, I was…a jerk. I didn't think I had to pay my tickets. But I didn't kill anyone. I sure as hell didn't kill my father, I swear it. I wasn't even there when he died. I was working, and then I went down and bought a hot dog from the vendor outside the office. You can talk to him if you want."

"Why didn't you tell anyone about the hot-dog vendor before?" Joe asked.

"I…I didn't think of it."

"What about the Sunday Lori Star was murdered?"

"I was at home."

"Sure you were."

"It's true." He reddened. "There were drugs involved. I admit it. But I was home." He brightened. "I saw someone then, too!"

"Who?"

"The window washer. I know he'll remember me. I had just poured myself a drink when I saw him out there, and I was joking around, pretending I was going to pour him a drink, too."

"Why the hell didn't you tell the police about this before?" Joe demanded.

Jared shook his head. "Because…because I'm Jared Bigelow. I shouldn't have to make excuses. I shouldn't need an alibi. I'm Jared Bigelow," he repeated in a small, defeated voice.

Disgusted, Joe turned away. Dammit. He believed the bastard. His story would be easy enough to prove. His building would have a contract with a window-washing service, and it would be easy enough to find whoever had been working there on a Sunday, of all days. No doubt the hot-dog vendor could be found and questioned, too.

But if it hadn't been Jared…

It had to have been someone with Jared. With Thorne.

That left two people.

Mary Vincenzo. But did Mary have the strength to do what had been done to William Morton and Lori Star?

Or…

The butler.

Or there had been two killers. A woman and a man, working together.

One with the strength to strangle someone. And one who could slip into a hospital room in a nurse's uniform, and not be noticed.

He suddenly remembered something. Something that had struck him as interesting a few days ago and then been forgotten in the welter of events.

Joe.

Someone had spoken his name, and it wasn't Jared Bigelow.

And he recognized the voice.

He looked up.

Matt, or a semblance of Matt, was there. Matt, his cousin and best friend.

His dead cousin. His dead best friend.

Joe, she needs you. For the love of God, hurry!

Fear and urgency set in. If Jared wasn't the killer, then the killer was still out there. And if Matt was urging him on…

She needs you, Matt repeated.

Joe ran past the officer on duty outside the door without bothering to explain why he was in such a hurry. His cell phone was in his hand as he sprinted for the street. Genevieve didn't pick up at her apartment, and she didn't answer her cell. He tried Eileen's number as he wondered why the hell you could never find a cab in New York when you really needed one.

"Joe!" Eileen said, pleased. "Are you joining us?"

His heart leaped. "Genevieve is with you?"

"No, but she may show up later."

"Who's with you?"

Eileen told him, and when she didn't mention one name in particular, he knew he had just figured everything out at last, knew what had niggled at him since the funeral until he'd remembered it just a few minutes ago.

He didn't want to panic Eileen, so he just said, "Ask Gen to call me if she shows up, all right? And don't leave O'Malley's."

He hung up. Where? Where the hell would the killer have taken her?

Where else, but...

He was within walking distance, but he didn't walk.

He ran.

Genevieve woke up slowly. Her head was pounding as if a thousand trucks were running through it. Worse than that, though, her arms hurt, as if there was a dead weight pulling on them.

Wherever she was, it was stuffy and it smelled funny.

She realized that there really was a dead weight on her arms. When she tried to move them, she heard what sounded like chains rattling.

It *was* chains.

She blinked, and her eyes adjusted to the semidarkness. But she was chained, and the weird smell was...

Mortar.

Someone was bricking her up behind a wall!

She fought back panic, reminded herself that she had been locked up underground by a maniac for weeks, and she had survived that. She had used her wits, and she had survived.

But this...

She heard the trowel moving in the concrete mixture, heard the telltale sounds as another brick was shoved into place.

Should she scream? Would there be any hope for her if she did?

Once the last brick went in, how much time would she have?

"She's awake, I know it," said a female voice.

Not Mary Vincenzo's.

It was familiar, but it sounded different, more confident than she had ever heard it.

"Yes, she's awake. Join us, won't you, Genevieve?"

A man's voice, and it was familiar, too.

She fought the panic setting in, trying to figure out the best way to play for time.

Time?

Time for what?

For help to arrive? What help? Joe was at the police station, convinced that all clues led to Jared Bigelow.

"Bennet, what a surprise," Gen said flatly.

"Bennet? Come, come. You know my given name. Why not use it...Miss Genevieve."

She lifted her head. The bricks that would eventually cover her face hadn't been laid yet.

"All right, Albee," she said. "I don't get it. Or maybe I do. I suppose you're furious because Jared gets the Bigelow money, even after you put up with *Thorny* for all those years."

Feminine laughter rang out, and Barbara Hirshorn popped her head up behind Albee's. "Don't be silly." Barbara had lost the Poe mustache she had been wearing, and though she still had on a man's nineteenth-century suit and a black wig, her sharp features were now easily recognizable. "It's not that at all."

"Okay," Gen said, frowning. "Then explain things to me. How did you do it? And why?"

"You really don't understand anything, do you?" Barbara demanded.

"She should. After that trip to Richmond and Baltimore," Bennet said.

How the hell had he known where she'd been? Gen didn't ask the question, but Barbara answered it anyway.

She giggled again, as if she were the most clever creature in the world. "Your mother told me where you were, of course. I mean, who would worry about what they said to poor, meek little nobody Barbara?"

Albee Bennet had stopped laying bricks for the moment, too busy grinning at her. Beaming with pride and pleasure. "We really are very clever, Barbara and I," he said.

"I'm sorry," Gen said. "But I still don't understand."

"You don't? You really don't?" Bennet asked her.

"No."

He smiled, setting his arm around Barbara's shoulders. "Actually, taking care of Thorne the way we did was Barbara's idea."

"Poison in the wine," Barbara said proudly. "My idea."

Her mother had been the one to say it first, but they'd all agreed that, statistically speaking, poisoning was a woman's method of murder.

"So clever," Bennet said again.

"It was nothing," Barbara said, blushing.

"He needed to die. It was justice, really. Just like those other two blowhards," Bennet explained. "Best of all, there's no way for anyone to prove that I had anything to do with it."

"I'm sure there *is* a way. They just haven't figured it out yet," Genevieve said as confidently as she could.

Barbara just rolled her eyes. "Bennet is the genius, don't you see? He knew Poe. He loved Poe. He can *be* Poe—far more effectively than I can. Once Thorne understood just how much Bennet knew about Poe, how he empathized with Poe, comprehended his work and everything about him, he would make Bennet come down for discussions. And everything Bennet said found its way into Thorne's work. He used him! My brilliant Bennet. Thorne was horrible. He deserved to die."

"What about Lori Star?" Genevieve demanded. "What about Sam Latham? He's just a nice guy with a wife and two little kids."

"Ah, yes, Sam." Bennet sighed. "It couldn't look as if we were only trying to kill Thorne, could it? I just happened to be on the road when I saw him pass me. I suddenly realized how easy it would be to engineer his death, so I drove like a bat out of hell to catch up. Unfortunately, he survived."

"But someone else died that night. You killed an innocent man," Genevieve told him. "A stranger who might not even have known the name Poe."

Barbara gave that awful giggle again. "If he didn't know Poe's name, he definitely deserved to die," she said.

"And that Lori Star... Well, I took care of her," Bennet said. "She was so easy. So desperate for fame and fortune. I rented the boat before I donned my costume, of course. I knocked her out first, then killed her on land. It ended up being a lovely recreation, don't you think?"

Genevieve's skin felt as if it were crawling with a thousand bugs. "Wait a minute," she said to Barbara. "You're supposed to be at O'Malley's. You called and asked me to go with you and Lou. Do you really think people won't notice that you left?"

"Are you really as stupid as you seem?" Barbara asked. "I conveniently developed a headache and decided to stay home." She turned to her partner in crime. "Albee, get busy," she urged.

"Wait," Genevieve said quickly.

"What is it?" Bennet asked impatiently.

"What about the other men?" she asked.

"That fellow in Richmond?" he asked, annoyed.

"Yes."

He shook his head. "Don't you see? It was the same thing! His research was faulty. He knew nothing. Everything he used in that book of his came from me. And did he so much as offer me an acknowledgment? He did not."

"They'll get you, you know," Genevieve said. "Sooner or later, they'll figure it out."

Barbara burst out laughing. "I'll swear Bennet was with me that Sunday morning, if anyone asks. And your dear friend Joe can vouch for his Sunday afternoon—you two came to visit."

"So you managed everything on Sunday morning," Genevieve said, looking at Bennet. "Impressive."

"I helped," Barbara said proudly. "I was ready with the car over in Jersey. Even that road will lead back to Jared, though. We rented the boat with one of Jared's credit cards. The Bigelows were always a bit careless. Too much money! They had so much, they never noticed little things like missing credit cards. But enough is enough. I think it's past time for you to be dead. Albee, get going," Barbara said shrilly.

"Someone's here," Genevieve said.

They both started.

"She's lying. She's trying to slow us down," Barbara said.

"It won't make any difference, dear," Bennet said.

"It could be Thorne Bigelow."

They both froze, staring at her.

She smiled sweetly. "Ghosts do come back," she warned.

"You're crazy. But if it makes you happy, feel free to come back as a ghost," Barbara said.

Albee started to slather on mortar so he could lay another brick, but suddenly he went still. "What's that?" he demanded, poised to listen.

"What?" Barbara asked.

"There's someone upstairs."

"There can't be. The alarm is on, and the door is locked," Barbara said. "Stop paying attention to her. She's playing games, trying to make us think Thorne's coming back to haunt us. She's just trying to buy herself time."

"I'm telling you the truth," Genevieve said. She managed to twist around a bit, and relieve some of the strain on her arms, but she couldn't help breathing in all the dust Albee's masonry was stirring up, and it was making her light-headed. She knew from the conversation that she had to be in Thorne Bigelow's basement, but it clearly hadn't been thoroughly cleaned in years.

And apparently they had built this special little niche just for her. When they were finished, no one would know there was anything behind it.

Oh, God. She had to keep them talking or she would panic.

Did it matter now whether she panicked or not?

"Albee, this is wrong," Barbara said, suddenly irritated.

"What is?"

"She's supposed to be begging and pleading and crying and all that," Barbara said peevishly.

"I'm sorry. Are my questions messing up your scenario?" Genevieve demanded. "You're so smug, but actually, you've messed up all your murders."

"What the hell is that noise?" Bennet demanded, stopping.

"Oh, shut up, and finish!" Barbara demanded. "You've only got five bricks to go."

Another brick slid into place.

Genevieve knew she had to keep him talking. Keep those last bricks out.

Someone would come. She knew that. Eventually, someone would come. But when? Long after her oxygen was gone...?

"Albee, I hear something, too," Barbara said suddenly. "And..."

Barbara's voice trailed off as she stared past him, and Genevieve strained to look in that direction, too.

There *was* someone in the room with them.

Someone, or...

Some*thing.*

She could make out a transparent, vaguely formed image of a person, and her heart leapt.

Leslie MacIntyre. And beyond Leslie...

Lori Star.

Leslie was trying hard to knock over the small pile of bricks that remained. Lori was staring at Bennet and tried to strike him, but her fist went right though him. He felt something, though, because he muttered fearfully, "What the hell?"

"It's Lori," Genevieve said.

He paused, staring at her. "What?"

"Lori's ghost is in here with us right now. I'm not lying. She's with a friend of mine, Leslie MacIntyre. You've heard of Leslie, of course. She saved my life before."

"She's full of shit, Albee!" Barbara cried.

Genevieve shook her head. "No, I'm telling you the truth. They're both here."

"Shut her up! Put that last brick in," Barbara demanded. "Do it!"

"Barbara, there's something... I can feel it," Bennet insisted.

Could he really feel it? Perhaps. Because they were both very real, and they were doing their best to help her.

Barbara still looked unnerved, but she shouted at him, "Put that brick in, you fool!"

Then, miraculously, there was another voice.

A real voice. Hard, loud, firm.

"Put that brick in and I'll shoot you right in the head!"

Genevieve's muscles gave, and she sagged against the wall.

Joe!

How had he known to come here?

"The switch!" Barbara yelled.

"No!" Joe shouted out.

But Barbara made a leap for the wall, and the single light in the basement went out just as a bullet exploded in the night, followed by the thuds and grunts of hand-to-hand combat.

Genevieve was powerless to help in any way. She wrenched desperately at her chains and with the help of a surge of adrenaline, freed one hand. She pressed at the bricks, trying to topple the wall of her makeshift prison, but they wouldn't give.

And then the light went back on.

With her limited field of vision, she could see Joe and Albee rolling across the floor, locked in a deadly struggle for life or death.

Genevieve stretched out as far as she could, found a brick and threw it.

Hard.

Barbara screamed and crashed to her knees.

Gen heard a sickening thud, and Albee screamed. He rose above Joe for a minute, then jumped back down on Joe in what looked like a wrestler's savage slam, but with one key difference.

Albee Bennet was dead from a bullet to the heart.

"Joe!" Genevieve gasped.

"I'm all right. He's just…heavy."

He shoved the body off, and as he staggered to his feet, she could see that he was torn and bleeding. And then, in the distance, she heard the blessed sound of sirens.

Joe tore down the wall Albee had built, then jerked the second chain from the wall, lifted her and held her close.

He didn't pull away until a dozen policemen hurried down to the basement. Even then, he didn't go far.

"How did you find me?" she whispered.

He looked into her eyes. Offered her a crooked grin. "'The Tell-Tale Heart'?" he suggested. "My heart is your heart, so I heard it from a distance?" His smile faded. "Matt told me," he said. "Matt brought me to you."

She leaned against him. "Leslie and Lori were here," she told him, then smiled. Dirty and disheveled, he smiled in return.

EPILOGUE

As I said, it's not easy being a ghost.

But it does get better.

The why of it, though, is something I'm just beginning to understand.

One of the reasons we stayed behind, Matt and I—one I see so clearly now—was so we could help uncover the Poe Killer—or Killers, as it turned out. Joe put the last pieces together when he remembered how hard Albee Bennet had clapped when Barbara Hirshorn had given her reading at Thorne Bigelow's funeral, a hint that that the man evidently had a crush on her. What he hadn't realized at the time was just how mutual and serious those feelings were, or how far they would go on each other's behalf.

The couple that kills together stays together?

They're not together now, though I suppose they may be in the future. I was there when Albee Bennet left this world, and, I assure you, he didn't go anywhere pleasant, with soft white clouds and harp music floating on a gentle breeze. Something came for him, something swift and oozing that reeked of brimstone and charred flesh.

Barbara Hirshorn, on the other hand, did not die that night. She's locked up now, and I expect she will be for quite some time.

As for Lori, though she did extremely well during her first outing as a ghost, she chose to leave us. That light is hard to resist. I hope she's finally gotten star billing. She deserves it.

Sam Latham made a full recovery and went home.

Sorting out some of the other details proved a more complex task. Apparently Barbara took a few days off from the library now and then, days that coincided with the Bigelows' travel schedule. It was easy enough for her to slip away to be with her secret lover. And for all that she adored and admired him, she would never have admitted to the affair, too afraid of what her fellow board members would say. A librarian was one thing. A librarian involved with a butler? She was certain she would have been ousted.

She encouraged Albee to kill William Morton, helped him with his costume and drove him around. The police believe now that Barbara was the one to lure Bradley Hicks to his death. It was easy enough to arrange a meeting in the cemetery, and from there...

Sarah was lucky she wasn't seen, or she, too, might have been found in a tomb. Hopefully no one will ever tell her that.

Barbara had extracted the arsenic that killed Thorne from rat poison. As a librarian, she had Internet access and lots of time to read, and the method wasn't hard to come by.

Larry Levine finally wrote a book. It was on the Poe Killings, and it was published by Brook Avery, in his first venture into book publishing. It was not only well-reviewed, it was a bestseller.

Don Tracy is scheduled to perform as Albee Bennet in an adaptation of the book that's coming to Broadway. It's going to be a musical. Go figure. It might be a short run. Then again, who knows?

Nat Halloway, executor of Thorne Bigelow's will, filed all the papers and did all the work. The New York Poe Society received a huge endowment. Jared, who inherited the bulk of the money, married Mary. She's still a closet drunk and a bit of a bitch. Which is sort of ironic and actually okay. They deserve each other.

At first Genevieve and Joe talked about running away to Vegas and doing something fun, like an Elvis wedding. But they both adore Eileen and didn't want to cheat her out of her chance to play mother of the bride, so instead they were married at St. Patrick's in a huge affair. Matt and I were there, of course, and I know they saw us.

They moved out to Joe's place in Brooklyn, but they're contemplating something a little wilder. Joe still has the urge to move out to Vegas.

Matt and I...

We're still learning. Learning as we go.

It isn't easy being a ghost, but it has its rewards. Matt and I have everything we need most, in life and in death. We love, and we're loved in return. And isn't that what everybody wants?